STAR TREK 36:
DOCTOR'S ORDERS

STAR TREK NOVELS

STAR TREK GIANT NOVELS

A *STAR TREK*®
NOVEL

DOCTOR'S ORDERS
DIANE DUANE

TITAN BOOKS
LONDON

STAR TREK 36: **DOCTOR'S ORDERS**
ISBN 1 85286 285 8

Published by
Titan Books Ltd
19 Valentine Place
London SE1 8QH

First Titan Edition June 1990
10 9 8 7 6 5 4 3

Printed and bound in Great Britain by Cox and Wyman Ltd, Reading,
Berkshire.

DOCTOR'S ORDERS

For Laura, Nita, Tom,
the good Dr. Spencer,
and the many other friends who worked (or work) in and
around Payne Whitney Psychiatric Clinic in New York City:

with happy memories of the Sixth Floor
and the Pros from Dover.

And for them all, this variation on a theme:

"Why would anyone want to rule the world?
They'd just have to do the time sheets."

"In the ancient names of Apollo the Physician, and Aesculapius, and by Health and Allheal his daughters, I swear this oath—though chiefly by the One above Them, Whose Name we do not know. I swear to wield my art in such ways, and only in such ways, as serve to preserve sentient life in its myriad forms, or to allow such life to depart in dignity. I shall turn aside from every act, or inaction, which would allow any being's life to depart untimely. Into whatever place I go for the healing of the sick, I shall hold such things as I see there to be as secret as the holy Mysteries. I swear to perform no procedure in which I am unqualified. Nor shall I use my position as a tool in the seduction of any being. I will teach this, my art, without fee or stipulation, to other disciples bound to it by oath, should they desire to learn it; and I shall hold the ones who taught me the art as close as family, and help them in their need should they require it. I ask the Power Which hears oaths to hear me swear this one. As long as I keep it, may I stand rightfully in the respect of my fellow beings: but should I break it, may the reverse be my lot."

—*Hippocratic Oath, revised ed.*

"I wish that blasphemy, ignorance and tyranny were ceased among physicians, that they might be happy and I joyful."

—*Nicholas Culpeper*
(specialist in alternative
medicine, fl. 1608)

Chapter One

"Do you remember," said Leonard McCoy, "when I stole your cadaver?"

The tall gray-haired man lying in the other lounger laughed. "Disaster," he said, "alas! Murder most foul, alarums and excursions, theft, buggery, barratry, incomplete perfusion!"

McCoy suspected that Dieter was trying to say that, at the time, he had gone into shock. It was always a matter of guesswork, figuring out what he meant. Dieter Clissman's grasp of English had never been less than perfect, but sometimes he seemed to want to make you wonder about that a little.

McCoy leaned forward a little to signal to one of the waiters looking out toward the hotel terrace. "Here, never mind," he said, "you've gone right through that. You and your milk drinks. Let me get you another."

The waiter glanced at McCoy, nodded, and went off. McCoy leaned back in his lounger and looked out through the railings of the terrace at the landscape. The old hotel sat on the highest shoulder of the little

1

plateau that held the town of Wengen against the Jungfrau, "the Maiden," queen-mountain of all the Bernese Alps. The sky was that perfect light clear blue of late Alpine summer, the color of the very end of July, just before the fall first begins to assert itself. Down below, among the dark green scattered pines, under the brown peaked roofs, lights were beginning to show in windows, as the day drew on toward sunset and the houses farthest west in town fell under the upward-leaping shadow of Schilthorn across the valley. A pair of lights down toward the Lauterbrunnen valley spoke of a train coming up the old cog railway, loaded with tourists and the day's commuters from Interlaken, Thun, and Bern. Nothing else moved down there in the streets of the town but people walking, and electric or horse-drawn carts; bigger ground vehicles and fliers came no farther up the mountain than Lauterbrunnen, a restriction that McCoy found hard to fault when the result was such perfect quiet, broken only by the bells on the horses' harness, and on the tuned bells of goats and cows on the green alp higher up the mountainside. High above everything, the razory peak of the Maiden was half-hidden in veils of wispy cloud, but that was the best possible news to McCoy. Cloud at the end of the day in Wengen meant incredible sunsets. They were one reason why McCoy was here. The other reason was to see Dieter.

It had been a long time since they were at medical school together. After graduation, they had gone their separate ways. Now Dieter ran the Xeno department at the University of Bern and was practically a legend among the xenomedics of the Federation; and McCoy . . . *Heaven only knows what I am,* he thought.

2

"When does it start?" he said to Dieter.

"In about an hour, I should think," Dieter said, looking down toward the valley. After a long, long drink, he added, "And whatever did make you steal my cadaver?"

McCoy laughed softly at that, and took another drink of his mint julep. "If I hadn't, someone else would have," he said. "I thought it would be better if a friend did it."

"Mmmmm," Dieter said. "We did have a few rogues among us, did we not."

McCoy nodded. There had been people studying xenomedicine in the same class as the two of them who turned out not to have been particularly well fitted for it. *Well,* he thought, *better they should find out in training, rather than in practicing on a patient.* But some of them had been less than kind to the hard-working, hard-studying man who got better grades than any of them, and made them look less than competent in the labs and on the wards. A lot of them had tried to make Dieter's life less pleasant than it might have been. That had annoyed McCoy. It annoyed him now, even though it was all a long time ago. But some memories would not lie down and be still.

"Rogues, yes," he said. "Well, they're all in other jobs, I hope and trust."

"What I don't understand is what made you put the cadaver in the Dean's office," Dieter said, leaning back to gaze at where the clouds around Schilthorn and Morgenburghorn and Niesen to the west were already beginning to crimson.

"Seemed like a good idea at the time," McCoy said, looking around him as the terrace slowly began to fill

3

up with tourists, people with stillshooters and cameras. Most of them had sweaters on—a good idea; it was cooling down, and McCoy wished he had brought his own jacket. "It also seemed to me," he said, "that the Dean would be forced by such a gesture to take a more personal interest in what was going on in our classes. That seemed like a good thing."

"But you were *flunking* anatomy," Dieter said.

McCoy blushed. That was one memory he had never quite been able to come to terms with. "Such only brought more attention to bear on you," Dieter said, ignoring the blushes. "Not a good thing."

"It's all relative," McCoy muttered. "And it all turned out all right in the end." Indeed it had, though it had meant the Dean of Medicine tutoring him within an inch of his life for the next three months. He had passed anatomy with a more than respectable grade, and the Dean had shook him by the hand and told him that she never wanted to see him again. "Getting a little thick up here, isn't it?" McCoy said, looking around him at all the tourists, who were beginning to gather expectantly at the railings.

"I decline to be distracted," Dieter said. "You went to great trouble for my sake. I have never forgotten it."

"Yes, well. What about that time—" McCoy stopped himself, then. *What's wrong with just letting a thank-you in?* he thought. "Never mind," he said after a second or so. "I was glad to help."

"I was glad to be helped. Which is one reason I wanted to see you before you went off again. Your last couple of letters—there was a lot of complaining about Starfleet bureaucracy."

McCoy chuckled. "You recruiting, Dieter?"

"Don't joke. You haven't my budget cuts to deal with. I just wanted to know that you are all right."

McCoy sighed, looked out at the darkening valley. "Well, good usually manages to triumph over bureaucracy, at least lately. But good has to be very, very careful. It can tire you out."

Dieter said nothing to that, just took another drink. "This mission that means you can't stay to dinner," he said, "will it take you away for long this time? I'd like you to come lecture, if you can spare the energy when you have some more leave. Your last few articles left the other department heads hot for your blood. That *Gastroenteriditis denebiis* one in particular. Old Kreuznauer threatened to feed you that article without a GI tube."

McCoy chuckled. "I don't know," he said, gazing out at the sunset. It was becoming magnificent; the late afternoon had become almost a recipe for splendor—high clouds in an otherwise clear sky, the reflected crimson light of a sun already gone down now lingering on the highest snow-covered peaks so that they blazed pink-orange against the deepening blue, as if lit from within by fire. "It's officially a post-survey survey. The First Contact people have been down to the planet in question and counted the species. Apparently they already have some knowledge of space travel. The survey has done the initial language analyses and so forth. Now we have to go in and do the fine calibrations for the Universal Translator . . . and evaluate them to see if they're Federation material. And if they want to be." He shrugged. "It's work we've done before. I'll be busy . . . there's a lot of xenopsych involved, as you might expect. Other than that—biological survey of flora and fauna, especially the germs—anatomical and medical analysis of the species involved—"

"Wait a moment. Species *plural?*" Dieter said, sounding surprised. "More than one?"

McCoy nodded. "It's unusual," he said. "They're not planted, either—not put there by some other spacefaring species earlier on in history. Three species on the one planet, all true convergent evolution. Starfleet is hot to find out what's going on . . . seeing that no such planet has ever been found before. *Enterprise* was headed somewhere else first, but this mission has pushed that other one farther down the list. So—off we go tonight, and not next week as I thought. Otherwise, I would come lecture for you, happily. There's no telling how many years it'll be this time. You know how it is."

Dieter made a little sound like a sigh. "Here we are in the prime of our careers," it said, "and we have no more time to ourselves than we did as first-year students. Something's gone wrong somewhere."

McCoy studied his drink. "At least we're not bored."

"We weren't then, either," Dieter said. He paused, and added, "You know, I think they may be starting early. Let's look."

McCoy got up and followed his friend to the end of the railing, where there was still a little room left. They looked out, down past the town, down the valley. There were sparks of light showing: not electric lights, this time, but fires, burning on the nearby heights and hills. One after another, they started to blaze up. Down in the valley, near Lauterbrunnen and

Murren and right down to Interlaken and Spiez by the lake: on the heights on the far side of Lake Thun and Lake Brienz, on the Brienzer and Sigriswiler Rothorns, and eastward to the Schrattenflue they shone, so that the fires doubled themselves in the still waters of the lakes; and right down into the lowlands, atop the hill-heights of Rammisgummen and Napf. And one tiniest light, farthest away, due north by Lake Luzern: not a bonfire, but a laserbeam starting upward straight as a spear from the peak of Mount Pilatus, and vanishing into the night.

"They just can't wait till midnight anymore," Dieter said. "The impatience of the young. But anyway, you understand why I wanted you to see this. This year in particular."

McCoy nodded. All around them, on every mountaintop, new fires were being kindled. One was lit down in the main square in Wengen; in response to it, another laserbeam lanced out upward from the meteorological research facility on the peak of the Jungfrau, pure white, casting a light like bright moonlight on everything around. The sound of singing began to drift up—at first a few voices together, then more and more of them, thin but clear, singing a simple tune in a major key, something that might have been mistaken for a music-box tune. But the translator handled the words without hesitation, even though they were in the oldest Swiss language, Rumansch, and made it plain that this was not a song for music-boxes. "Freedom or death, that is our will; no foreign rule, for good or ill; Free folk are we, in a free land—"

"Almost a thousand years since they spoke those words first," Dieter said, "in the middle of the night, in the Rütli meadow up north by Luzern. Thirteen stubborn people, annoyed with the local representative of a foreign empire."

McCoy nodded again. That pact, the Perpetual Alliance, had been the seed of the formation of Switzerland: the declaration that the Swiss belonged to themselves, and each other, not to whatever empire felt like conquering them. And the Swiss Articles of Confederation had been one of several useful models for the Articles of Federation of the United Federation of Planets—a loose association of fiercely independent parties bound to help one another in distress, to protect the group against threat or interference from outside, and otherwise to leave each other pretty much alone. It was all history, and well enough known. But a little thread of suspicion woke up in McCoy and wouldn't go away. "How much of it really happened?" he said. "All the William Tell stuff?"

Dieter chuckled. "Willem Tell certainly lived," he said, "but he didn't kill the tyrant with his bare hands, or shoot any apples off his son's head. He was a stubborn man with a talent for withholding his taxes in protest, and getting his neighbors to do the same. Among many other things. And as for the Rütli meadow, it's there, all right, but who knows what happened nearly a thousand years ago, in the dark? All we have is the signed Pact in the Bundesbriefarchiv in Schwyz. And its results."

Some of the people up on the terrace were singing, now, in German or French or Italian; the words all came out the same in McCoy's translator, though it often had trouble with the Rumansch, and kept trying to treat it as if it were a sort of worn-down Italian with

8

pig-German mixed in. "Our homes, our lives, no one's but ours: our earth, our blood, no foreign power's—"

The song chorused up to its end. Applause and cheering broke out as more fires flared up on the heights. Glasses were raised, drained, but not smashed—this was Switzerland, after all; smashed glasses were untidy—and people went in search of refills. In McCoy's back pocket, the communicator cheeped.

He sighed, yanked down suddenly from the odd elation that had been building in him. "At least I got to see this," he said to Dieter, and pulled the communicator out. "McCoy," he said to it.

"Doctor," Spock's voice said to him, *"The Captain has asked me to say to you, 'All aboard that's coming aboard.'"*

"Tell him I appreciate the extra time, Spock," McCoy said. "Tell Uhura I'm ready."

"Noted." There was a brief pause. *"It is a most notable sight, Doctor. And a bit of a curiosity."*

"Oh? Why's that?"

"I had not thought of you as much of a historian."

McCoy chuckled a bit. "It's personal history, more than anything else. And besides," he said, "those who ignore the mistakes of the past usually wind up treating the resultant bullet holes in the future. Just consider this as prophylaxis. McCoy out."

He could hear Spock's puzzlement as he closed the frequency down, and he approved of it. "A longer stay next time, old friend," he said to Dieter.

Dieter raised his glass. *"Grüsse Gott,"* he said.

"Mud in your eye too," said McCoy. He drained his

9

julep, putting it down just before the transporter effect started to take him. "And *ciao*."

James T. Kirk leaned back in the helm and appeared to take no particular notice of the predeparture checks going on around him. That appearance was one he had cultivated for a long, long time. It didn't do for a Captain, in terms of the everyday running of a ship, to let his crew think he was watching them too closely. Such scrutiny only made them nervous, or gave them ideas about their Captain's opinion of their competence. No, it was better to lean back, enjoy the view, and let them get their jobs done.

At the same time, Kirk knew every move of the predeparture ritual, for every station of the Bridge. He paid scrupulous (though low-key) attention to it, for the same reason that old-time parachutists used to pack their own chutes, having first signed the silk. With the back half of his attention he listened to the checks on the warp and impulse engines, and the OKs from the various departments around the ship, and assured himself that everything was proceeding correctly. But in the meantime, the front half of his attention was busy with a philosophical problem.

Am I lonely? he wondered.

He had had a birthday not too long ago, and some of his congratulatory mail had just caught up with him. One card that had come from an old friend on Earth had made some mildly humorous remark about wondering when he was going to settle down with someone. Kirk's first reaction, after chuckling at the question, had been to think that he already *was* settled down with someone: with the *Enterprise*. But a moment later, some annoyed part of his brain had very clearly said to him. *How long are you going to keep feeding yourself that answer? You made it up a long time ago. Is it still valid? Was it* ever *valid? And how come it's been so long since you even gave it any thought?*

Because it was true then, and it still is, he had answered the mouthy part of his brain. But the derisive silence that was the only reply had brought him up short. Slowly, over years, Kirk had learned to pay attention to the things his brain said to him without warning; accurate or not, they tended to be worth considering. So he was considering the question, regardless of the fact that it made his brain hurt.

This is all McCoy's fault somehow, he thought, a bit sourly. *I never used to be this introspective. He's been contaminating me.*

"Sickbay," he heard Lieutenant Uhura say behind him, as she went down the checklist.

"Sickbay ready," he heard Lia Burke say: she was acting as McCoy's head nurse while Christine Chapel was out doing her doctorate practicals. *"Doctor McCoy's on his way in from the Transporter room."*

"Ask him to come up to the Bridge when he has a moment," Kirk said suddenly, deciding in momentary wickedness that if he had to be philosophically uncomfortable, he was going to spread some of the discomfort back to the source.

"Certainly, Captain. Anything in particular?"

"I'll discuss it with him when he gets here," he said. *Let him sweat,* he thought with mild amusement. "Ah, Mr. Chekov. Thank you."

He reached down and took the datapadd Chekov was offering him; he looked it over, saw nothing on the day's schedule that he hadn't been expecting, signed the padd, and gave it back to Chekov. "Your briefing today, I see," he said.

"At 1900 hours," Chekov said, "yes, sir."

"Done all your homework?"

"I should think so, Keptin," Chekov said mildly. "It *is* a Russian inwention. Like many other things."

Kirk smiled. "Carry on, Ensign," he said.

"Sir," said Chekov, and went back to his post.

Spock stepped down beside the helm from where he had been going through his own checklists. "We are ready to leave, Captain," he said. "All personnel are accounted for, and all departments report ready."

"Fine," Kirk said. "The usual notifications to orbital departure control, then. Mr. Sulu," he said, glancing at the helm console, "take us out at your discretion."

"Yes, sir," Sulu said, and started the departure procedures.

Kirk stretched a bit in the helm. "A quiet time out this time, I hope," he said to Spock. "A little pure science will do us all good."

Spock looked speculative. "It would be dangerous to attempt to predict events in advance without sufficient data," he said, "but one may certainly wish for ample time in which to do one's research."

Kirk looked sidewise at Spock. "Is there something you know that you're not telling me?" he said. "Some reason to suspect that things *won't* be quiet?"

"Indeed not," Spock said, with a slightly scandalized expression. "I would inform you immediately of any such. Preliminary data about this mission are all negative as regards any significant problems."

"A hunch, then?" Kirk said. His teasing mood was refusing to confine itself to McCoy.

"Really, sir," Spock said, "it is *most* undesirable technique to hypothesize without data—"

"Of course," Kirk said. "Never mind."

The Bridge doors hissed. "Can't leave for a moment," McCoy said. "Place goes to pot the minute I turn my back on it. Evening, Spock."

"Morning, actually," Spock said. "It is point three six—"

"Spare me the decimal places," McCoy said, leaning up against the center seat. He was carrying a datapadd, and looking cross. "Jim, have you seen these?"

Kirk took the padd and scanned it. It was a list of crewmen who had been seen in Sickbay over the past week, while the *Enterprise* had been on layover. "Yes. So?"

"These numbers are *twice* what they should be. Maybe three times. Look at this. There were five people down with colds—"

"It's not their fault that you haven't found out how to cure the common cold yet," Kirk said.

McCoy scowled at him. "You know perfectly well that diet and exercise and a generally healthy immune system are the only things that're going to stop minor upper respiratory infections. These people go on shore leave, and all their health training goes out the window."

"Oh, come on, Bones," Kirk said. "One of the reasons for shore leave is to cut loose a little."

"Indeed," Spock said, "just last week you were lecturing us on the beneficial effects of shore leave in minimizing the effects of long-term stress." He paused for a beat, then added, "In those species that *experience* stress, of course."

McCoy merely snorted at Spock in genial disgust, and said to Kirk, "The numbers are *much* higher than they ought to be."

Kirk sighed and stretched a bit in the helm. "Yes, well. We can't have everybody on the ship in perfect health, can we?"

"Yes, we can!" McCoy said, with surprising force. "That's what I'm aiming for. Nothing less."

"But if that happened, you'd be out of work."

"Jim, every doctor and nurse from here to the Rim lives in hope that one day we'll wake up and find that everybody in the Universe is perfectly healthy and in possession of a signed certificate from God saying that they're going to die peacefully in their sleep. Then we can all retire and go fishing."

"You don't like fishing. You said it was barbaric the last time I took you. You made me throw back a ten-pound trout."

McCoy scowled at Kirk. "Now you know what I mean, dammit. We all want some other job. Any other job. In any case, it's not likely to happen this week."

"Not *any* other job, surely," Kirk said, feeling the teasing mood get stronger.

"Not *his,* anyway," McCoy said, glancing at Spock. "Give me an ulcer for sure."

"Not *mine,* then?!"

"Don't tempt me," McCoy said. "Your chair's a lot more comfortable than the one in my office. I think it was designed by Torquemada. Anyway, look, Jim," McCoy said, "these figures need to be handled at the next department heads' meeting. They're too high right across the board; they were too high for the last two missions. Heads need to take a little more responsibility for helping their people follow their regimens, especially as regards shift scheduling and making sure people don't run themselves into the ground out of sheer enthusiasm. I can't be everywhere."

"No?" Spock said, lifting one eyebrow.

"No," McCoy said. "Doctors couldn't be everywhere, so the Lord invented Vulcans. I thought you knew."

Kirk smiled a bit. "Anyway," McCoy said, "we'll go into this in more detail at the heads' meeting. Jim, I need your backing on this."

"You've got it, of course. Anything else?"

McCoy looked meaningfully at Kirk's middle. "I'll be wanting to see you sometime tomorrow," he said.

"Just me? Not Spock?"

"Spock is logical," McCoy said with entirely too much relish, "and takes good care of himself. Besides, he's not due for his hundred-thousand-kilometer oil change yet. 0800 tomorrow, Jim. Be there."

McCoy headed for the Bridge doors. "Good to see you too, Bones," Kirk called after him. "I had a nice leave, thank you for asking!"

"Mnnnhhhhnnn," McCoy said, and the Bridge doors shut on him.

Kirk and Spock looked at one another. "He's in a prime mood," Kirk said. "I guess he wasn't done with his leave yet."

"It is frequently difficult to tell what is occupying the Doctor," Spock said, "or perhaps 'preoccupying him' would be a more accurate assessment. I suspect the medical model of behavior is at fault; it seems to require its adherents to keep their true concerns to

15

themselves. But I daresay the Doctor will let us know in good time."

Kirk nodded, watching Earth slip hurriedly away behind them as Sulu took them up out of the plane of the ecliptic and out of the system. "You're probably right," he said. "Now what about those mass conversion ratios you wanted to discuss with me? . . ."

"The planet's name," Mr. Chekov said, "is 1212 Muscae IV: the fourth body out from 1212 Mus, an orange type-F8 star with no spectrographic or historical anomalies worth mentioning. The star was initially cataloged by the Skalnate Pleso stellar survey on Earth, the edition dated epoch 1950, and the Bayer number and classification then assigned have been retained under the new IAU survey. Galactic coordinates and the nearest Cepheid-wariable tag beacons are in the ephemerides listed to your screens."

Kirk leaned back in his seat at the head of the table in Main Briefing, noticing that the list of coordinates was about half again as long as it would have been if Spock had been doing the briefing; evidently Chekov was taking no chances, for Spock was down at the other end of the table, his cool regard resting on the screen with the calm interest of a teacher waiting to see how a star pupil performed.

"The planet," said Mr. Chekov, "was surveyed in the first Southern Galactic Boundary Survey. Initial readouts from the non-landing survey indicated a planet in the broad M-type classification, that is to say, metallic core, largely silicon-bearing crust with significant carbon deposits: the atmosphere middle-reducing, with oxygen at no more than 20 percent, nitrogen no more than 70 percent, and noble gases within Federation medical tolerances for carbon-based life."

He touched a control on the data panel in front of him. The image showing in the screens changed to show a green-blue planet of a very Earthlike kind, the picture taken from about three hundred thousand kilometers out. Soft white brushstrokes of cloud stroked across its surface; the continents were separated by wide seas, and were mostly islands not much bigger than, say, Australia, to judge by the scale of miles down in the corner of the image. The polar caps were tiny scraps of ice, hardly there at all.

"As you can see," Chekov said, "the planet is presently interglaciated; overall planetary average temperature is sixteen degrees Celsius. Weather patterns are generally unremarkable except for their mildness; no wind during the survey period of twenty-nine days exceeded force four, even in the polar areas."

"What's the mean daytime temperature in the temperate zones?" Scotty said from down the table.

"Twenty-one C in the winter," Chekov said, "Twenty-three C in the summer."

"Ahh," Scotty said, "just like Aberdeen."

Several people around the table laughed.

"That's as it may be, Scotty," Kirk said. "Mr. Chekov, this planet sounds like a nice place for a holiday."

"It might be, sir, if people weren't living there. But more of that shortly. If you'll look at the next image—" and it changed in the screens, to a small-scale tactical layout showing the relative position of Federation space—"you'll see that the system is in so-called 'debatable' space, to which neither Federation nor any other aligned group has laid any serious territorial or 'buffer' claim. Neither Klingon nor Romulan interests have ventured much in this direction, probably for economic reasons; this part of space is fairly star-poor, it being in a gap between the Sagittarius and Perseus arms of the Galaxy, and systems with sufficiently exploitable resources, like asteroid belts, are few and far between."

Kirk nodded. "A long way to come for just a holiday planet," he said.

Chekov nodded. "In any case, the warious indigenous species would complicate a holiday," he said. The image changed again, to show a diagram with three line-drawn figures, compared for size: one like a collapsed sack, one vaguely treelike, and one that was merely a squarish dotted outline somewhat taller than the human figure that stood nearby for comparison.

"There are three intelligent species native to the planet," Chekov said. Some glances were exchanged around the table, from those who had as yet heard nothing of this. "This is extremely unusual, as some of you have guessed. So far this is the only planet found by any Federation survey that has so many species living together that were not brought there by some other species, like the Preservers. The First Survey team confirms that they are genuine products of evolution on the planet; the DNA-analog samples taken early on give a better than six-sigma probability to the thesis. One of our mission objectives will be to get absolute confirmation of the evolutionary situation, which is certainly historic in space exploration so far, and which will certainly be actively questioned by the scientific community when we bring our data home."

"We have our honor to defend, hm?" McCoy said from down the table.

"The truth is worth defending, Doctor," Spock said calmly. "As long as it *is* the truth. It is our business to find out."

"The three species show an unusual spread of morphotypes," Chekov said, very calmly continuing and paying no particular attention to the backchat. Kirk smiled a little to himself. "The first one to be contacted—"

The image on the screens changed again. It now showed something that looked surprisingly like a plastic bag full of some clear liquid; but the surface of the bag shimmered with iridescent color, like glass left for years in the sun. "This species," Chekov said, "identifies itself as one of a people called the Ornae—the singular and adjective form appears to be Ornaet. They are one of the first true theriomorphs known to Federation science, even more so than creatures like the Alariins or the amphibian gelformes of Sirius B III. There are apparently about five million of them on the planet, which they describe as a normal and stable population. The creatures' interior, according to the survey team, is pure undifferentiated protoplasm: the outer membrane seems to be a standard semipermeable, such as is possessed by simple one-celled animals like the amoebae. However, the outer skin or pellicle is highly radiation-resistant, and its relative permeability seems to be consciously controllable. It is also completely malleable; the Ornae seem able to take any shape they choose, for limited periods, and they use their own bodies as tools."

"They're not shapechangers, though," Scotty said.

"No; their appearance remains the same, regardless

of the shape they take," Chekov said. "They seem able to absorb energy directly from their surroundings, in any form awailable." He began to grin a bit. One of the younger Ornae took one of the survey team's phasers and ate it. The team member got the phaser back physically undamaged, but completely drained of charge."

Scotty put his eyebrows up at that.

"The survey team found the Ornae friendly and communicative, if a bit obscure," Chekov said. "They weren't sure whether to attribute the obscurity to difficulties with the uncalibrated universal translator, or species-specific difficulties. We're expected to find out which."

McCoy looked interested. "What were they obscure about?"

"The survey team reported most of their difficulties with terms having to do with physicality," Chekov said. "Body shape and so forth. It was thought that polymorphs might have difficulty understanding why an alien didn't change shape as often as they did themselves."

"Makes sense," McCoy said. "Probably the language is at least as flexible: a psychology like that would find it normal for *everything* to change constantly, including symbology. I think we'll be able to find a way to handle it."

"The second species—" The image changed again. This time Kirk found himself looking at something that resembled a small forest—except that he couldn't get rid of the idea that it was looking at him. "This is a Lahit—"

"Singular?" Uhura said in surprise.

"One entity," Chekov said, "yes. These people

20

obviously bear some physical similarity to dendroids like the Lusitanii, but there the likeness ends. The Lusis are individuals; the Lahit are more like a hive economy than anything else. They are vegetable in habit, and move slowly over the face of the planet in large colonies, some of which willingly inhabit the parklands in the Ornaet cities. In many cases, the Ornae seem to create those parklands specifically for them. There are about twenty million Lahit on the planet, which is described as an under-usual population due to some disaster in the recent past, the nature of which the survey team was unable to establish. Each Lahit entity is connected to its own subgroups and to its immediate supergroup by a dendritic system that usually resides under the soil, and moves through it with great rapidity, in the same sort of way used by the sporulating tubules of brachiophytic fungi like the fairy-ring mushrooms. The network of dendrites functions as a nervous system, though the survey team remarks on the apparent slowness of transmission along the network. Asking a Lahit a question can mean waiting a few days for the answer."

"I talk to the trees," Uhura sang softly under her breath, "but they don't listen to me . . ."

A little chuckle went around the table. "Apparently that was pretty much what the survey reported," Chekov said. "Very few of the Lahit would even acknowledge their presence, much less have any kind of conversation with them. But the Ornae seemed to think that the Lahit were somehow more important to the planet than they themselves were. It's another of the puzzles left us to solve."

The image on the screen changed again. "The third species—" said Chekov.

Kirk squinted at his screen. The image there was a vague one—a large, oblong, palely colored shape, seen as if through a fog. "Bad weather that day, Mr. Chekov?" he said.

"No, Keptin. The image was made in full daylight under clear conditions. That is an ;At."

"Say again?" Uhura said to Chekov.

Chekov shook his head. "That's the approved pronunciation of the species' name for themselves—as close as the survey's linguist could get to it, anyway. The IPA orthography is in the full report—maybe you can make better sense of it than I have. Anyway, the ;At are the planet's third species. We have no count of their total numbers, and this is the best image the survey could come up with."

"Some kind of gaseous entity?" Scotty said.

"No, sir. They simply seem not to be *there* sometimes; their physicality is selectively variable. The survey reported that members of the ;At with whom they were having conversations would fade in and out without warning, and without any seeming correlation to the subject being discussed. Images of them seem not to come out, no matter how clearly the entity in question is manifesting."

Chekov sounded a bit embarrassed by what he was having to report. "The survey team," he said, "reports that the ;At received them with great courtesy and were willing to converse with them at great length— much greater than the other two species. However, those conversations were all rather problematic . . . since it seems from the transcripts in the report that the ;At did not believe in the survey party."

There were some bemused glances exchanged around the table at *that* one. "Didn't *believe* in them?" McCoy said. "Like not believing in Santa Claus? Sounds absurd."

Chekov shrugged. "The transcripts repeat that basic thread several times," he said. "One member of the survey party asked the ;At in question whether it doubted the evidence of its senses, and its reply, as closely as the translator could render it, was that 'it always distrusted perception, and if its senses gave it unacceptable data, it exchanged them for new ones.'"

McCoy sat back in his chair with his arms folded and a look of great interest spreading over his face. *Aha,* Kirk thought, pleased, *that's got him.* There was nothing better calculated to catch Bones's fancy than a bizarre new psychology, and this certainly sounded like one.

"No more information was obtainable about the ;At," Chekov said. "Again, the survey party found them sociable and voluble, but also found great difficulty in understanding what they meant. The report suggests that a more advanced or complex translator algorithm may be necessary."

Uhura nodded and began making notes on her datapadd.

"That concludes the survey's report, Keptin," Chekov said.

"Thank you, Mr. Chekov." Kirk looked around the table.

"This mission leaves us with some interesting work to do," Kirk said. "We're well away from the conflicts of more populated areas of the Galaxy, so we should have leisure to concentrate on our work. Starfleet's orders to me indicate that we may stay in the area as long as we require to do a more thorough survey— subject to recall, of course." All around the table, eyes rolled. The *Enterprise* had a way of being dragged out of the most interesting assignments to save someone's bacon halfway across the Milky Way. Everyone was used to it by now, but no one liked it.

"All the same," Kirk said, "I think they may let us be on this one. My orders make it plain that the *Enterprise* was assigned to this mission because of the considerable scientific expertise aboard her. Half of our brief is straight scientific investigation; the Federation scientific community desperately wants all possible information on this world's evolution, on as many of its species as we can catalog, both sentient and nonsentient, and as many informed theories as we can come up with on how this world got this way . . . and why only *this* world, among the tens of thousands of inhabited planets we know. What we discover here, what these species can tell us about themselves, will profoundly affect all the biological sciences. So all the departments of Science aboard ship are going to be stretched to their utmost." McCoy stirred a little in his seat. "I want to remind you all not to let your people overextend themselves," Kirk said. "Tired researchers miss clues that may be right under their noses, and may prove to be vital. I'll be vetting all lab schedules and landing party assignments daily, once we arrive. Please consult Dr. McCoy with any questions you may have."

Heads nodded all around. "The other half of our mission," Kirk said, "is diplomatic. Or at least we hope it will be. The survey merely identified its members as explorers; they were able to get very little actual information about how the planet is administered, how the three species interact with one another, and so forth. Our business is to find out—to make sense of their cultural structures and government, if they have one—and to make formal contact with all three species on the Federation's behalf. We must discover whether they want to be affiliated with us, some or all of them, and to what degree. Also, we must discover whether it's even appropriate to ask them. There is some emphasis in my orders," Kirk said, looking a little grim, "to try to make sure that it *is*. Considering the political implications of this kind of evolutionary situation—whatever they are—the diplomatic people are apparently edgy to have this world in our camp rather than in some other, and have put some pressure on us to that end. Nonetheless, I intend to see to it that this secondary survey is carried out with the utmost probity. What *matters* is that these species be offered a well-informed choice, and left free to make it. I expect all departments to act accordingly."

He paused for a breath or two to think. "One of Science's main tasks will be the correct calibration of the Universal Translator for this planet. Obviously the initial survey team couldn't do more than a quick and dirty calibration, with the time they had to work in. A great deal rests on making sure we have good translation: otherwise much of the 'hearsay' data we collect will be corrupt. And everything in the later stages, especially the diplomacy, will rest on the correctness and completeness of translation, for all three species; we, as well as they, must have the correct data with which to make our choices." He looked at Uhura and Spock. "I expect all the other departments of Science to defer to Linguistics for use of computer time and other necessities. Note it, everyone."

"Noted," several voices murmured.

"With any kind of luck," Kirk said, relaxing a little, "at least two out of the three species will elect to be associated with us, in some way or other, and give us the leisure to know that some other ship can come back and fill in what we miss. But we can't count on it, and the sheer uniqueness of this planet demands that we treat this survey as a once-and-never-again opportunity. Starfleet has kindly used this short layover to install an extra eighty terabytes of storage in the Library computers. I want to come home with that memory *full,* ladies and gentlemen. Be advised. In the worst case, at least we'll have enough raw data to have made the trip worthwhile . . . and found out that little bit more about the Universe that we didn't know. At best, one or more of these species will join us, and after completing the agreement between the Federation and the people of 1212 Muscae, the rest of the mission will degenerate into rubber-chicken banquets. Or rubber-whatever they use on 1212 instead of chicken."

Another chuckle went around. "Any questions?" Kirk said.

"How soon do we get there?" Uhura said.

"Three days. Three days, Scotty?"

"At warp six, aye. Unless you want more."

"What, and deprive the departments of time to get ready? Seems unwise. Three days let it be. Anyone else?"

No one spoke.

"That's the story, ladies and gentlemen," Kirk said. "Dismissed for now. There's an informal reception at 2100 hours, for those of you who have time to attend."

They all rose, all but McCoy. Kirk kept his seat too,

waited until the room cleared and the doors had hissed shut for the last time. "Problems, Bones?" he said. "Was that enough backing?"

"More than enough." McCoy stretched a bit. "Thanks, Jim."

"Something else, then?"

McCoy smiled a bit. "They handed you the hottest potato they could find, didn't they?"

Kirk shrugged. "It's not Starfleet's style to hand you easy jobs once they find you can handle the tough ones," he said.

"I bet I know what your orders looked like, though," McCoy said. "The only commander with sufficient diplomatic and exploratory experience for the job. Incredible importance to the Galaxy. Severe consequences for the Federation if anyone else should acquire influence in this sensitive part of space—"

Not for the first time, Kirk found himself wondering if the command ciphers controlling access to his personal terminal were as secret as he liked to think they were. "Listen, Bones, they're not—"

"Yes, they are."

"Are *what?*" Kirk said. McCoy's favorite mind-reading game always annoyed him.

"Entitled to depend on you to pull their bacon out of the fire *every* time it falls in," McCoy said. —*annoying, especially when he* does *know what I'm thinking, dammit,* Kirk thought. "Jim, want some advice?"

"Is this a free sample, or will you bill me later?"

McCoy snorted. "Jim, listen to me. Just try to relax and enjoy yourself."

Somehow that wasn't the advice he had been expecting. "Oh really?" he said, a little weakly.

27

"Yes. Because for a good while, if I read this mission correctly, you won't have any decisions to make; you won't have enough data to *make* them. Sit back and let your people do their jobs." There was a wicked twinkle in McCoy's eyes. *"We're* going to have the worst work to do on this mission, anyway. Make a change for you."

Kirk laughed softly. "You're always telling me how to do my job . . . now you're telling me how to *not* do it, too?"

"May be the last chance I get for a while," McCoy said. "Psychology and Xenopsych are going to be real busy this mission, from the look of things. Working on the people on 1212 . . . and on our own people, who may have their own problems interacting with them. Culture shock works both ways . . . and always worst the first time."

"I thought you were a surgeon, not a shrink," Kirk said, teasing.

The Doctor looked ironic for the moment. "Probably in a couple of weeks, I'll wish that were true," he said. "Hell, since when did a ship's doctor get to wear just one hat? If our people get busy enough, I may find myself staining microscope slides. It's happened before."

"Not this time, I hope," Kirk said. "Don't *you* over-tire yourself. I might have to relieve you of duty."

"Threats, idle threats," McCoy said, grinning a bit as he got up. "Are you coming down to the rec room later?"

"If I have time," Kirk said, getting up too. "Paper-work."

McCoy rolled his eyes. "What about that administration-free starship they promised us about ten years ago?" he said. "The one where we all have secretaries from telepathic species, who know what we need done without asking us, and do it?"

"They got it worked out, finally," Kirk said. "Then they stuck it in Earth orbit and called it Starfleet Command."

Laughing, they went out together.

Chapter Two

"I CANNOT BELIEVE THIS," McCoy said, first under his breath, then more loudly, for the benefit of his staff: "I can't *believe* this! Lia!"

"Mmm hmm," Lia said from the next room of Sickbay, without much enthusiasm. Possibly this was understandable, since she had been responding to expostulations of this sort for two days now.

"What are you going to do about this damn report from Bio?"

"I'm going to let it sit there until," there was a brief pause as if options were being considered, "someone else does something about it. I'm busy with Uhura's thing at the moment."

McCoy put his head in his hands and groaned. "Can't you get Lieutenant Kerasus or somebody in Linguistics to handle that?"

"Not when Linguistics has sent the translator algorithm to us for a psych assessment."

"Damn," McCoy said, and sat down at his desk again. This did nothing to improve matters, since it merely called to his attention the pile of tapes, datapadds, cassettes, floppies, and other debris all over the top of his normally tidy desk.

He groaned softly and leaned back in his chair. The preliminary work for the mission was spread among departments all over the ship, but one way or another, they all seemed to wind up on his desk for approval or adjustment. The microorganism cataloging and the antibiotic/antigenic survey: well, those would naturally come under Medicine. But spending hour after hour looking at pictures of slides of germs, and wondering which might be biologically active, and which you should have the Lab people culture, was no fun: any more than thinking that should you miss some unprepossessing organism because of a flaw in your thinking, or the way you felt that afternoon, the humanities might be cheated of a pandemic cure for cancer. *Or the common cold,* McCoy thought sourly. And no matter what he did, people were going to have to run all over that planet picking up samples of dirt, and the lab people were going to have to be told which to culture out for likely organisms; and McCoy knew that they were going to rediscover penicillin at least three hundred times on this trip.

Then there was the flora and fauna survey. You would think that would come under pure Science, the Biology department. But no, all the flora on 1212 Muscae, from the simplest to the most complex, were apparently a little on the hyperactive side—*walking trees, for pity's sake, whose good idea was that?*—so all the plants wound up in Xenobiology, and hence in Medicine. *A surgeon I may be,* McCoy thought, *but a tree surgeon?*

31

And then the linguistics work; no translator program could begin to work without some knowledge of the psychology of the species in question—not that the survey team had done more than give the slightest inkling of what any one of the three species in question liked to think about, or the way they did it. *Who picked that survey team, anyway? Some damn civil servant with thinking like a New York sidewalk, all concrete and no abstracts. About as much depth to the interviews as a frog pond in August, no invitation to introspection or analysis, nothing! 'How do you get around?' 'What do you eat?' Dammit, no species lives by bread alone—*

And that was just the beginning. Atmospheric surveys, taxonomy, etiology of local diseases, once they managed to talk enough to the local species to find out what their diseases were—once they figured out *how* to talk to the species—if the species even *wanted* to—

McCoy rubbed his head. "Nurse," he said, not for an audience this time, "my brain hurts."

"It'll have to come out," Lia said from the doorway. She was standing there with her hands full of tape cassettes: a slender little curly-haired woman, her normal cheerful look very much muted at the moment. It looked rather as if it had worn off.

"Take it," McCoy said. "Lobotomy sounds like just about what I need."

"We're having a special," Lia said. "Prefrontal with a ten percent discount on a vasectomy."

"You just shut your mouth," McCoy said, straightening up a bit. "Uppity nurses anyway. Pretty soon you'll start thinking you run this place."

Lia merely smiled. "You asked about the crew

health summary," she said. "It's done. Do you want to read it?"

"Should I? Will it tell me anything I want to know? Or don't know already?"

"No."

"Then sign the damn thing and send it to the Captain. Let *him* read about what the crew brought home from leave." He snorted. "Athlete's foot! Only place you should be able to catch *that* these days is in a museum."

Lia looked resigned. "Are you happy with what you've got for Linguistics?" McCoy said after a moment.

Lia nodded. "It should do for the time being. We need to get someone skilled in interviewing techniques down there in a hurry, with the first party, if possible. The present Translator algorithms are pretty shaky without more verbs and without the causal relationships tables filled in. If these species *believe* in causal relationships, and I'm beginning to have my doubts, especially in the ;At's case."

She made a sort of click before the vowel sound. McCoy cocked an ear. "Is *that* how you pronounce it?"

"Don't ask me," Lia said. "That's how most of the survey people pronounced it most of the time. But that's hardly a guarantee of anything. I want to hear one of those creatures say it." She paused and added, "If hearing's even involved. Some of those audio records are pretty strange. Staticky."

McCoy nodded and sighed. "I'll have a listen later . . . things are a bit busy now. Anything else I need to know?"

"Lieutenant Silver's in for his physical," she said. McCoy raised his eyebrows. "That bone still behaving itself?"

"Good knit," Lia said, "no sign of metastasization or edema."

"Keep an eye on it. His marrow's gone funny on us once before."

"Want me to do a broad-spectrum histological on it?"

McCoy nodded. "Go on," he said, "let me get back to this. Spock's going to be jumping down my neck for this damn taxonomy proposal in a matter of minutes."

Lia went off about her business. McCoy sighed and turned to his own data terminal again. "Restart," he said. "Display previous listing."

The screen came up with a long list of Greekish and Latinate names, and the desk comm whistled stridently, both at the same moment. "Damn," McCoy said, and hit the button. "McCoy!"

"Spock here, Doctor—"

"Of *course* you're there," McCoy said, with exaggerated politeness that at the moment he definitely didn't feel. Where *else* would you be? I'm not done yet; you can have it in an hour."

There was a longish silence on the other end. *"Doctor,* Spock said, *"I was not inquiring about the taxonomic parameters list."*

"That's a relief."

"My interest was in your assessment of the survey's fungal data in the preliminary microbiological catalog."

"Spock, my boy," McCoy said, "between you and me, I don't think those survey people would know a

34

toadstool if one jumped up on them and gave them warts. There's one spot here"—for a moment he riffled through the cassettes on his desk, then gave it up—"never mind the reference, but there's at least one mycete listed as four discrete species, and another three of what look like different species to *me* seem to have been mistaken for different sporulating forms of the same one. Heaven knows how many times this kind of thing happened in the one prelim catalog—not to mention all the others. And since the divergent-evolution problem makes it crucial to tell the difference between mutative and allomorphic forms on this particular planet, I think we may have to reassess almost everything the survey team gave us. But certainly *this* report is best suited to somebody's compost heap."

There was another brief silence. McCoy braced himself. Then Spock said, *"Doctor, we are in perfect agreement. Am I to understand that you are finding your department somewhat overloaded at the moment?"*

McCoy let a breath out. "Spock, that would be a correct understanding. To say the least."

"In examining the assignment rosters," Spock said, *"it would seem possible to reassign some Science personnel to Medicine, once we have made planetfall and had time to do some initial assessment. Perhaps two or three days after arrival."*

Now is when I need them, McCoy thought. *But Science needs them too, and needs them now; the study and classification plans they're making now will determine what they do for the next several weeks. . . .* "That would be very nice of you, Spock," he said, "very nice indeed."

There was another of those brief silences. *"It would only be logical, Doctor. Nice is—"*

"Oh, for gosh sakes, shut up and go count electrons or something," McCoy said, though he was smiling a little. "That'll do just fine, Spock. Anything else?"

"No. Spock out."

McCoy shook his head and picked up the offending report, tossing its cassette off his desk into the antique "wastepaper basket" his daughter had sent him. He stared at it for a moment.

"Doctor," Lia called from the next room, "do you want to come have a look at this histo?"

Not really, he thought. "Coming," he said, and went to check the bone marrow test.

The planet was even prettier than its images had made it look. They came out of warp on the far side of its system, so that its tiny far-off disc shone like an evening star in the slightly brassy light of its primary.

Kirk sat there and watched idly as Sulu worked the ship in close, slipping past several of the system's inner planets that were in fortunate conjunction. This approach wasn't absolutely necessary, but Kirk admired the fact that Sulu had done it, and wondered whether he was thinking strictly of the scenic value of such an approach, or the scientific opportunities . . . for Spock was even now getting spectroanalysis on each of the inner worlds as they passed. *Knowing Sulu,* Kirk thought, *he probably did it for both reasons.*

Two of the three inner planets were rocky and barren; the third had an atmosphere, but it was one of the Venusian type, full of reducing gases at high pressure. Spock dropped a radar-mapping buoy into the nitric-acid soup of its atmosphere in passing, and then turned his attention to the fourth planet out, their object.

"Flyspeck," Sulu said, under his breath, and chuckled.

"Pardon, Mr. Sulu?" said Kirk.

Sulu laughed. "It's a nickname, Captain," he said. "A lot of the Science people are using it. Because the system is so small."

Kirk chuckled too. Musca, the star's constellation of record, was Latin for *fly;* the name was one of the original ones given the constellations as seen from Earth by the old astronomer Bayer. The tradition of Latin naming had been continued when the explorers had hit the Southern Hemisphere, but when they ran out of animals and insects, some of the later names had been comical. "Just as well we're in this part of the sky," Kirk said. "It's harder making puns out of words that mean things like *airpump.*"

"Yes indeed," Sulu said. "Planetosynchronous altitude, Captain. Shall I hold here, or take her in on standard orbit?"

"Mr. Spock?" Kirk said. "Anything you need from this orbit?"

"No, sir." The Vulcan stood up and looked calmly at the screen.

"Standard then, Mr. Sulu."

"Aye aye."

They slipped in close to the planet, began to circle it. The seas were about twice as blue as the images had made them seem; the clouds in the high atmosphere caught the slightly golden color of the planet's star, looking less like clouds than swirls of Jersey cream. The continents, as they passed over them, looked almost impossibly verdant.

"A lot of nitrogen in that atmosphere?" Kirk said. "Or CO2?"

Spock shook his head. "No more than usual. The visual effect is not due to diffraction. I would speculate that the forms of chlorophyll or phyllanalog here are more intensely colored than those on the usual M-type planet. There are probably cellular or chemical differences that will be quite fascinating, once we have time to look into them."

Chekov, next to Sulu at the helm, was monitoring preliminary mapping at his console. "No signs of cities," he said, sounding slightly puzzled. "No energy output. Some geothermal—"

"The cities were quite small," Kirk said, "according to the report, and the lifeform calibration that the survey gave us was very tentative—I seem to remember the report stating that calibrations they made one day sometimes didn't work the next."

"Correct," Spock said. "There may have been a problem with their instrumentation; we shall have to look into that. Our own equipment is functioning properly, of course."

"Of course," Kirk said. Beneath them another continent gave way to another sea, impossibly blue; then they slipped around through the planet's terminator into its night side. A little moon looked down greenish silver on the clouds there. Its light was the only thing on the night side that shone.

Kirk nodded to himself. Another day, another world; but the same old excitement was there again, new again, as it always was . . . thank Heaven. "All right, Mr. Sulu," he said, "give Mr. Chekov a mapping orbit until he and Mr. Spock are satisfied with the results. Then standard equatorial. Mr. Spock," he said, "have you got your First Contact party picked out?"

"Yes, Captain." Spock stepped down by the center seat, handed Kirk a padd.

Kirk scanned down the list. "Hm. Kerasus for Linguistics, good; Morrison and Fahy from Science; Chekov for Exo—" He nodded at Spock. "That's fine. Pinpoint one of the Ornaet settlements the survey mentions—they seem the most approachable of the three species at the moment—and have the landing party go say hello."

"The settlement has already been chosen," Spock said. "I will meet them in the Transporter room."

Kirk nodded, waved Spock away. "We'll be watching," he said. "Good luck."

Spock nodded gravely, and headed out. Kirk rubbed his hands on his pants a bit. Starfleet had been getting quite outspoken these days about Captains going down with first landing parties, even when there had been a prelim survey through the neighborhood in the recent past. His orders had been explicit: his value to this mission was primarily in terms of data synthesis—seeing what happened, trying to make sense of it—and in his diplomatic capacity. No one else aboard ship but the commander was empowered to work out the Inclusion Agreement with one or more of the indigenous species. He was to sit tight until it was plain that things were safe, and then to confine his visits downplanet to those necessary for diplomacy's sake.

At least, as far as the Fleet people could tell. Kirk smiled a little. There was always room to cheat a *little*.

The Bridge doors hissed open again. "Pretty place,"

39

McCoy's voice said, a moment later, over Kirk's shoulder.

Kirk looked over at him in mild surprise. "Thought you were going down with the landing party," he said. "I would have thought you wouldn't want Spock to mess it up."

McCoy chuckled. "Not very likely," he said, and rubbed his eyes for a moment. "Nope, got too much work on my plate at the moment. I'll go down in a day or two."

Kirk frowned a little. "How much sleep did you get last night?"

McCoy's eyes opened wide. "Now don't you take that tone with *me,* Jim. I bet I got more than you did."

Kirk smiled slightly and nodded. "Probably you did," he said. It had always been a problem for him—not a serious one, of course—that excitement at the prospect of seeing a new world tended to keep him up later than usual, the night just before. All the same— "You've been working too hard," he said.

"Not yet, I haven't been," McCoy said. "In about two days, I will have, though. *Then* you can yell at me, and I'll envy you your nice easy job here."

Kirk choked genteelly. "Easy—!"

McCoy laughed at that, too, then. "Well, everything's relative, I guess."

The communicator whistled. *"Transporter room,"* it said, *"Lieut. Renner here. Landing party reports ready to beam down, Captain."*

"Beam them down, Lieutenant," Kirk said.

The Bridge screen came on just then and showed them the images being transmitted by Ensign Morrison's tricorder: Lieutenant Renner behind the Transporter console, making a few last adjustments, then slipping the levers upward; a storm of glitter as the effect blanked out the room; and then the glitter fading.

Through it the screen showed them all what seemed to be a clearing in a forest. Bright yellowish sunlight came lancing down among the wide branches to lie in bright pools on a ground surface that alternated between what looked like scuffed heaps of leaf mold and other material greener than the greenest grass Kirk had ever seen. The trees were all impossibly green, even to the trunks, which were quite smooth, like some kinds of birch. One after another, the landing party stepped into sight and looked around.

Spock produced his tricorder and began to scan in the traditional manner. The others moved around slowly, touching a branch here, a plant there. The woods were very quiet, except for a soft scratching sound in the distance that might have been the stridulation of some insect—but Kirk immediately put that thought away; on a new planet, there was no predicting anything at all without data, and your suppositions could kill you without warning.

"Readings," Spock said softly to Chekov and Kerasus, who had their tricorders out as well.

"Life signs, sir," Chekov said. "I think. Two one four mark six. Not much movement."

Spock studied his tricorder. "Ms. Kerasus," he said.

The tall, cool-looking young woman nodded. "I concur. The readings are very mixed—animal and vegetable. But they would be."

"Correct. Landing party, let us work toward that bearing. There appears to be a rough path here."

"Looks like a deer trail," Morrison said to those

watching on the Bridge. "Occasional broken branches —about waist height. A fair amount of traffic, I'd say."

They worked through the woods. Kirk sat back and watched as the green-gold lighting changed almost completely to gold. The landing party came out into a clearing and paused there for a moment, looking around.

What the—Kirk thought, for in the middle of the clearing stood what seemed to be a large amorphous lump of crystal about the size of a shuttlecraft.

Until it moved.

The lump of *crystal* came apart into about fifty pieces, which began to roll and hop toward the landing party with the most peculiarly fluid kind of motion that Kirk had seen in a long time. There were a few gasps around the Bridge, but Kirk ignored them, wondering for a moment about what the creatures were using for musculature, since they were supposed to be nothing but protoplasm. They certainly weren't having any trouble moving, though this particular brand of locomotion looked mostly as if thick plastic bags were pouring themselves along the ground, and occasionally doing a forward roll to make a little better speed.

"No phasers," Spock said softly to the landing party. They nodded.

The tumbling, pouring shapes slowed down as they came close to the landing party, surrounding them. Spock looked down at them with his usual calm— none of them came much above his knee—and waited to see what would happen. Slowly a circle formed around the landing party, and the creatures settled where they were, shifting or wiggling slightly.

Morrison turned slowly to show the circle of creatures, like so many lumps of iridescent glass, but quivering and alive, and thinking who knew what.

"Good morning," Spock said. Kirk took a second to flash a grin at Bones; sometimes Spock's formality could tempt you to laugh. "Are you members of the species called the Ornae?"

There was another tremor of movement through the layered circles of creatures, and then a sound: something scratchy, not quite the "insect" sound that Kirk had heard before. The Bridge's Translator circuitry immediately cut in and rendered the sound as oddly high-pitched laughter.

One of the creatures in the front circle shook itself all over and, still shaking, moved very, very slowly toward Spock. He didn't move a muscle. The creature put out a long slender pseudopod, gleaming in the sunshine like suddenly blown glass, and poked Spock's boot with it. Then it made the scratchy sound again, more laughter, and said a word:

"Gotcha!"

It jumped back to its place. All the other creatures began to echo the scratch-laughter. Spock looked around him with mild bemusement. "Captain," he said, "I suspect we have found a kindergarten at recess, or something similar."

Kirk laughed. "Whatever," he said, "they're certainly Ornae."

"That they are." Spock bent down a bit to the Ornaet who had gotcha'd him and said, "We are visitors here. Do you suppose you might take us to see the same people who greeted the last visitors who looked like us?"

There was more scratchy laughter at this, and some

of the Ornae began to shuffle out of the way of the landing party, opening a path for them toward one side of the clearing. "Thank you," Spock said gravely, and headed in that direction. The Ornaet who had spoken to him went hopping and rolling alongside him, bumping him occasionally to show him the right way to go.

They watched the Ornae lead the landing party into the woods again, onto another path, a wider one this time, with more broken greenery at the sides, seeming to indicate a heavier traffic load. The landing party was led through several more clearings, though none of them had Ornae in them; then they burst out into one last clearing, the biggest they had seen so far. And this one had structures in it, the size of small houses; more iridescent glass built into surprisingly graceful structures—curving towers and spires, glass-webbed domes, open-roofed mazes of uncertain purpose. More of the Ornae moved in and out of the buildings as they approached.

McCoy let out a soft breath. "The report didn't say anything about buildings like that," he said.

"Indeed not, Doctor," Spock said. "I suspect the half was not told us . . . as I mentioned to you."

Kirk made a mental note to compose a sharp memo to Starfleet about the report from the original survey team. The last three days of reports from the *Enterprise*'s various departments had been making it plain that the survey report had been about as incomplete and error-ridden as one might imagine. *What are they sending these people for if not to make our job a little easier? Heaven knows what dangers they missed on this planet that we might have to deal with before we leave . . .*

"Holy smoke," McCoy said suddenly, "look at *that.*"

Kirk did . . . and understood the exclamation. One of the buildings had quietly begun to come apart; its tallest spire, some fifty feet above the ground level, was slipping down around the remaining structure of the spire as slowly and gracefully as a drop of glycerine . . . but a drop containing about twenty gallons.

"They build their buildings out of *themselves,*" McCoy said, delighted, almost reverent. "Jim, this is incredible. Is it a permanent job? Do they take turns?"

"Ssh," Kirk said, watching the single Ornaet slip down the structure built of its presently less mobile fellows. It came to rest in front of the landing party, at Spock's feet, and looked up at him. Visibly looked up at him, by putting up two eyestalks out of what had been a blank smooth curve of body.

"Greet," it said.

Spock's eyebrow went right up.

"Greetings to you as well," he said, giving the creature just a fraction of an inch's worth of bow. "I am Commander Spock of the Federation starship USS *Enterprise.*"

"Federation," the creature said, and the translator gave the word a slightly meditative tone: "mmf."

Spock looked over at Lt. Janice Kerasus, whose big dark eyes were thoughtful. As head of Linguistics, she was perhaps best equipped of anyone on board to understand the vagaries of the Universal Translator. But this situation, with the calibration only half done, and apparently incorrectly done as well, was likely to be twitchy for days, perhaps months. Heaven knew what they were saying to these creatures; Heaven

45

knew (until they heard a great deal more of it) what the creatures were saying to them. And the whole mission rode on that point.

"Our landing party," Spock said calmly: *he* wasn't sweating. "Lieutenant Kerasus, Ensign Morrison, Ensign Chekov."

"Mmf," said the Ornaet. "Greet, greet, greet. Federation?"

"Yes," Spock said, as the others nodded or rumbled or spoke their own greetings: "We are all with the same organization. Our commanding officer has sent us to make initial contact with you. We should like to visit your planet for a while, and participate in discussions with you, if you have no objections."

The Ornaet stretched its eyestalks a little farther up toward Spock; there was something quizzical about the expression . . . and Kirk warned himself again against anthropomorphization. "Only objections ;At," it said.

Kirk raised his eyebrows. This was news to him. McCoy glanced at him, and the quizzical expression on the Doctor's face was not in any danger of misinterpretation. "Uh oh," he said.

"Let's not panic just yet," Kirk murmured. "A bit early for that."

"Welcome," the Ornaet said then. "Stay, talk, be here, yes." It let its eyes plop back into its main body, rather as if holding them up so high for so long had been a strain.

"We thank you," Spock said, with a nod of acknowledgment. "We would also like to examine you and your people, to see how you are like us, and how different. The examinations are noninvasive. May we do this?"

The Ornaet goggled up at Spock again, though without putting the eyestalks up quite so far this time. "Examine," it said thoughtfully. "Yes. Examine you?"

Spock glanced at Kerasus as if to ask silently whether she understood the creature's syntax in the same way as he did. She nodded. "Yes," Spock said, "most certainly. Gentlemen?" he said, to Chekov and Morrison.

"Of course, sir," Morrison said, and "Certainly," said Chekov.

Next to Kirk, McCoy twitched slightly. "Like to know what they're going to be examined with first," he said softly, for Kirk alone to hear. "Don't know how noninvasive *their* techniques are."

"Spock will keep an eye on things," Kirk said. "So will we. And it's a fair request."

McCoy sighed and nodded. "Uhura," he said, "make sure their tricorder readouts go straight to Sickbay. I want to get a running start."

"No problem, Doctor."

"Can't imagine how they even move," McCoy said softly. "The report said that was undifferentiated protoplasm. Doesn't have anything like enough ATP or analog for motility on this scale—"

"The report said a lot of things," Kirk said, "and I'm going to have a word with Starfleet about that. Never mind it now."

He was more interested in what was going on on the screen; understandable, as the landing party was led into that astonishing structure. The building was not terribly big inside, by human standards; it was perhaps the size of the briefing room, with a rather low ceiling. But the relative transparency of the walls kept the effect inside light and airy, as if one were inside a room built of glass blocks. The only difference, of course, was that there were no blocks, but the rounded shapes of Ornae, each stretched or compressed to fit the particular spot it occupied, a sort of bas-relief mural of flowing rounded shapes. And all the shapes were *looking* at the landing party, with eyes either hidden inside their bulk, or projecting. It would be enough to give a person of nervous disposition a serious case of the jitters.

Spock, of course, was not even slightly concerned with nerves. He sat down in the middle of the room's floor, unslung his tricorder, and started making fine adjustments in it, while still talking calmly to the Ornaet who had led him in. The other members of the landing party strolled around, struck up their own conversation, and examined their surroundings. It began to be difficult to follow what was going on with the party as a whole, since only Morrison's tricorder was transmitting, and he was concentrating on examining the structure of the walls at the moment. The Bridge screen became dominated by the image of several pairs (or triplets) of shiny black Ornaet eyes staring at the tricorder, or poking it gently with pseudopodia.

Kirk sat back and rubbed his eyes a bit. "This is going to be fascinating," he said, "to coin a phrase."

McCoy sighed. "You said a mouthful. I'd better get down there and make sure they're getting the data I need. What those critters are using for energy transport, I *can't* imagine . . ."

"Let me know when you find out," Kirk said. "I've got to sit tight for a good while yet, otherwise certain people at Fleet will have my britches for breakfast."

"Poor Jim," McCoy said. "The burdens of duty. Having to sit in a nice soft chair and watch the rest of us run around and bust our—"

"Don't you get started," Kirk said. "Life's hard enough. Get your body down there, and have fun."

"Fun!" Bones snorted, and headed out of the Bridge.

Kirk sat back, and slowly, slowly, began to smile.

The medical side of the situation was turning into a circus, that was all it was. People just could *not* function without close supervision anymore. McCoy didn't know what they were teaching them in school these days.

"Come on, Mr. Chekov," he said to the air in his office, as he started flinging together a rock-bottom kit of the things he would need downplanet. "Let Lieutenant Kerasus handle the verb problem for the time being. We've got other fish to fry. I'm going to be down there in ten minutes, and if you haven't got waiting there for me a group serology analysis, a tegument series with scrapes, a neural series with pertinent EEG, and a percussion-and-auscultation set—"

"No problem, Doctor," Chekov said cheerfully.

McCoy snorted genially. "See to it. I'll be there in ten minutes. McCoy out."

From the next room, Lia called, "Do you want me to come down and give you a hand?"

"No, thanks," McCoy said, picking up an inverpalliator, considering it, and then tossing it back in its drawer and pulling out a miniature polariophthalmoscope instead. "The Captain hasn't authorized

49

any other people downplanet but department heads until the Translator is better calibrated. Doesn't want to multiply the possible errors."

"Sounds like your advice," Lia said, peering around the corner of the door.

"It was."

"Just another excuse to overwork yourself, I see," she said.

"No, indeed," McCoy said, closing his little black bag, then opening it again and tossing in a radio-laparoscope, and a tongue depressor. "You get your work done here, and make sure all this data is safe."

Lia sighed. It was plain she had heard this sort of thing often enough before, and had learned there was no use in trying to argue with it. "Have a nice time, then," she said.

McCoy grunted, picked up his little black bag and headed for the Transporter room.

He found Spock still sitting on the floor of what seemed to be the Ornae's main building in this clearing. Scan had since found many more of the clearings, with similar structures; but there were apparently also structures here and there that were made of local wood and stone. *One of the other species?* McCoy thought. *Or not? Why would sentient trees need houses? And the third species is supposed to be nonphysical. Well, one thing at a time—*

"Ah, Doctor," Spock said, glancing up from his tricorder. "I wondered whether you would find time to join us."

"Didn't have much choice," McCoy said, "data is coming in at such a miserable damn trickle—"

Spock gave him a look more of pity than anything

else—if a Vulcan would in fact admit to pity. McCoy suspected that Spock might, as long as *he* was involved. "You mean *medical* information," Spock said. "We have been giving more attention to linguistics at the moment, I fear—"

"I'll just bet you have. How's it going, Lieutenant?" McCoy said over his shoulder.

Janice Kerasus glanced up from her own tricorder, which the Ornaet she was talking to was examining with interest. "I need more verbs," she said, sounding a bit desperate.

"So do we all, my dear," McCoy said, "so do we all." He strolled over toward Chekov, pausing a moment next to Morrison. "How're we doing?"

"I'm being examined, this lad says," said Morrison, from where he sat crosslegged on the floor. Sitting, if that was the word, across from him, was an Ornaet that seemed to be rolled right up into a ball, with no eyes or other features showing. *"I* can't feel anything."

"Don't complain," McCoy said. "At least, don't phrase it like that. You don't know what they use to test lack of sensation here. Might be a bit solider than a reflex hammer. Well, Mr. Chekov?"

"Here's what you wanted, sir," he said.

"Mmf," McCoy said, as he squatted down beside Chekov and began running down the list of readouts. The results of the group serology tests he had asked Chekov for were confusing, to say the least. The creatures barely had a circulatory system per se, so there was no telling exactly how much of the fluid running around in it was perfusion material, and how much was just temporarily fluid, having been solid "muscle" material a little while before. McCoy had seen a few protoplasmic creatures in his time, but few quite so undifferentiated as this. Usually by the time a being got to this size, it had managed to develop at least a little multicellular structure. The situation was puzzling, but it was probably also grounds to write another paper. *Poor Dieter,* McCoy thought, smiling slightly, *he thought they got upset about that last paper! These people are going to set the xeno crowd on their ear.* "Hmm," he said again, scrolling past the obscure serology results and looking at the tegument test and scrape instead.

"Hmm," the creature said to him, quite plainly. McCoy glanced at Chekov, then at the Ornaet. "Sorry about that, son," he said, "I've been ignoring you. McCoy's my name; I'm a doctor."

The Ornaet said something scratchy, which the translator rendered as, "What son?"

"Doctor," Kerasus called from across the room, "for pity's sake, key your translator to overlink to mine, will you? I can use the extra vocabulary."

"Right." He made an adjustment to his tricorder and then turned back to the Ornaet. *"Son* is a term of affection," he said. "You know, when you like somebody?"

There was a pause, and the Ornaet said, "Like?" It bumped McCoy's leg from one side, like a friendly cat.

"That's right. Or like this. May I touch you?" he said, catching himself before actually doing it.

"Touch, yes."

He very much wanted to, having seen the first part of the tegument report. McCoy patted the Ornaet's hide in a friendly fashion. "There," he said, "that's one of the ways we show we're friendly to each other."

"Friendly, yes!" said the Ornaet cheerfully. It put

out a blunt rounded pseudopod and patted McCoy back.

He chuckled a bit and stroked that beautiful iridescent hide. *Hide* was a misnomer, of course, since the scrapes reported that the creature's tegument wasn't any more multicellular than the rest of it. It was one thick piece of selectively permeable membrane, no different than what separated one blood cell, or skin, or muscle cell in a human, from another. It was just about five thousand times thicker. *Now how did this evolve?* he thought. *How is this tissue kept correctly perfused, not to mention fed? No vascular structure. Then again, if you posit permeable-membrane behavior, any spot in it has access to enough fluid—after all, it's all just sloshing around in there. But at the same time it doesn't make sense—*

"Do you have a name?" McCoy said, turning a bit to tell Chekov's tricorder to scroll down to the next set of readings.

"Name?"

"You know: what others call you." He stopped to look at the neural series. It made even less sense than the tegument test. "The way they call me McCoy."

The Ornaet made another scratchy noise, once that didn't translate. *Oh boy,* McCoy thought, since that noise could mean either that the creature's name had no equivalent in any language known to the Translator, or that it had misunderstood his question and said something else that the Translator wasn't able to handle. "Hmm," McCoy said. "Would you mind repeating that?"

The Ornaet produced the scratchy noise again, exactly the same as before. "Well then," McCoy said, "you won't mind if I call you Hhch, bearing in mind that that's the best I can do with that noise you just made, and I have no idea what my pronunciation's like, and I don't know how well you're able to understand me, or whether that's even your name to begin with. Pleased to meet you, anyway."

The Ornaet bumped him again, perhaps by way of acknowledgment. "What do you call this part of you, Hhch?" McCoy said, patting the creature's hide once more.

The Ornaet made another sound. "Skin, would that be?" McCoy said, pulling up a bit of skin from his own forearm to illustrate.

"Yes, skin," said Hhch.

"There's one for you, Kerasus," he said, and went back to looking at the readouts. "Now then, let's see what the rest of your insides are like. Good God, son, a potato has more of an EEG than you do. But you obviously think and move, and you're a carbon-based life form. What are you using instead of bioelectricity? Unless you're all chemical neurotransport, like a Denebian? That wouldn't make any sense, not with your physical structure. Such as it is."

"I have structure," said the Ornaet, rather suddenly. McCoy looked at it, wondering exactly what it meant.

"You have indeed, Hhch, my lad. But not like anything I've seen in *this* month of Sundays. Here, Chekov," McCoy said, feeling around behind him, "do me a favor and do a chemical study. That looks like a neurotransmitter site to me, you see that microstructure there?—no, on the next screen—right —put the molecular analysis module on that and see if there are any compounds at the end of that structure that look willing to unravel. Or unwilling," he added, bemused. "Anything goes in this lad's insides, it looks like. Heavens, what a report I'm going to write . . ."

"Doctor," Spock said from across the room, where he was still talking to the Ornaet who had first greeted them, "to write a successful report, one must first understand what one is writing about—at least well enough to form theories that have a chance of standing up."

"You just be quiet now, Spock," McCoy said, feeling cheerful for the first time since the mission had started. "By the time it comes time to start writing, you can bet I'll have a few theories." *I dearly hope,* he thought.

Spock raised an eyebrow and said no more to McCoy, but went back to his conversation with the Ornaet. McCoy smiled and turned back to his work. "Now then," he said to Hhch, "let's see what kind of nerves you've got. . . ."

"Where's Dr. McCoy?" Kirk said, looking up and down the table in the briefing room with some surprise.

It was late evening, ship's time. The landing party had returned some hours before, and another one had been sent down to do surveys on the local flora and other nightside activities. All the members of the original party were around the table now, with their department heads, all but McCoy. "Lieutenant Burke," Kirk said, "where is he?"

She looked flustered. "Captain, the last I heard from him, about an hour ago, he was still down on the planet's surface. He knew when the meeting was, and told me he'd be here for it. I assumed he was going to meet me here."

Kirk sighed. This was something he'd had to deal with before, in McCoy; he might complain about overwork for his department, or other departments aboard ship, but he didn't even think about how he drove himself. Kirk touched the communications switch on the table and said, "Bridge? Lieutenant Brandt."

"Sir," the evening communications officer's voice came back.

"Find Dr. McCoy. We're waiting on him down here."

"Yes, sir."

Kirk sat back. "We can at least do some of the preliminaries. Spock? The diplomatic situation, as it stands."

Spock folded his hands. "Sir, as we knew, serious efforts must wait until the Translator is better calibrated. But we are certainly better off tonight than we were with the information from the survey report, and our data is of a much finer degree of accuracy." Kirk smiled; there was Spock making his position clear. No one aboard more thoroughly loathed inaccurate data.

"I spent most of my time downplanet attempting to refine our knowledge of the Ornae's concept of themselves and their relationship with the other sentient species on the planet," Spock said, "with special attention to anything we might be able to discover about their organizational and political structures. There is a great deal more to discover—waiting again, as I said, on the improvement of the Translator

56

algorithms—but briefly, I believe we can rely on the following information. First of all, the Ornae seem to perceive almost everything as fluid: relationships, language, as was mentioned before, and structures both physical and nonphysical. They are quite surprised by our rigidity, and it was my sense that they find us not necessarily unacceptable, but certainly rather abnormal. However, they have what for us would be an unusually accepting nature, for beings that have never until recently seen another sentient species—possibly again a function of their own fluidity and the way it affects their thinking. They do not mind us being as rigid as we are, but they do look narrowly at us, expecting us at any moment to give up our present physical forms for something different."

"I hate to disappoint them," Kirk said. "They're going to have to deal with it. Does it seem like a problem to you?"

"It does not," said Spock. "There will be problems enough elsewhere, I should think. After some discussion, it became plain that these beings have no organizational structure anything like ours. No one rules the planet: decision making is strictly a personal matter, which is probably wise, since anyone may change shapes or plans at any given moment. There are periods of cooperation, as we saw in the *buildings* down on the planet—structures for which I have as yet been unable to discover a purpose. These creatures seem to have no need for shelter in the classic sense. Their environment is generally unable to harm them, and they seem to need no protection from it. But at any rate, each individual decides whether to be part of a community or not; they have little influence over one another, and none over the other species, whom they describe with words for which we have as yet no referents."

"Does the tone seem friendly?" Uhura said from down the table.

"Difficult to tell," Spock said. "We have not yet enough vocabulary information to do the autoemote calibration on the translator. It may be some days yet. These people are not purposely obfuscatory, but their mindset is very different indeed from the hominid, and common ground will take a while to establish."

Uhura nodded.

"The Ornae," Spock said, "seem to have no concept of work or the need for it. They survive apparently by direct energy acquisition from the surrounding environment, though we are as yet uncertain as to the mechanism by which they achieve this. They do not eat, drink or excrete; they need no shelter, as I have said; besides accidental trauma, there really appears to be nothing on the planet that can affect them adversely. They have no physical needs as we normally consider them. They seem to have a rich social life, but as to what *does* occupy their days, we have little sense as yet. They are not idle, by any means. But most of the concerns that we find important, I suspect will seem useless or foolish to them. This will of course affect the diplomatic outcome somewhat."

Somewhat, Kirk thought ruefully. *What incentives to community do you offer a species that doesn't need anything, and doesn't understand why you do?*

"I should take it from here, I think," Uhura said. Spock nodded at her to let her know he was finished for the moment. "Captain, their language, as much of it as we've got so far, makes it plain that the Ornae would be a wonderful addition to the Federation—if we could just persuade them to join. These people have a higher verb density in their spoken language than *any* species in the Galaxy. Given differences in sentence structure, the relative density is something like ten verbs to every two nouns. Their *pronouns* are all verbs—which I suppose shouldn't surprise us, when you consider that these people make tools and buildings out of themselves. They cannot imagine *not* acting on their environment. Which begs the question, how *do* they act on it?—since they don't need to eat, drink, or work. Or apparently to sleep, either."

Burke looked thoughtful. "That rich social life, maybe. They act on each other."

"So it seems. That building behavior we saw today may be some indication of it. Or they act on the other species."

Lt. Kerasus nodded. "When we started getting onto the interspecific topics," she said, "we got a whole flood of new verbs, more than we could handle—"

"You asked for more verbs," said McCoy as he came in, "you got them. Better watch what you ask for. Sorry for being late, everyone."

"Sit down, Bones," Kirk said. "We're not that far along." *He looks awful,* Kirk thought. McCoy looked drawn—the look that Kirk had learned to recognize as the dehydration of someone who hadn't stopped for food or drink for some hours.

Kerasus smiled a bit ruefully at McCoy. "You're right about that, anyway," she said. "The interspecific verbs were of great complexity and length—verbal action piled on action, so that a whole sentence's worth of activity takes place in one concept."

"Lieutenant," Kirk said, "how close are we to a

level of translation that we can trust enough to start making some advances on the diplomatic side?"

Kerasus and Uhura looked at one another, then in unison shook their heads. "I'd be lying if I gave you any concrete time or date," Uhura said. "Sir, we need a great deal more vocabulary before we'll be ready to talk about anything more advanced than the weather."

"Well," Kirk said, "we can't rush this, so do what needs doing, in your own time. Doctor," he said, "doubtless you were deep in data gathering, and must have something fascinating to tell us."

"Well," McCoy said, glancing at the datapadd he had brought in with him, and then pushing it away as if annoyed with it, "fascinating it is, but not necessarily illuminating. The Ornae have one of the most mutable physiologies I've ever seen or heard of. I carried out four examinations on the same being— each about three hours after the exam before it—and major portions of its interior physiology changed between each examination and the one before. Energy transport mechanisms, plasma flow, neural currents, you name it. I was trying to discover whether this is a voluntary or involuntary change, but the good creature seems not to know the difference, or believe in it. Whether this is a translator problem or not, I don't know." He glanced at Uhura and Kerasus.

They both shook their heads again. "Doctor," Kerasus said, "we've been chasing that question in circles too. The Ornaet idea of causality is peculiar enough to begin with. They seem to think they are the cause of everything that happens to them. Even things that they didn't know about, and couldn't have. Like the arrival of the original survey party . . . and our own." She chuckled. "They were surprised to see us, but they told us they had made us come. Or something to that effect: without more vocabulary and more feeling for the verb structure, it's still hard to tell whether that's what they actually mean, or whether we've just misplaced a subject/object pair."

McCoy nodded. "I was afraid of that. Well, all I can say is that if any of the other species on this planet share this mutability, we're going to have a nightmare in front of us in terms of understanding their physical setup. I desperately hope there's a pattern to the physiological changes I've been seeing, but it's going to take some days of monitoring to tell whether that's the case. We are going to need a *lot* of physical exams done each day, since one horrible thought that's occurred to me is that each individual Ornaet may have its own pattern of change, or kinds of changes."

Kirk nodded. "Noted. Spock? What about the other species?"

"We asked the Ornae if they would arrange meetings with some representatives of the Lahit and ;At," Spock said. "They agreed, as far as I can tell; at least, the individual with whom I spoke said it could be done, and would be. But there seemed an atmosphere of reticence about the other species, the ;At in particular. I have no idea why, and asking the wrong question at this point in an attempt to get to the bottom of the issue could do more harm than good."

"All right," Kirk said. "We'll take it as it comes. But it's going to be interesting negotiating a document of association with these people, if they're all as disorganized—" He caught himself. "Excuse me, that term's a bit judgmental. If they're as nonorganizationally oriented as the Ornae seem to be."

"It may be impossible," Spock said, "at least, impossible to make an agreement for the whole planet. No one species may contract for the others."

Starfleet had made it very plain in Kirk's orders that they wanted all the species represented in an agreement, and would consider a one- or two-species agreement a very poor second indeed. Kirk sighed. *Sometimes politics gives me a pain,* he thought. *We'll do our best for them. Anything else, they'll just have to deal with it.*

"I understand that, Mr. Spock," Kirk said. "When did the Ornae think the Lahit and the ;At would be by?"

"Their time words are rather peculiar," Spock said, "but I gather they thought something could be arranged for tomorrow or the next day."

"Very well, then. We'll shine up the company silver. Ladies and gentlemen, anything else that needs to be covered here, for the department heads? The Sciences briefing will be tomorrow morning."

Heads shook up and down the table.

"Dismissed, then. Doctor—"

The room cleared out slowly. McCoy stretched in his chair, and as the door closed, said, "Do I have to stay after school for being late?"

"I thought you were the one carrying on at me about overwork," Kirk said.

McCoy looked guilty, but only for a moment. "Jim, you've got to bear in mind, this situation is like nothing we've ever seen before—"

"Like most of the other situations we see," said Kirk. "You just calm down a bit and let your staff take some of the weight. The situation seems stable enough; larger landing parties can go down tomorrow, and more of them."

McCoy nodded and yawned, then looked annoyed at himself. "Sorry—it's blood sugar. I missed a meal."

Kirk wagged a finger at Bones as he got up. "Shame, shame. Physician, feed thyself. Better still, come on down to the rec room with me. I missed dinner too."

McCoy said, "How are you supposed to stay healthy if you keep skipping meals—"

Kirk told McCoy that he was a pain, and in nonclinical detail began describing where it was as they went out together.

Chapter Three

McCOY STOOD THERE in the very early morning sunlight, the next day, shaking his head. "Old Will Shakespeare would love this," he said softly.

Next to him, big blond Don Hetsko, one of Sickbay's other nurses, looked up from his tricorder bemused. "How so?"

"Look," McCoy said. "Birnam Wood is coming to Dunsinane."

They were standing in the clearing, surrounded by Ornae again, and by other *Enterprise* crewmen. Until now, the main sounds to be heard had been morning noises of the local forest—the soft, repetitive piping of a large local winged insect that looked surprisingly like a winged iguana—and the cheerful scratchy voices of the Ornae themselves, overlaid with the conversation of the various Sciences people talking to them. But now there was another sound, growing louder: a swishing noise, like branches rustling rhythmically. And so they were. A party of Lahit were moving slowly into the clearing.

None of them was less than six feet tall, and most of them more like ten. They had definite trunks, and branches, and their general shape was tall and pointed, like a pine tree's. *At least* this *bunch is,* McCoy thought, for the survey's pictures had made it plain that there were quite a few forms of the Lahit— it wasn't clear how many. The "leaves" on the creatures' branches were soft and feathery that in shape resembled pine needles, but were longer and finer, and moved in the slightest touch of wind. The trunks were a bright green, like the more stationary trees of the forest; the leaves were darker, a slightly blue-green "spruce" color. Hidden among the leaves were small bright round shapes, like berries. At first, McCoy thought that was what they were. Then he realized that they were eyes, and that some of them were looking at him.

He commanded the small hairs on the back of his neck to go down. Next to him, sounding very impressed, Hetsko said softly, "Goodness. The Day the Christmas Trees Struck Back."

"Don't give them ideas, son," McCoy said, watching the Lahit method of locomotion with interest. Walking trees they might be—or rather, *it* might be; this could be just one creature, though there seemed to be about fifteen main trunks involved, and they seemed to be moving independently. At any rate, their roots never came very far out of the ground. That made sense, if their roots did indeed function like the roots of more conventional plants; no point in suddenly cutting off your source of nutrients every time you moved. The mechanism of perfusion in this species was probably going to be even more interesting than in the Ornae.

Stop saying "their", McCoy told himself silently. *Don't superimpose your own prejudgments on the situation. The reality is going to be weird enough.*

He said to Hetsko, "Better store that last group of readings; we're going to have a whole 'nother batch to deal with shortly. Uplink the new Ornaet stuff to the ship; I'm going to have to go up there and have another run at the Translator algorithm later."

"Right," said Hetsko, and went off to do it, leaving McCoy to watch Kerasus ambling over to talk to the Lahit. She looked slightly uneasy, and McCoy could understand why. She had just gotten to the point where she was beginning to feel mildly confident in translating elementary Ornaet correctly . . . and now she was going straight back to kindergarten, having to start from scratch with another species, and make who knows what mistakes.

He ambled over too, thinking that he might as well get some initial physiological readings that he could trust, without having to wonder later whether whichever crewman had taken them had been holding the scanner by the correct end. McCoy glanced at her as he unlimbered his little personal scanner, and said, "Courage. There's only one more new species after this."

"We hope," she said softly. "Good morning," she said to the Lahit.

The Lahit rustled, a sound that McCoy's Translator rendered as white noise.

"As a preliminary to courtesies," Kerasus said, "how many of you is/are there?"

The trees seemed to bend together for a moment, then sway upright again. "We are one," said the Lahit.

That's a big help, McCoy thought sardonically. Yet

another species that was confused about plurals. *Heaven knows how many of us it thinks there are. Oh well . . . it takes all kinds to make up a universe . . .*

"Thank you," Kerasus said. "While we're talking, would you mind if one of our physical specialists examines you? He needn't touch you if you don't want him to."

There was more rustling. "Him?" the Lahit said.

And gender confusion too, McCoy thought. *Nothing about this mission is going to be easy, is it?*

"Uh, I'll explain in a while," Kerasus said.

The Lahit rustled together again. "Yes," it said finally, "examine."

"Thank you," McCoy said, and turned his scanner on, walking slowly around the Lahit. Absently he looked over the torn ground in its wake. Various squiggly life was moving in it. *Or were those in fact independent life forms? Was it possible those were actually just more roots, newly detached by the act of "walking"? Did the creature possibly propagate itself this way?* "Lieutenant Siegler," he said, glancing up and beckoning a Medicine crewman from across the clearing, "I can't look at these just now. Get some readings, will you? I want to know if they're independent of our friend here."

Lt. Joe Siegler hurried over, making some adjustments to his tricorder, and McCoy went back to what he was doing. The mediscanner was sopping up raw data as fast as it could, and McCoy could only abstract a little of it while the thing was in rapid-gather mode. *Very low systemic pressures,* he thought; *might as well be trees, that way. Maybe the standard exovegetative model will be more useful than we originally thought. Hmm—interesting echo reading there—a structure*

67

something like a heart, but stretched right up and down the inside of each "trunk"—cylindrical, gravity-run mostly, like a human venous system more than anything else—pockets and traps in the "veins," the actual movement of the creature pushes the fluid back up into the circ system, the way walking does with humans. Funny, I would have expected something more strictly capillary—the parallel with xylem and phloem in trees back on Earth is close enough, there are those two sets of "muscular" layers inside the trunk with the fibers running in opposite directions—

His communicator bleeped. McCoy swore. The Lahit and Kerasus both looked at him, the Lahit with considerably more eyes and less expression.

"Sorry," he said, "got carried away." He took out his communicator. "McCoy."

"Doctor," Spock's voice said, *"the Captain has asked me to find out whether your interim physio report on the Ornae is ready. Starfleet is apparently becoming impatient."*

McCoy thought of several things he could say, but there was no point in it, because Spock was out of visual range, and he wouldn't have the pleasure of watching him resist changing expression. "I'm about to do the final polish on it," he said. "Can it wait half an hour?"

"In my estimation, no."

"Dammit," McCoy said, "they're five hours away by subspace radio, it's got to be the middle of the night at Starfleet Command; don't those people ever sleep? It's bad for them. Never mind, Spock, I'll be up in a few minutes. I didn't want to go away without a bit of Lahit data, that's all."

"They have arrived?"

"Big as life and twice as natural. You ought to get down here yourself. Then again," McCoy said, "maybe you'd better not just yet. I don't know if I'd want to tell one of these creatures that I was a vegetarian."

"Regrettably," Spock said, *"I too am in the throes of report compilation, and must defer the opportunity for some time yet. I shall tell the Captain you will be here soon."*

"You do that. Have the Transporter room give me a beam-up in forty seconds, will you?"

"Affirmative."

"Out."

He put the communicator away and finished his walk around the Lahit. Kerasus was still talking to it, asking question after simple question, listening to the answer, and then coming up with another question, in a clear, patient voice. She was one of those people with a very mobile face that revealed every passing thought as it went by; and from the way her eyebrows were jumping around and her mouth was quirking, it was plain she wasn't entirely pleased with the results she was getting. Fortunately the Lahit was in no condition to read her expressions . . . at least McCoy sincerely hoped not.

"How are the verbs coming?" he said, as he packed up the mediscanner.

She threw him a look of extreme desperation. "Haven't hit one yet," she said.

"Keep at it."

A few seconds later the world shimmered out, and McCoy found himself in the Transporter room.

He hurried to Sickbay, which was slightly crazed when he arrived there. Several people were in having routine examinations, and one of the previous day's landing party was being seen for some scratches on his arms. McCoy stopped next to Morrison and had a look at them. The scratches were puffy and inflamed; one set on the forearm was even slightly edematous and showed some small vesicles, blisters filling with clear fluid. "When did these start to bother you?" McCoy said.

"Last night, pretty late. I'm not even sure how I got them; I didn't bump into anything that I can remember."

"Hmm. Do you have problems with cortisone? No, of course you don't. Lia, give him some CorTop cream and a prospray of the euthystol. That should clear this up. If you don't see any improvement by this evening, stop in again and we'll try something more aggressive."

"He's had the euthystol," Lia said, coming up from behind McCoy and handing Morrison an applicator tube. "You think we sit around here waiting for you to diagnose things? That report is in your office, on your terminal—better hustle."

"Nobody needs me," McCoy muttered, "everybody rides me, I think I'll go eat worms." He headed into his office and sat down at his desk, staring at the terminal. "Scroll," he said to it, sighing.

It showed him a report that was essentially a written version of the previous night's debriefing on the Ornae. In a couple of places he stopped the machine and added a bit of data, or clarified a statement that could have been misunderstood by the more inflexible minds at Starfleet. In McCoy's opinion there were far too many of them—armchair officers who had forgotten how to really understand the sciences—but he couldn't do much about that at the moment.

It took him about twenty minutes to get the report into shape, and finally he told the machine to send it along to Spock's station on the Bridge. He was just reaching out for the button when the communicator went off.

"McCoy here."

"Doctor, I really must ask you—"

"No, you mustn't, because it just went to your machine."

There was a moment's pause. *"So it has. My apologies, Doctor."*

"No problem, Spock. If you need me for anything, I'll be back down on the planet. It was just getting interesting."

"I dare say it was. Spock out."

Now, was that the slightest little bit of annoyance there? McCoy thought, as he headed out of his office, through Sickbay again, and out. Just outside the door, he turned and poked his head back in. "Lia, did you get that last set of readings on the Lahit?"

"No."

"Damn, did the uplink go on the fritz? Wait a moment." He pulled out the mediscanner and pushed it into one of the reader bed's ports, activating it. The scanner poured its data into the bed's memory. Lia looked up from noting something in Morrison's records and gazed with interest at the picture the screen above the bed drew of the Lahit's internal structure.

"Just echosound, that reading?" she said.

"Yup. Interesting, eh?"

"Good thing I've got a green thumb," Lia said, clearing her padd off. "By the way, the Captain was down here earlier. He wanted to see you after you finished that report."

"Did he sound urgent?"

"Not particularly."

"Good—then it can wait another hour or so. I've got to get back down there and talk to the trees."

When he reappeared in the clearing, it looked as if Birnam Wood really *had* come to Dunsinane. There was a whole group of Lahit there now—or perhaps a whole grove of them would be a better word, or orchard—and the Sciences people were all talking to them as fast as they could, running scanners over them and waving tricorders. McCoy smiled a bit at the sight.

Something bumped into him about knee level. He glanced down and saw that it was an Ornaet. "Good morning," he said.

"Good morning to you too," the Ornaet said quite clearly; or at least that was what the Translator made of it. McCoy raised his eyebrows. Kerasus and Uhura must have been up all night doing algorithm work.

"Is there something I can do for you?" McCoy said, going down on one knee. He hated talking down to people, and with the Ornaet it was difficult to avoid it.

"Will you examine?" it said.

"Ah," said McCoy. This then was the gentleman he had been working on yesterday. *Or lady,* he added, *if gender is even an issue with these people. Something we'd better find out pretty quick.* "Gladly," he said, and pulled out his mediscanner, touching its controls first to make sure that this set of readings would add itself to the set already stored aboard ship. Sometime in the next hour the scanner would call the ship's library computers and dump its newly acquired data, emptying its temporary memory to make room for more information. "How have you been feeling since yesterday?"

The Ornaet was quiet for a moment. McCoy began to sweat a bit as he ran the mediscanner over it. No matter how good the Translator got, it wouldn't stop you from asking questions that had no cultural referents, or were somehow insulting. But the Ornaet shook itself a bit and said, "You inquire of method? Or condition?"

Thank heaven, McCoy thought, *they've got the first-stage idiom sorter installed. At least these critters won't have to be relentlessly literal . . . and neither will we.* "Condition," he said.

"No complaints," said the Ornaet.

McCoy chuckled a bit at that. "You're about the only one I've seen today who seems willing to say that," he said. "Except maybe for them." He nodded at the Lahit, waving a hand at them for good measure in case the Ornaet might not know how to read the head gesture.

The Ornaet put up eyestalks for a moment and gazed at the Lahit. "They don't complain either," it said after a moment.

Now *this* was interesting. "How can you tell?" McCoy said. "Oh, and leave those eyestalks out for a moment, would you? I want to look at them."

The Ornaet kept looking. "Just know," it said. "Feeling."

"Hmm," McCoy said. There was no direct way to test esper ratings in a new species, except to have a known psi-talented crew member do an assessment; and the only one he would really trust to do that was Spock. But Spock had his hands full, and besides, McCoy hated to ask him to do psi evaluations on

73

other entities. From what he understood of the Vulcans' code of mental privacy, asking something of this sort was like asking a doctor to test for diabetes mellitus the old-fashioned way. Not very pleasant at all, either sensually or esthetically. Better to wait for more vocabulary, and then run a rhine series.

"I take it that you and the Lahit see one another pretty frequently," McCoy said. "I mean, you socialize." *This is amazing,* he thought. *The optical tissue is actually multicellular. That's recognizable retinal tissue, there, with rods and cones. And a compound lens, very sophisticated. But it all goes away at will—* "Would you mind terribly making one of those eyes go away? Can you do just one? Not too quickly, please."

"Of course," the Ornaet said, and slowly the left-hand eyestalk was subsumed back into the Ornaet's main body mass. "Yes, we socialize."

"What about?" McCoy said. "If I may ask. What kinds of things do you do together?" *Damn, look at that. The cells just melted away. Not all at once, either, but one at a time. I wonder, if we found the right words, could we teach these creatures to synthesize new organs for themselves? Would they want to, though? Or need to?* He shook his head and put the mediscanner away.

"We talk," said the Ornaet.

"Can you tell me what about?" said McCoy, sitting down next to the Ornaet. And then added, "I'm sorry. I was calling you Hhch yesterday. Was that really your name? Or was I mispronouncing it?"

The creature made that scratchy noise again that the translator clearly rendered as laughter. "You mispronounced," it said, "but no harm. You have words slowly, yes?"

"Yes, indeed," McCoy said, and laughed a bit himself. "We'll get more as we go along."

"My name is Hhhcccccchhhhh," said the Ornaet, and then he and McCoy both laughed together, because it was clear the words weren't there yet.

"Maybe tomorrow," McCoy said. "But what do you and the other species talk about?"

There was a pause. Then, "Life," said the Ornaet.

McCoy nodded. "This means yes," he said. "Well, so do we, my friend. The details will come out with time."

"What do *you* talk about?" said the Ornaet.

McCoy stretched, thinking. "Work," he said, "play, relationships . . . the things that happen in the world . . . things that we can do something about, and things that we can't."

The Ornaet was quiet for a moment. "Yes," it said. "What is *work?*"

Oh brother, McCoy thought. "Work," he said, "is when one must do things one doesn't always feel like doing, because they need to be done, for some reason. If you're lucky, you like doing work most of the time. Not everyone's that lucky."

Another long silence. "Yes," it said. "I know. Some of us work."

"Really?" McCoy said, surprised. "Doing what?"

The Translator emitted several short blasts of static.

"Oh well," McCoy said, "never mind. We'll have more words in a while."

"No," said the Ornaet. "I can show you."

"Really?" McCoy was on his feet in a moment. "Where?"

"Come," said the Ornaet.

They went off through the clearing, the Ornaet

leading the way, McCoy following, trying not to trip over other Ornae—they did seem to be everywhere this morning—and zigzagging around more copses of Lahit. There were more and more of them, too, rustling and hissing, and looking at the *Enterprise* people with all their eyes.

The Ornaet led him out of the clearing, into the forest again, by one of the many paths. This was a broadish path that seemed to have seen a lot of use recently, to judge by the broken branches on either side of it. Also, there seemed to have been something rather larger than the Ornae using it. "Tell me something," McCoy said as they went along. "Do you have animals around here?"

"Animals?"

"Other creatures able to move about, like you. But not talkers, not intelligent."

"Oh yes," the Ornaet said. "But we keep them away."

"How?"

There was another static attack. "Never mind," McCoy said again. "I'm much more interested in *work* at the moment."

"Here," said the Ornaet.

They came out into another clearing. This one was wider than the one where most of the *Enterprise* people were. There were none of the wonderful self-built buildings as in the other clearing. But there was a large stone, set right in the middle of everything: a tall, oblong stone, brownish colored, roughly cylindrical, well set into the ground.

McCoy walked up to it with interest, then looked around the clearing, and finally at the Ornaet. "Where is the *work,* then?" he said.

"Here," said the Ornaet.

"You mean someone set this stone up, as work? Hmm." He turned to look at it. There were certainly marks on it that could be construed as tool-marks. *Chipped stone?* he thought. *Metal, perhaps?—Or maybe—what need does a species have of tools, when it can make tools out of itself?*

"No, no," the Ornaet said. And it laughed at him, so that McCoy looked at it in astonishment and confusion. "This *is* work." It paused a moment, then said, "This is *working.*"

"It is?" McCoy said, looking up at the stone, very bemused. *Some kind of machine, inside the stone? Wouldn't be the first time we've found something like that—*

And then the stone moved.

Not much. McCoy backed away in the time it moved about a foot, leaning toward him. But somehow it had *not* moved. There was no change in the earth at its foot: no crumbling, no change in the grasslike plants that grew there. The rock was suddenly simply a little closer to him than it had been.

"Wait, wait," said the Ornaet, clearly pleased with itself. "Not, it-*indefinite-pronoun* is working. It-*personal-noun* is working."

McCoy's breath caught somewhere south of his breastbone.

"And I can't pronounce your name either," he said to the ;At. "Not even the name of your species."

There was a long silence. The ;At looked at him. How McCoy knew it was looking at him, he couldn't say. But he knew it was; and he was too surprised, and—to his own bemusement—awestruck, to do anything but stand there.

77

The creature was not fully physical. On these grounds at least, the initial survey report had been correct. It was not a question of the creature being somehow vague, or misty-looking. It was not. It was as solid as any Swiss mountain seen from its lower slopes against clear sky . . . and there was an equivalent feeling of weight to it, solidity, *there*ness. But at the same time, you had the feeling that that *there*ness might suddenly stop—a feeling you did *not* get with any mountain. McCoy knew that no matter how many times he might say to the Jungfrau, in the old words, "Be thou removed," it would stay right where it was. But looking at the ;At, one was left with the impression that it might remove itself without warning, and take a great deal with it if it wanted to.

"At any rate," McCoy finally managed to say, "good morning."

"Good morning to you, Doctor," the ;At said. No hesitation, no difficulties with the syntax; though the voice itself, even translated, tended to drive thoughts about syntax away. It was a voice with overtones of earthquake about it, of avalanche—of great force, controlled, but force that could be suddenly unleashed to some huge effect.

McCoy took a deep breath or so to help him manage himself. Then he said, "Sir or madam or other, do you understand the meaning of the concept *doctor?*"

"It is not a concept we use ourselves," the ;At said, "but I believe we understand the general sense."

No syntax problems at all. *Oh dear. Kerasus is going to have a fit. In fact, I'd have one myself, right now, if there was time.* "Then may I examine you as I have done with my friend here?"

"You may."

Nothing else: just the sound of the wind in the trees. McCoy cleared his throat, pulled out the mediscanner, and did a hasty recalibration on it—he wanted all its available bandwidth working for *this* scan. He keyed it on and began walking around the ;At. "Would you mind if I touched you?" he said.

"Feel free."

Idiomatic, too. Good Lord on a bicycle. He paused halfway through his circuit to put a hand on the stone. It was warm. The mediscanner was ingesting data much too fast for him to be able to tell anything from the sound of it; he was thrown back on his physical senses, which told him nothing except that the creature's outer surface looked very like an igneous stone, granite or something similar. He wondered idly if there was any radioactivity that would indicate genuine igneous formation, and resolved to check later. "May I ask you a question, please?" he said.

"Ask." The rumble sounded good-natured enough.

"How many of you are there on this planet?"

"All of us." Was there an edge of humor there? Was he being joked with? McCoy cleared his throat again.

"Ah, yes. Do you have a problem with our number system?"

"We understand it well enough, I think. Our numbers in manifestation vary between nine hundred thousand and one million."

Vary why, and how?—but it would have to wait. "My friend here, whose name I can't pronounce," McCoy said, "said to me while we were coming here that you were doing work." He finished his circuit. "May I ask what you were doing?"

His communicator went off.

He didn't swear this time; it seemed as inappropriate, somehow, as swearing at the Jungfrau would have been. "Excuse me, please," he said, and pulled it out. "McCoy here—"

"Bones," Kirk's voice said, *"what do I have to do to get a word with you these days?"*

"Jim," McCoy said, as politely as he could, "I promise you on my Oath that I'll be up there in a minute. I just need to—"

"Sixty seconds," Kirk said, *"and I'm counting."*

"But—"

"Your Oath, you said."

"McCoy out," he said. He looked longingly at the mediscanner and shut it down. "Sir or madam or other—"

"As I understand the term," said the long slow rumble through his Translator, "I think 'sir' would do."

"Thank you. I have to go. I'll be back as soon as I can. Will you still be here?"

There was no answer for a second or so. Finally the ;At said, "That is a philosophical question of some complexity—"

The golden shimmer took McCoy away. This time he *did* curse, as soon as he couldn't see the ;At anymore.

"Though perhaps," it added then, " 'madam' would have been correct as well."

McCoy burst into the Bridge so torn between delight and wild annoyance that he didn't know which to let go with first. For the first moments, at least, the need to choose was aborted. Kirk was sitting there in the center seat, facing the elevator doors.

"You made it," he said, "just."

"Jim," McCoy said, "we've got a breakthrough on our hands here. It's the ;At."

"Are you catching cold?" Kirk said, looking suddenly concerned.

"No, I am *not* catching cold! Jim, I think we're concentrating on the wrong species here. I was just talking to one of the ;At, and—" He paused for a moment and looked around the Bridge. It was surprisingly empty for the time of day: the only ones there besides Kirk were a Communications officer and someone from Navigation, sitting in Sulu's spot. "Where is everybody?"

"Down on the planet, most of them, or coordinating data. Or off shift. Sulu had just done two back to back, and I remember what I'm told about shift relief."

"Oh. Well, good. Jim, the ;At translation algorithm seems to be OK, they have idiom and everything, and this one said to me that it was—"

"*Doctor,*" Kirk said, "you have been overworking yourself just a bit. I think it's time you got some rest. But not even your own staff seems able to get you to slow down. Nurse Burke has been complaining to me."

I'll kill her, McCoy thought.

"You say a word to her and I'll dock your pay," Kirk said, wagging a finger at him. "I want you to sit down here and write me a decent report, not like that whitewash you did for Starfleet a little earlier today. They may be suckered in by all your long words, but

81

you can't hand *me* that stuff and expect to get away with it. I want an analysis of what's going on down there."

"But I can't do that without more data—"

"Give me what you've got, and make sense of it. If you just sit still and think for a while, you're bound to come up with something that will do me some good. And you stay out of Sickbay to do it, too. You go down there, you'll just start treating someone for something. Sickbay is off limits to you except for legitimate medical emergencies, until further notice. That's a direct order. Understood?"

McCoy glowered. It was best to humor Jim when he got in these moods. They passed quickly enough. "Understood," he said.

"Good. And just to keep you out of trouble—" He got up from the center seat and stretched. "Here. Sit down."

McCoy stared at him.

"Come on," Kirk said. "Have a seat. It's nice and comfortable; you can sit here and dictate your report. But anyway, I'm leaving you the conn."

McCoy was outraged. "You can't do that," he said. *"I* can't do that!"

"Of course I can," Kirk said, "and of course *you* can. You've had line officer's training. Not the full Command course, naturally, but enough to know what to say at the right times. Not that you'll need to. And I can leave anybody with the conn that I please, most especially a department head and a fellow officer. There's no need to be in the direct chain of command at all—that's a common misconception. I could leave an Ensign Third-class with the conn if I liked, and the situation seemed to call for it. Well, at the moment, it seems to call for Captain's discretion."

"Uh—"

"So sit down," Kirk said.

"Uh, Jim—"

"I am *leaving the Bridge,* Bones. Then I am going to get something to eat. And then I am going to go down to the planet and have a chat with Spock, who is also overworking, and who I've also got to yell at; and then I'm going to meet some of these people we're supposed to be talking to. I've stood it up here about as long as I can. And *you,* Doctor, are going to sit in this comfy chair, and have a nice relaxing time, and coordinate data, which you are better equipped to do at the moment than *I* am, and then you're going to call me on the planet's surface and give me sage advice. You got that?"

McCoy nodded.

"Then get down here."

Slowly, McCoy walked down to the center seat, and very slowly, very gingerly, lowered himself into it. It was indeed very comfortable.

"You have the conn," Kirk said. "I'll be back at the end of the shift. Have fun."

"Mmf," McCoy said as Kirk walked away, and the Bridge doors closed on him.

Leonard McCoy sat in the command seat of the Starship *Enterprise* and thought, *I'm going to get him for this.*

Kirk had a sandwich and a cup of coffee, grudging the time for anything more complicated. He then took himself straight off to the Transporter room, and down to the clearing on the surface of Flyspeck. The sweet taste of the fresh air made the hair stand right up on his neck, as usual. It was one of the small, secret delights that he had never really managed to tell anyone about—the scent of a new world's air, for the first time, with its particular compendium of strange new aromas. This one smelled as if there had been rain recently; and there was an odd edge of spice to the air too, as if the growing things here were mostly aromatics.

He glanced around him at the business of the clearing—all the Ornae and Lahit rolling or trundling or wading around through the ground—and at his crew, doing their jobs, talking, examining, collecting data. *Spock must be around here somewhere,* he thought, and looked around for him, but couldn't see him anywhere.

"Morning, Captain," someone said behind him; he turned and saw that it was Don Hetsko, one of McCoy's people. "Looking for anyone in particular?"

"Oh, Spock, if you've seen him."

"Not for a while. The Doctor went off that way just a few minutes ago, though," Don said, pointing toward one of the paths that led out of the clearing. "You ought to be able to catch him."

"Thank you, Mr. Hetsko," Kirk said, and went off that way, smiling slightly.

His businesslike stride slowed to a stroll as he got into the forest proper. The quality of the light here was unusual, somehow: more intense than he had been expecting. It was as if some photographer had purposely lit the place to look both warm and coolly enticing; a curious effect, caused by the brassy gold of the planet's sun, probably, and the extreme greenness, almost blue-greenness, of its plants' dominant chlorophyll. The science of the situation aside, it was a very pleasant effect, restful, and he was in no mood to get out of it in a hurry.

The path gave onto another clearing, bigger than the first one. Kirk paused on the fringes of it, looking at the great stone shape in the middle. He remembered the pictures of the ;At from the briefing; he remembered McCoy's insistence that the ;At were the people he wanted to talk to. But at the same time an odd reluctance came over him, almost a shyness. There was a sense of remoteness about this creature, somehow, a feeling that it knew things that might make it wiser not to disturb it . . .

Odd feelings, and baseless, of course. Kirk shook off the slight case of nerves and stepped out into the bright sunshine of the clearing.

The ;At saw him coming, Kirk knew, though it had no eyes that showed, and seemingly no other sense organs. *I wonder if Bones managed to get a scan on it,* he thought. *Have to ask him about that later.* Some feet away from it, Kirk slowed down, and stopped.

"I beg your pardon," he said.

There was a long silence before the ;At said to him, "I am not aware of your having done anything that requires pardon."

The voice was astonishing: it rumbled like a landslide. But there was nothing threatening about it. Rather, its tone of voice was so grave, and at the same time so humorous, even through the Translator, that Kirk smiled. "That's good," he said. "The phrase is an idiom of my culture, often used when one person interrupts another. I didn't want to take the chance that I might have been interrupting you in the middle of something important."

"You have not interrupted me, Captain," said the ;At.

"I'm glad." He paused and said, "You must have been the one with whom the Doctor was talking."

"We did speak," said the ;At.

Kirk hesitated. "I hope you'll excuse my ignorance," he said, "but I have no name to call you by. Not even a gender designation, if you use such things."

"The Doctor would have called me Sir," said the ;At.

Kirk nodded. "If I may, then. Did the Doctor speak much to you of why we are here?"

"He began to," said the ;At, "and I said to him that the matter was one of some philosophical complexity. He then disappeared."

"He went back to our ship," Kirk said. "The vessel in which we travel, and by which we came here."

"Enterprise," the ;At said.

"That's right."

"I see it," said the ;At. "All silver, but it shines gold where the sunlight touches it. And it has lights of its own, for the dark."

"Yes," Kirk said, while thinking with some excitement, *These creatures must have a sensorium that we've never seen the like of. I know the sound of a direct perception when I hear one. Anything that can see a starship, somehow, from the surface of a planet—what else can it see?* "Sir," he said, "did he speak to you at all of why we came?"

"No," said the ;At. "No more than did the first party who arrived here, though they asked us many a question. They were cautious. But we knew well from the sight of them that they did not come of this world, and had traveled from some other."

Kirk shook his head, thinking, *There has to be a better way to get these initial surveys done. Dammit, these are intelligent species we're dealing with, not idiots. They figure out what's going on quickly enough. How does it make us look?*

He glanced up. The ;At had not moved, but the sensation that it was looking closely at him grew quite strong—in fact Kirk was finding it a little difficult to breathe normally, with the closeness of that regard acting almost like a physical pressure on him. There was nothing angry or threatening about it. It was merely a level of interest so intense that it was actually affecting his body.

"Sir," he said, "that ship up there, and the people who are here with your people and the Ornae and the Lahit, are under my command. We have all come here to see how much we can discover about your people, and how much we can tell you about us. Once that is done, we have some questions we would like to ask all three species as a whole—if that is even possible. That is one of the things we need to discover."

"Many questions," said the ;At. "And what questions do *we* get to ask?"

"Any you like," said Kirk, just a bit nervously.

"So we shall," said the ;At, and fell silent.

Kirk stood in that silence and felt the hairs rising on the back of his neck again, but this time for no reason that had anything to do with the sweetness of the morning air. That intense interest was bent on him, and on his ship, and all his people. He could feel it on his skin, like sunlight, but it was not a warming or calming feeling at all.

"When will we start?" he said at last, when the silence became too much for him.

"We have started," said the ;At.

McCoy sat in the center seat and yawned.

He was tired, and annoyed, but at the same time he felt a certain smug satisfaction. Kirk had counted on his being terrified by this experience. Unfortunately he had not reckoned with McCoy's great talent for learning to cope at high speed. It was probably the first important thing a doctor or nurse learned—how to turn the sudden surprising or annoying situation into a commonplace.

He had been playing with the buttons on the center seat's arms. There was quite an assortment of links into the library computer, so that even without a Science officer at his or her station, you could display all kinds of information on the main Bridge screen, and even do things like voicewrite reports. McCoy had finished the report that Kirk had asked him for, and then had gone back to playing with the machinery, pulling various information up out of the library computer and annotating his report with it.

The Bridge intercom whistled, and McCoy glanced over to the communications officer on post, Lieutenant DeLeon, to say that he would take it himself. He pushed the appropriate button on the seat console and said, "Bridge. McCoy."

"Heaven help us, Doctor, what're ye doing up there?" Scotty's shocked voice said.

"Blame the Captain, Scotty," McCoy said. "He stuck me with the conn two and a half hours ago."

Scotty chuckled a little at that. *"Well, it'll do you no harm, I suppose. Himself is downplanet, I take it."*

"You take it right. Anything I can help you with?"

"Not a thing. He had asked me to do a reset on the warp engines, and I have the figures for him on how long it would take and how much antimatter we would need. It can wait till he gets back up."

"Why did he want a reset?"

"Ah, I talked him into it. It's a matter of maximizing our fuel consumption, is all. He was looking to save some power by resetting the fusion timing. I found a better way, but I shan't trouble you with the details."

"Thanks, don't," McCoy said. "I'll let him know you've got the figures for him."

"Right you are," Scotty said. *"Engineering out."*

McCoy pushed the button with satisfaction, and sat back in the center seat. "DeLeon," he said, "would you get me the landing party? I want to see what they're up to down there."

"Yes, sir," said DeLeon. A moment later the screen was showing the main clearing down on Flyspeck and crewpeople all over the place, busily doing their work.

McCoy saw Spock, and Lia, and various other people he knew; but there was no sign of Kirk.

"Off gallivanting again," he said. "Pinpoint the Captain, would you, Lieutenant?"

"Sure, Doctor." DeLeon touched a few controls, then peered at his board. It was a curious look.

"What's the matter? Did he turn his communicator off? Just like him," McCoy said, grumbling.

"No, Doctor," said DeLeon. "I can't find him."

McCoy got up and stepped up to the Communications station, looked at the scanner screen, and frowned. No trace of the Captain was showing at all. Even if Jim had dropped his communicator, the scanners would still clearly indicate where it had fallen.

But there was no trace of it at all.

McCoy swallowed hard and called Spock.

Chapter Four

WHEN SPOCK ARRIVED on the Bridge, McCoy was so utterly glad to see him that he was tempted to jump up and hug him. Instead, he just said, "Spock, your damn scanner's gone on the fritz again."

Spock favored him with an expression that was skeptical at best. "Doctor," he said very gently, as if to a brain-damage case, "that hardly seems likely. Nonetheless, I will run some checks."

The Vulcan went over to the Science console and began touching controls with the swift certainty of someone who barely even needs to look at them. "I take it matters are sufficiently under control in Sickbay as to not require your presence there," he said.

McCoy humphed. "Fat chance, Spock. Kirk handed me the conn and told me to stay out of Sickbay except for medical emergencies."

That made Spock blink. He looked up from his console—though he did not stop keying in instructions—and said, "Forgive me, but I should not want to misunderstand you. You say the Captain left you in command?"

"His idea of a little joke. Ask DeLeon, he was here."

"It will be on the Bridge procedural recording as well," Spock said, and turned his attention back to his work again. McCoy turned away and watched the front screen for a moment. There was a little forest of Lahit in that clearing now, and about two hundred of the Ornae seemed to have gotten together to build a much larger structure than had been there the day before—more ornate, with plenty more room inside. They were considerate hosts, if nothing else about them was very clear as yet.

McCoy turned back to Spock to see the Science Officer staring at his console with a concerned expression. "Doctor," he said, "we have a problem."

He had known that, but hearing Spock admit to it somehow made it much worse. McCoy sat down in the center seat, more by reflex at this point than by preference, and said, "He *is* missing."

"The instruments are working correctly," Spock said. "The Captain's communicator is not on the planet. According to the instruments."

"Never mind the communicator, Spock, *where is he??*"

"Doctor," Spock said, stepping down to the center seat, "calm yourself. There are ways to explain why we might not be able to find the Captain."

"Such as?"

Spock raised an eyebrow. "The Captain may be in an area having a high concentration of some other rare earth element, so that the communicator's signal is washed out in the background radiation—"

"And did you locate any such?"

"Well," Spock said, reluctant, "I must admit—"

"So? What else then?"

Spock looked at him with as close to a helpless expression as McCoy had seen on him for a long time. "Nothing," he said.

"Well, the hell with *this*," McCoy said. "I'm going where I can be of some use . . . down there, to help look for Kirk. *You* mind the store."

He was halfway to the Bridge doors when Spock said, "Doctor . . . I am afraid you don't understand the situation."

McCoy stopped and looked at Spock in surprise. "What part of it?"

"Your part, at least," he said. "Doctor, you are in command. You cannot leave the ship under these circumstances."

"Dammit, yes I can! I'm turning command over to you! Where it ought to be, by the way. You're the one who went all the way through Command School, and you're the second most senior officer aboard ship. *You* sit in the damn chair."

"Doctor," Spock said quietly, "as the Captain might put it, it would not matter if I were Commanding Admiral of Starfleet and had a note from God. I could not accept command from you under these circumstances. Nor could anyone else. Fleet regulations are most specific in this regard. An officer placed in nominal command of a vessel *must retain command* until relieved by the commander of official record. The Captain is not around to relieve you. Anyone who exercised command in your place would be liable to court-martial—and would not have a leg to stand on, as it were, in court. And any effort by *you* to leave your post—in this case, the *Enterprise*—

would also be a court-martial offense . . . especially in these circumstances, when the Captain is missing. An emergency, to say the least."

McCoy sank down onto the Science station chair and stared at Spock in dismay.

"You are 'stuck,' Doctor," Spock said. "I am very sorry." And he sounded it.

McCoy looked over at Spock. He took a deep breath or two, thinking, *Calm yourself, boy. You're going to need your wits about you today.* "All right," he said. "You'd better go down there and get a search started. Find out who saw him last . . . take it from there."

Spock nodded and headed for the Bridge doors himself.

"And by the way," McCoy added, "can I at least have a restroom break?"

Spock nodded. "Give the conn to Lieutenant DeLeon," he said, "but don't be away too long. Though," he added, from just inside the turbolift, "I believe the Captain would say, 'You should have gone before we left.'"

"Why, you—"

The lift doors closed.

McCoy looked at DeLeon and said, "Take it, son. I'll be back in a few minutes."

"Yes, sir."

"And see if you can get Uhura away from her business downstairs. I need some advice."

"Right, Doctor."

When he came back to the Bridge, she was there waiting for him. "Lieutenant," McCoy said to the young Comm officer, "go take a break or something. When does your shift end?"

"In about an hour, Doctor," said DeLeon.

Lord, where has the day gone? Time goes fast when you're having fun. He glanced at Uhura; she nodded, and McCoy said, "Never mind coming back, son. You go on ahead."

"Thanks, Doctor," he said, and headed out.

When the lift doors shut, Uhura said softly, "I hear we have a little problem."

"You bet your sweet—well, never mind. Yes, we do. Do many of the crewpeople down there know?"

"All of them do, now. Search parties are working their way through the area." She looked worried. "But the trail may be getting a bit cold at this point. Nobody's seen the Captain since this morning, and only very briefly then."

"Where was he going?"

"Off through the woods, on one of those paths. That big one that seems to get a lot of use."

A sudden suspicion flowered in McCoy. *The one that led to the clearing where the ;At was*—"Has anyone seen any ;At around there?" he said.

"No," said Uhura, sounding faintly surprised. "Doctor, I think it's more of a glottal stop, that noise."

"Never mind the pronunciation. Anyway, I want to hear one of *them* say it. Uhura, I saw one this morning. I was talking to it when Jim made me come up here. I think he may have met it too."

"You were talking to it?" she said in surprise. "But we have hardly any of the algorithms for their language yet. The survey party could hardly get anything out of them. Was it fairly easy to understand?"

"As easy as you are. I was surprised."

Uhura looked very concerned. "Doctor," she said,

95

"this is very odd. It can't be happening this way . . . unless that species knows a lot more about us than we think it does."

McCoy thought of that slow, silent regard bent on him, the feeling of concealed, controlled power, and shivered a little. "I wouldn't put that past them. Uhura, we've got to find at least one of them and see what it knows."

"It would help if we had some scan information," she said, sounding dubious. "On the outside, they just seem to look like big rocks. There are a lot of rocks on this planet."

"Not that many rocks that *move*," McCoy said. "And only about a million of them, according to the ;At I was talking to this morning. Never mind that; I've got a scan. Here." He reached down for his instrument pouch, which had come straight up to the Bridge with him, and handed Uhura his mediscanner.

"Good," she said, and went over to her station, popping the scanner into one of its input ports. She touched a button on her board, then squinted for a moment at the readout screen. "Uh-uh," she said. "It's dumped its memory."

McCoy muttered. "Yes, it would have. Check the library computer; the file should be in there."

Uhura nodded, touched a few more controls, and waited. "Here we are," she said, gazing at the screen; then started to shake her head.

McCoy's stomach began to tie itself into a little knot. "What's the matter?"

"I've got your uplink here," she said, "but there's trouble in the visual component. What's this?"

She touched another control and brought what she was seeing up onto the main screen. In the background of the shot, McCoy could see the other side of the big clearing, the view changing as he carried the mediscanner around something in the center of the shot. What the something was, though, there was no telling. All the screen showed was a silvery vagueness, foggy, an oblong shape with no detail.

"Damn," McCoy said.

"Your scan information is gone too, I'm afraid," Uhura said. "Not wiped; the scan bands are just blank, as if your scanner didn't record."

"This isn't my day for machinery, I can see that," McCoy said.

"Not the machinery's fault," Uhura said promptly. She had been doing something else with her console. "I get faint scan artifact in some of the bands from the background life forms—too faint to be of any use for data collection, naturally. But your scanner was picking up some of the fluid movement in the plant life in the background, for example."

"Yes, it does that . . . but usually the life form it's being directed at simply drowns out the background readings, by proximity. Now what does this *mean?"*

Uhura shook her head and took the scanner out of the reading port, handing it back to McCoy. "Your guess is as good as mine," she said. "Probably better, since you saw the ;At, and I didn't." She looked very curious. "What did it sound like?"

"Trouble," McCoy said, only half listening. "Like something you wouldn't want angry at you." His stomach went cold at that thought; he had to consciously push the fear away. "Never mind. Maybe," he said, thoughtful, "it didn't *want* to be scanned?"

He looked at Uhura. She tilted her head to one side, eyes narrowed. "Possible," she said. "Species that are good at handling energy flows can do that sometimes. Take our scans of the Organians, for example, before they revealed themselves. We thought we were dealing with hominids . . . and they manipulated our instrument readings to make it look that way. We never thought to question what was going on. These people—" She looked at the screen. "That," she said, "is energy management of great virtuosity, if your theory's correct. A creature that could do that could do all kinds of other things."

"But it didn't try to trick us, as far as we know," McCoy said, trying very hard to keep strictly to the facts. "It just concealed its own readings. Why would it want to do that, I wonder?"

"Privacy taboos?" Uhura said.

McCoy sighed. "Until we talk to more of them, we'll never find out. And they don't seem to be quite as forthcoming as the other species."

Uhura laughed at that, a short sound, and slightly sarcastic. "Don't bet on the others being any more 'forthcoming,' Doctor. I spent all morning discussing the nature of reality with some of the Ornae. They don't really believe in us."

McCoy blinked. "This theme keeps coming up," he said. "'Don't believe in us' how? Are we against their religion? Or is there something they don't approve of?"

"Not that, exactly," said Uhura, sitting back and sighing. "They just don't think we're real. Or no, that's not exactly it. They know we're here. But they don't think we're human."

"What? Two arms, two legs, one head, what else should 'human' be? More or less."

"Not that way. They don't think we're *people*. It's

not prejudicial on their part. They like us well enough; they like talking to us. But they don't think we *matter,* particularly. The things we find important seem laughable to them. And why not?" Uhura said. "In their worldview—theirs and the Lahit's both, they seem to share this—the basic survival needs, air, water, food, are all there for the taking—or don't even need to be taken, in the Ornae's case. You just *live.* They simply start at a higher rung of the self-actualization ladder than we do. They have all those basic physical needs met already, and don't have to deal with them consciously. Their concerns are all social. They may be the most social species the Federation will ever have encountered, in fact."

"Be a nice change from some people we've run into over the years," McCoy muttered.

"Well, yes. They understand the idea of a Federation, too—more or less. They just don't understand our reasons for having one. They might join us just to chat. But they would never think of joining us because we had something they wanted. As far as I can tell, we have *nothing* they would want or need—except perhaps ourselves, to talk to. The language of any association agreement would have to be changed to reflect that, and I'll be telling the Captain so—"

"When we find him."

"Yes," Uhura said, and concern showed in her face. "I must admit, I'm worried."

"You think *you're* worried," McCoy said. "Well, never mind that at the moment. I suppose Starfleet is going to want to hear from us sooner or later and find out how we're getting on." He groaned. "This is one conversation I'm going to love having."

"It won't be a conversation," Uhura said, "not at

five hours' subspace radio distance, it won't. You put together a report and get it ready for me—our next scheduled transmission should go out in about an hour and a half, and you don't want them getting any ideas that you're having trouble with things by being late with the news."

"I *am* having trouble with things, dammit!" McCoy said. "I'd be delighted if they'd relieve me. Here, quick," he said, "get me a padd. I'll certify myself unfit to command. Stress, that's a good excuse. Then they'll put Spock in this miserable chair instead of me—"

"Doctor," Uhura said, her voice full of pity, "don't you just wish. But there's no way they'll do it. Relief of command by 'remote control' is very rarely done, specifically because it very rarely works out. On this ship in particular. The time or two that Fleet has done something so dumb, they've regretted it. And think how it would look on *your* service record."

"Mmf," said McCoy unhappily. "Hadn't thought of that."

"Think of it," Uhura said. "Poor Doctor. You've got the tiger by the tail this time."

He nodded. "Nothing to do but hang on, I guess."

"You do that. We'll all help you."

"Find me the captain," he said. "That would help."

Uhura nodded and turned back to her station.

McCoy sat there drumming his fingers on the arm of the seat. He shifted uneasily. The cushions were feeling a lot less comfortable than they had earlier.

Spock came back from the planet surface some three hours later, looking, to McCoy's practiced eye, very drawn—not physically tired, but showing the effects of not having produced any results whatever.

"We're going to have to have a department heads' meeting in a while, I guess," McCoy said to Spock, "and record it and send it along to Starfleet."

"I would not do that," Spock said, sitting down at his station and dropping a couple of tricorder tapes into one of its reader ports. "Call the meeting, certainly. We must intensify our search for the Captain. But Starfleet does not require the details of our decision-making process. Also," and there was a slight glint of humor in his eye as he glanced over his shoulder at McCoy, "there is no point in giving the, ah, bureaucratic elements at Starfleet any more insight than necessary into how we arrive at our decisions."

"How I arrive at my command decisions, you mean," McCoy said.

Spock nodded. "The bureaucratic mind," he said, "will always find some way to meddle if at all possible. If faced with a decision-making process that they find too . . . original . . ."

"Too intelligent, you mean. Or too consultative."

"Precisely. Under such circumstances, you could find yourself issued orders which you would be required to carry out, but which would be most . . . distasteful."

"You mean stupid."

"I believe I said that," Spock said. "Though perhaps not in so many words."

"Spock," McCoy said, in a moment's gratitude, "when this is all over, I'm going to cancel your next physical."

The look Spock gave him had more than a trace of mischief about it. "Dereliction of duty, Doctor?" he asked. "I could never allow you to behave in such a manner. I will take my physical in good part."

"And find some other way to ride me about this for the rest of my life," McCoy said.

Spock didn't quite smile as he turned away.

"All right," McCoy said. He looked over his shoulder. "Uhura, call the department heads . . . tell them we should meet in the briefing room in an hour. Special attention to Linguistics and Biology; I want everything we've got on all the species so far. I also want a report to the *minute* on when the Captain disappeared. Starfleet is going to want at least a *few* concrete facts."

"Yes, sir," Uhura said, and started calling around to the various departments of the ship.

McCoy looked over at Spock. "I take it," he said, "that no one has seen anything of the ;At today."

Spock shook his head. "Uhura was kind enough to give me your mediscanner's readout file for signal analysis," he said. "I must admit that at first I thought you might have mishandled the device somehow. But two thoughts suggested otherwise: the fact that you are most intimately familiar with the equipment after years of using and even improving on it; and the certainty that even you could not misuse an instrument so selectively and skillfully."

McCoy sat still for a moment doing mental sums in his head and trying to work out whether that sentence, taken as a whole, came out to a compliment. He decided it didn't, and decided to ignore it. "Thank you," he said. "Were you able to tell anything useful from the scan?"

"Something not useful," Spock said, "but certainly odd. Your scanner picked up some incidental radiation in the neighborhood, for which it was not specifically calibrated, but which it recorded nonetheless."

"Radiation? Anything dangerous?" McCoy said, alarmed.

Spock shook his head. "Merely odd. There was an over-threshold amount of high-energy particle decay: some Cerenkov radiation, and Z-particle remnants. Most peculiar."

"But Cerenkov radiation is associated with black holes," McCoy said. "There aren't any of those here."

"Indeed not. Cerenkov radiation, however, is also associated with the sudden deceleration of a superrelativistic body in atmosphere."

"Someone traveling faster than light, and slowing down—"

"Or some *thing.* Mere subatomic particles can be responsible. The number your scanner recorded was very small, too small to indicate a spacecraft or anything of the kind."

"But still above the threshold amount," McCoy said.

"Yes."

He shook his head. "What about the Z-particles?"

"Again," Spock said, "I am at a loss to understand their presence. Naturally occurring Z-collisions and decay are rare enough that it has always taken great amounts of sensitive equipment to detect them. But here they do not seem to be rare. Or did not while you were scanning. My own scans, conducted over the past hours with much more sensitive equipment, showed no such collisions taking place."

"Then it's something associated specifically with the ;At," McCoy said.

Spock nodded. "I feel that is a safe assumption. But

what it can mean, I have no idea. It is a pity the rest of your scan was not more revealing, but it was most skillfully interfered with."

"You think it did that on purpose?" McCoy said.

Spock frowned a bit. "We have no direct evidence of that," he said, "but on the other hand, if the ;At in question had not wanted its internal workings to be known or theorized about, it could hardly have managed it better. Statistically, I would find this data at least suspicious."

McCoy sighed. "All right," he said. "I'm going to go take a break. Have everybody get their notes together, and I'll see you in an hour."

He went down to his quarters. The sound of the door closing behind him filled him with a wild sense of relief, which he knew was completely spurious. In an hour he would have to go out and sit at the head of the table in the briefing room and pretend to run things.

He sat down in his favorite chair, probably the oddest thing in his quarters, certainly the most expensive. It was an antique, and he had given up most of his personal-possessions space allowance for it. It was a genuine Shaker rush-back rocking chair, circa 1980; not the most venerable of its kind—the really old ones were all in museums—but good enough. It was good for back problems, and the rocking was soothing.

I need some soothing now, he thought, as he sat down. The motion was physically comforting. His mind, of course, was running around in little circles, screaming and biting itself in the small of the back, but then that was understandable—and the more clinical parts of his mind weren't troubled by the fact. If he kept rocking long enough, the body would affect the mind eventually. It had no choice.

"Take about a year at this rate, though," he muttered. He ran a quick check on himself. Palms clammy, pulse elevated, some fine muscle tremor, general malaise. Stomach spasm. *Physician, feed thyself,* he remembered Kirk saying. *When did I eat last? Was it really this morning? Not like me to miss meals. My blood sugar must be down in my socks somewhere.* He reached out, tapped the intercom button, and said, "Commissary."

"David here."

"McCoy. Can you have somebody send me up a sandwich and a coffee? I'm in my quarters."

"He leaned back again and sighed, glancing around. The room seemed smaller than usual. Was this the way Kirk felt when he took a break during a crisis? As if the whole world's trouble was pressing on the outside door, and would come rushing over him the minute he opened it again? He could understand why sometimes he had to tell Kirk to take a sleeping tablet. Sleep wouldn't come anywhere near *him* until all this was resolved.

Yes, it will, said one of the clinical parts of his brain. *A mind that isn't rested is useless. Lowering your own efficiency won't get Kirk back. If you have to sleep, you take the damn pill, or get Lia to hit you on the head with a hammer, or whatever. You don't get to indulge yourself in staying awake and feeling miserable . . . not this time.*

He sighed. All the times he had given Kirk his

advice, and had been so sure he was right, while Kirk sat in that center seat and joked with him, and sometimes took the advice, and sometimes ignored it. . . . Often McCoy had been sure that things would have worked out better, more elegantly, more simply, if Kirk had done what he told him. They had worked out anyhow, as a rule, and McCoy had shrugged and tended his own business in Sickbay, and made that part of things work.

But now there was more business to tend to than just Sickbay, and it was all his responsibility. And no matter who gave *him* advice, and no matter how good it was, the responsibility for the choices he made would lie with *him*.

And if he had a good idea, and acted on it, and it didn't work, that would be his responsibility too.

He found himself wondering how Kirk had ever been able to accept his advice with such good humor, when he did accept it.

He found himself wondering whether any of his advice had ever been good at all, all those times he had hung over the back of the center seat and made off-the-cuff suggestions.

Well, he thought, *at least* some *things are going right around here. I've gotten all introspective again. First time I've had the leisure for it in hours.* Not that being introspective was bad for a doctor at all, especially when he had the kind of psychiatric responsibilities that McCoy had, with the whole gestalt of a starship more or less in his professional hands. But overdoing it could be a mistake, and sometimes McCoy veered that way. It was a tendency he had learned to watch out for.

Someone touched his door signal. He got up and answered it. There was no one there but a tray, hovering on its automatic transport pad. McCoy chuckled a little: apparently Meg had gotten Scotty to teach her transport pads a new trick or two.

He picked the tray up, and the pad silently zipped off down the corridor and around the corner, out of sight. "Just as well," he muttered, taking the tray inside. "I was out of change for a tip."

The sandwich vanished in short order, followed by the coffee. McCoy began to feel better almost instantly. *Blood sugar,* he thought. *I've got to eat bigger breakfasts if I'm going to be stuck in this job for long. Tea and toast doesn't make it.*

His intercom whistled then. "McCoy," he said, finishing the last of the coffee.

"Doctor," Spock said, *"five minutes to the meeting."*

"What? Never. I just got here," he muttered. "Oh, hell, I guess time *does* fly when you're having fun. I'll be right down, Spock."

"Acknowledged."

McCoy took just long enough to change into a fresh uniform tunic—no time for even a sonic shower, it would have to wait—and headed out.

"All right," he said, looking around the concerned faces at the table in Main Briefing. "One at a time, from best to worst. Engineering."

"No problems, nothing to report," Scotty said.

"Bless you. Keep it that way. Communications."

"Same as Mr. Scott," Uhura said, "with the exception of our inability to find the Captain by the usual means."

"We'll get back to that. Recreation."

Harb Tanzer, the big silver-haired rec room chief, said, "No operational problems. Crewmen coming in on their off-shift time are a bit nervous about the Captain's disappearance, but it isn't a serious situation as yet."

"Mmf. How are they viewing the present, uh, command?"

Harb smiled a bit. "With some amusement," he said, "but positively. You've bandaged up too many of them for them to doubt your general expertise, and they know you're getting good help."

McCoy allowed himself a breath or so of laughter. "All right. Science."

"We have a huge body of data to add to what we gathered yesterday," Spock said, "especially as regards plant life and subsoil flora and fauna. It may interest you to know—it will certainly interest Starfleet—that this planet is one of the most promising sources of medicinal substances that we have ever found."

"That's wonderful," McCoy said, meaning it, "but it also means that Starfleet is going to put that much more pressure on us for a three-species agreement. My delight knows no bounds.—What else?"

"There is also much more information about the physiologies of the Ornae and Lahit. We are coming to some conclusions that may shortly lead to theories that will explain how such very different species evolved here. On that count, at least, our present information agrees with that of the original survey."

"You mean, they were actually right about something." There was muted laughter around the table.

McCoy smiled sardonically. "Noted. What have you been finding? Any fossil records?"

"Surprisingly, yes. One of the landing-party teams, from Geology, has been concentrating on some submerged strata off the northern coast of the continent where most of our research is taking place. There is a possibility, bizarre as it sounds, that the Lahit and the Ornae have a common ancestor-species."

McCoy shook his head. "That would be an eye-opener. Anyway, I take it that this information has all been packed up for the next transmission to Starfleet."

"It has."

"Good. Security."

Ingrit Tomson, the tall, blond security chief, said, "Nothing to report shipside, sir. On the planet, we have search groups combing the entire area where our contacts with the Ornae and Lahit have been concentrated, and then spiraling outward. Nothing has been found as yet, though we've covered some fifty square kilometers. There is no sign whatsoever of the Captain, but there have also been no overt signs of foul play."

"There is also something rather peculiar," Spock said. "Doctor, after you furnished me with the coordinates to which you beamed down, I was able to get a temperature scan of the area—even when some hours have passed, there are infrared heat-traces of the passage of the human body." Spock reached out and touched the data terminal in front of him. A second later, everyone's terminal was showing a picture of the clearing, seen from above, its colors processed by the computer to indicate areas of latent heat.

There was a wavering line that came from one side of the clearing, circled around one spot, and then vanished.

"That's what Jim did?" McCoy said.

"No, Doctor. That is what *you* did. *This* is the Captain's trace." He pointed to another fat smudgy line, off to one side of the clearing, that entered it at the same point . . . and faded out.

Glances were exchanged around the table. "Somebody else's transporter beam?" McCoy said.

"Unlikely, Doctor. That too leaves some slight thermal trace, and some characteristic background radiation. This fade-out is atypical, and does not resemble a beam-up."

"Great," McCoy said. *"Something* grabbed him and spirited him away. Something subtle enough for us to need methods like this to find out about it." He sighed. "Any theories?"

"None as yet," Spock said.

"All right. Defense?"

"Nothing to report," Chekov said. "All ship's defense systems at normal and on standby."

"Good. Medicine?"

Lia, sitting down toward the end of the table, said, "Business as usual, Doctor. Routine small interventions. It looks as if Morrison's problem was some kind of allergy, by the way. No one else has reported a similar problem, and his skin irritation is almost gone."

"That's good. Communications—"

"Linguistics and I have been working closely together," Uhura said, "trying to improve the level of translation a little faster than would be the norm.

Unfortunately, we're having some difficulties—not with vocabulary so much, at this point, but with conceptualization and very different mindmaps. I have a recording I'd like you all to see."

She touched a control on her own terminal. Their screens came alive to show her sitting on the ground, chatting amiably with an Ornaet, while Kerasus sat next to her taking notes.

"I have a question to ask you," said Uhura in the recording.

"All right," the Ornaet said.

"One of our people is missing down here," she said. "Do you understand *missing?*"

"Not to be found," said the Ornaet. "Why did he do it?"

"He didn't do it himself," said Uhura. "Someone else did it."

"That's ridiculous," said the Ornaet.

"How so?"

"No one does things, except by themselves. He must have wanted to go away, if he went somewhere."

On the tape, Uhura thought about that for a moment, then said, "Where do you think he might have gone?"

"I don't know. Why would he want to go away at all?"

"That's what we're trying to find out. Have any of your own people gone missing this way?"

"Oh, lots. But they were all right here."

"Here, close by? Or here, on the planet?"

"Yes."

Another long pause. The Ornaet, sitting next to her, turned slightly in the sunlight, and its iridescence flashed bright. "Why are you asking these questions?" the Ornaet said.

"We're worried about our friend."

"Why? He's all right."

"How do you know that?"

"Nothing ever happens to anyone here. The ;At make sure of that."

In the recording, Uhura raised her eyebrows. "Yes," she said, "let's talk about that. Where *are* the ;At today?"

"They're here," said the Ornaet.

"What? Here with us, right now?"

"Yes."

"I can't see them," said Uhura.

"Neither can I," said the Ornaet, "but they're here."

"Do you think they know where our friend is?"

"Probably," said the Ornaet. "They know most things."

"Could you ask them?"

"When they get here," the Ornaet said, "yes."

"But you said they were here."

"They *are*," said the Ornaet, sounding faintly cross.

"Is there a reason you can't ask them now?"

"Yes," said the Ornaet.

A long pause. "What is it?" Uhura said.

"Because [static]," said the recording.

One or two people around the table groaned. McCoy resisted the temptation. They had a real problem here; one of those alien-point-of-view differences that might take months to understand and resolve. Somehow he doubted Starfleet was going to give him months.

112

"All right," said Uhura in the recording, "we'll come back to that. When you *can* ask them, will you?"

"All right." There was another pause. "It doesn't matter, you know," said the Ornaet. "Your friend is all right."

"But how do you know that?" Kerasus put in from the side.

The Ornaet put up its eyestalks at her. "Nothing happens here," it said. "And your friend must have wanted to go."

At the table, Uhura reached out and froze the frame. "That went on for about an hour," she said; "I've just shown you the highlights. We talked with various other of the Ornae and a few of the Lahit— our work with their language is coming along very satisfactorily, though we'd still like to know how the two species can speak completely different languages and understand one another without benefit of translation. There's no telepathic component—we think. At any rate, everyone we talked to was certain that the Captain must have *wanted* to vanish, that he was just fine, and that the ;At probably knew something about it, and would tell us everything we wanted to know when they arrived. Despite the fact that they were already here." She sighed. "Several of them insisted that the Captain was in fact there *now,* and that we were making a big fuss over nothing."

"What are the odds of that?" McCoy said. "Spock?"

"Doctor, we are moving among many unknowns here." Spock laced his fingers together and gazed at McCoy over them. "I have no way to give you odds on such an improbability. We must obviously continue

113

searching in the orthodox fashion, but we must also take great care with our other data gathering so as not to miss some small piece of information that might make all these seeming contradictions plain. Most urgently, the linguistic work must continue to go ahead at its best speed."

"We concur," Uhura said. "We're keeping our people on it."

"I just want to remind you all of that line that the first landing party heard yesterday," McCoy said, "something to the effect that the only ones around Flyspeck who had objections to things were the ;At. We have yet to find out what that means. Uhura, I'd like you and Lt. Kerasus to follow that up. And we have some other mysteries to solve; for example, the ;At I spoke to this morning claimed that there were nearly a million of them. Where are they all? How come the initial survey had no problem finding them —lots of them? What's making them fight so shy of us? We need *answers* about this stuff."

Heads nodded all around the table as people took notes. "And there are other problems," McCoy said. "As soon as they get this news, Starfleet is going to get antsy, and want to know what we're *doing* about getting the Captain back—knowing them."

"We have no diplomatic recourses," said Spock, "since as yet there is no diplomatic agreement. Starfleet will doubtless suggest some kind of display of force."

"They can just go to bed early on *that* one," McCoy snapped. "These people barely understand the concept of death or injury, as far as I can figure it out. *I* don't want to be the one to teach them what it means. Neither would Jim, if he were here in my place. I'll refuse such an order if they give it. Or find some way to weasel out of it."

Spock's expression was calm, but there was warning hidden in it. "If we are successful in finding the Captain," he said, "Starfleet may well forgive you that . . . eventually. If not . . . your career in Starfleet may be short."

"That's as may be," McCoy said. "I have oaths to follow, the same as they do. The discipline of the service be damned." He paused, and then said, "We *have* stopped recording this briefing, haven't we?"

"No one will hear," Spock said, "what was certainly a casual remark made after the meeting proper." He looked at Uhura.

"Of course not," she said to Spock. "I'll just look around and see if I can't find my sewing scissors."

McCoy chuckled. "All right. Anyone have anything to add?"

No one said a word. "Good enough," McCoy said. "Let's all get back to what we were doing. Keep calm, keep your people calm, and be nice and slow and methodical—"

That was when the red-alert siren went off. McCoy leaped straight up out of his seat. He had never been good with sudden loud noises. "Holy Christmas, what's that??"

"Red alert, red alert, this is no drill, this is no drill," said the voice of the automated alert. And right afterward came the voice of the junior Communications officer, Mr. Brandt. *"Proximity alarms activated,"* he said calmly, *"vessel dropping out of warp and incoming to orbit. Early ID indicates Klingon battle cruiser—"*

People scrambled out of the room at speed. McCoy

stood there with his mouth open for a bare second, then said, "Hell." He ran out into the corridor, turned down toward Sickbay—

And stopped. And cursed. And turned, and ran after Spock, toward the turbolift, and the Bridge.

Chapter Five

HE COULD HEAR the bedlam of the Bridge before the turbolift doors even opened for him. Alarms were whooping, people were running in all directions, but what astounded McCoy most was the sheer *noise* of it all. Red alerts in Sickbay were a much quieter business; they had to be, or they might wake the patients. *This noise would wake the dead,* he thought in mild amazement.

The doors opened for him, and McCoy stepped out. All over the Bridge, heads turned; eyes looked at him speculatively. He could practically feel the thoughts. *How is he, is he, going to be able to manage this, what if he can't . . . ?*

But this at least was a position he had been in before; on a planet's surface, or in some operating room, where the staff had looked over at him, wondering, *Can he save this one, or will we have another wrap job in a few minutes? . . .* He had usually managed to surprise them all. He would do it again.

He hoped.

He stepped down without hesitation, as he had seen Jim do so many times, sat himself in the center seat, and said, "What's the situation?"

"Shields are up," Spock said, coming down to stand beside him, "and weapons systems are ready."

"All right, then. Do we have an ID on this clown?"

"Yes, Doctor—ah, sir," Sulu said. "Positive identification as KL 818, Imperial Klingon Vessel *Ekkava.*"

"No one we know personally, then," McCoy said.

"No," Spock said. "The vessel has assumed a standard orbit around the planet, slightly above ours, and is pacing us some two thousand kilometers behind. Just outside firing range," he added.

"Mmm hmm. So the gesture is overtly . . . noncommittal. So far." McCoy looked at the screen, which showed the faint white blip well back behind them. "No communications as yet?"

"Nothing yet, Doctor," Uhura said. "They're probably busy scanning."

"Confirmed," Spock said, glancing over at his station.

"All right. Why wait to be friendly? Uhura, hail them. The usual niceties."

She nodded, and did it. McCoy looked up at Spock and said, "I remember Jim mentioning a rumor that he'd heard, something about an increased incidence of Klingon 'moles' inside Starfleet. You think there's anything to that?"

Spock looked abstracted for a moment. "Difficult to say. Certainly one can understand the reasoning behind it. But it strikes me as information that both sides would desire to keep hidden. At least, accurate versions of the information."

"Mmm hmm. Spock, we're a long way from any-where out here. Funny that they should just come coasting into the system like this, a couple of days after we do."

"'Funny' is not the word I would have chosen," Spock said. "But it certainly does strain the limits of probability somewhat."

The Bridge fell quiet, waiting. McCoy wiped his hands on his trousers. *Here we go,* he thought. *I just wish I had some better idea of what to do. Nothing to do but wing it, I guess. . . .* Then Uhura said, "Coming on screen, Doctor. Ready for visual?"

The question almost made him laugh. He had never really had to worry about how he looked at work before. "Ready," he said.

The screen shimmered, and the starfield it had been showing gave way to the bridge of a Klingon ship, all dim red lighting and cramped, crowded-together con-soles. In the center of the screen, a Klingon glared at them: a man with a rather noble face, McCoy thought, with excellent bone structure. *Pity he has to ruin the effect by glowering like that. Then again, I guess it's an occupational hazard for Klingons in command posi-tions. Look tough or get shot—*

"*I am Commander Kaiev,*" the Klingon said. "*Is your vessel's identification correct?*"

McCoy leaned back in the center seat and was visibly amused. Among the Klingons, as on Earth, there was no surer way to discommode a very serious person than to refuse to take the individual seriously. "Well now," he said, "and why wouldn't it be? We're not in the habit of running around playing Galactic Twenty Questions."

"*Then you* are *the Starship* Enterprise?"

"Yes," he said to the Klingon, and nodded, "we are. Who wants to know?"

Commander Kaiev stared into the screen, and at McCoy, with an expression that McCoy thought was supposed to be fierce eagerness. *"I have long waited my chance to meet the famous Kirk,"* he said.

Not another one, McCoy thought. *How the hell does Jim stand it?* "Sorry," he said, lacing his hands behind his head and leaning back. "You just missed him."

"Missed him?" the Klingon said, looking for a moment slightly bemused. *"We did not fire."*

There was a suppressed snicker somewhere on the Bridge. McCoy shot a warning glance around, then said, "Uh, excuse me, Commander. Syntactical difficulty. I mean, he's not here."

The Klingon looked actively disappointed. "Commander Leonard McCoy, at your service," he said, before the Klingon could pick up the conversational ball. "Now, Commander, would you mind telling me a little something about what you're doing in this part of space? Not exactly a crowded neighborhood, as a rule."

"Ah," Commander Kaiev said. *"We have been— exploring this part of space for some weeks now—"*

Lie, McCoy thought. He knew that much Klingon body language, even when the man was sitting still, and trying to keep his face still as well.

"—and when by chance we detected your ship here, so far away from Federation-frequented space—"

Lie, McCoy thought. And, *Ambulance-chaser!* They just want to see what we're up to, and see if they can't find a way to get a bit of the action if it's anything good. He kept smiling.

120

"—we thought we would stop and investigate."

Now, McCoy thought, *he waits to see if I'll tell him to get out of here.* "Well, you're more than welcome here, Commander," he said. "Four planets, no waiting. Make yourself right at home."

Commander Kaiev actually blinked. McCoy had a hard time keeping his face straight, but managed it somehow. *Now he lets us know that he would have anyway,* he thought.

"So we have done," said Kaiev, with a sort of air of jovial threat that McCoy had to admire. *"We shall send down landing parties to investigate the planet."*

"Well, go ahead," McCoy said. "But I should warn you, things are pretty weird down there. We've lost some people in odd ways. Trees eating them, mostly."

The Bridge crew all looked at McCoy in fascination. He ignored them. "But don't mind that," McCoy said jovially. "You go ahead down there, have a good time. Our people will show you around, if you like."

An expression of suspicion did not so much creep across Kaiev's face as run across it, shouting and waving placards saying *I don't believe you, you're up to something!* McCoy was delighted, and kept his own face straight. *"No, thank you, MakKhoi,"* Kaiev said. *"We will manage our own investigation of this planet. Shall we speak further of this?"*

Or in other words, 'Wanna fight?' "No, heavens, why should we?" McCoy said, waving a hand languidly. "You go right on ahead. But listen," he added, "you watch out for those trees, now. And the *rocks.*" He leaned forward a little as he said the word, and waggled his eyebrows at the Klingon.

"MakKhoi," said Kaiev, looking slightly discom-

moded by McCoy's strange expressions, *"I must ask you. What has happened to Kirk?"*

McCoy paused for a moment, then sighed heavily and leaned back in the center seat again, looking down. "I killed him," he said. "In a duel. Very sad."

And he looked up then, and gave Kaiev a long cool look from under his brows. "I do *so* hate killing my friends," he said.

Kaiev looked at him for a long moment. He opened his mouth, but before he could say anything, McCoy sighed again and said, quite cheerfully, "At any rate, Commander, if we can help you with any little thing, don't hesitate to call. *Enterprise* out." And he glanced over at Uhura, who killed the circuit. The screen went back to showing starfield again.

There was a rather stunned silence on the Bridge. Then the laughter broke out. McCoy let it go on for a few moments, then said, "All right, everybody, hush up now!"

They got quiet. "That should give us a few minutes to breathe," he said, "since they'll now think the *Enterprise* is being commanded by a raving loon. Perhaps even a homicidal raving loon, which would be even better."

"I think you are wise," Spock said, "not to let them know that the Captain is missing. They would certainly perceive that as a weakness, perhaps a fatal one, on our part."

"Spock," McCoy said, smiling a bit, "I may be just an old country doctor, but I know enough not to tell my patients that I don't know how to cure them. Why, half of them cure themselves just because they think I'm doing it. Saves me no end of trouble, and it's cheaper than placebos."

"In any case," Spock said, "there is nothing we can do about their presence here. Under the Organian Peace Treaty, they are entitled to explore planets that they find us exploring, even the populated ones. Of course, the 'exploitation' part of the agreement does not apply here."

"And a good thing. I'd hate to see this planet Klingon-dominated. The Ornae are too good-natured, and the Lahit are just too strange; I have a feeling neither species would long survive a Klingon settlement."

Spock nodded. "However that may be," he said, "we now have a more interesting problem: how to conduct our searches for the Captain without letting the Klingons know."

McCoy nodded. "Our own efforts can be disguised as land surveys and so forth," he said. "But I worry that the Ornae might tell them. Or the Lahit. They wouldn't understand the need not to, I think."

"I don't think they would either, Doctor," Uhura said. "The whole concept of fiction and falsehood seems to have passed them by."

"Sad that they'll miss fiction," McCoy said, "but as for the rest of it, they may be into a good thing. Never mind. We have a little protection in that the Klingons won't have much in the way of translator algorithms."

"Doctor," Sulu said suddenly, "if you're right in your suspicion about moles in Starfleet, the reason the Klingons are here might well be that the whole initial survey report was leaked."

That was a bad thought. McCoy mulled it over for a moment, then said, "That may be. We've had the whole linguistics resource team of this ship working on those languages for two days now, and we're just

123

beginning to make progress. It's going to take them a while to catch up. By then, we may have found the captain."

"And if not?" Spock said. "What then? Or what if they come to us and ask us in a friendly fashion for our algorithms? You have set the tone for this encounter, Doctor, and have practically invited them to do so."

McCoy had been thinking about that. Now he grinned evilly. "Simple," he said. "Media mismatch. Our software won't talk to their hardware."

"But it will," Spock said.

"No, it *won't*," McCoy said. "Think about it. When's the last time the Klingons had access to our data transfer methods? Goodness, Spock, *anything* could have been invented since then."

Spock got a glint in his eye that McCoy had seen before, and always enjoyed. "I take your point, Doctor," he said. "But that aside, we must get back to business. We have our own work to do, not least of which is finding the Captain."

"Right. Spock, you coordinate the landing parties, and Uhura, make sure everybody gets the word about what's going on. Utmost courtesy to our guests, give them anything they want—except data—within reason. The old Galactic Unity game."

"Yes, Doctor," Uhura said.

"I would have thought," Spock said, "that you approved of Galactic Unity, Doctor."

"I do," McCoy said, "with those who mean it the same way I do. The Klingons just have a little convincing to do, as far as I'm concerned." He sat back and smiled.

Spock nodded and went about his business. McCoy stood up. "Keep an eye on our friends here," he said to Sulu. "If they do anything sudden, call me. I've got to catch forty winks. Uhura," he said, "if the landing parties that are staying down tonight find anything, call me right away. Or if anything else happens that you or your relief judge to need my attention."

"Yes, sir."

He headed for the turbolift, waited for the doors to close.

When they did, he collapsed against the back wall and shut his eyes, and tried very hard not to moan out loud.

"Deck five," he finally said, when he could trust himself not to say something that would confuse the lift's audio sensors. It began to move.

He was shaking all over. *Like a mouse at a cat show,* he thought. *I hope I get used to this fast, because Lord, I'm not used to it now, and if I misstep because of nerves, a lot of people could die.*

He fell into the deep-breathing exercise routine that did him the most good for an attack of nerves. *I need a good long spell of anti-stress exercises tonight,* he thought, *and then maybe I should get Lia to come hit me on the head with that hammer. Lord, Klingons, whose good idea was* that? *Not funny, God!*

The Deity declined to respond, possibly being on a break. The deep breathing began to work; the trembling started to ease off. *I may need something else to eat,* McCoy thought, as the lift slid to a stop. *I only had the one sandwich, after all. I wonder if Jim sometimes eats to distract himself from the stress?*

It was an interesting thought, one that McCoy had

had before, and usually discarded. He was now less willing to discard it. *Jim may need better stress management. I should have noticed that before, if that's the case. Getting sloppy,* Leonard my boy . . .

His room door opened before him, and closed behind him. He sat down in his rocking chair with a feeling of vast relief. Unfortunately, behind the relief was a formless terror that insisted on reminding him that there was no way to tell how long the relief would last. He sat there and finished his breathing exercises, and then thought about ordering something else to eat. *No,* he thought then. *Stress reduction first. If I try eating anything with my stomach in its present state, it's going to be sent back with extreme prejudice.*

He composed himself, made sure his breathing was settled, closed his eyes, and set about imagining the private place where he did his mindwork.

About five seconds later he fell asleep.

"Here," he was saying to Dieter, "I've spilled your drink; let me get you another," when the soprano shriek of the Jungfrau cogwheel train's horn abruptly turned into the intercom's whistle. McCoy's eyes flew open. He sat up straight in the chair from his original slumped position, and grimaced at the feel of his back—no matter how orthopedically sound straight-back rocking chairs are, they aren't made for sleeping in. McCoy reached out and hit the intercom button.

"McCoy."

"Bridge, Doctor. It's Ensign Vehau, on Communications. We've got something in from Starfleet for you."

He groaned. "At this hour? Tell them to take two aspirin and call me in the morning."

Vehau laughed softly. *"I wish I could. Unfortunately,*

you're going to have to come up here and sign for the miserable thing, and right away, too."

McCoy sighed. "On my way," he said.

He made his way up to the Bridge through the subdued lighting of night shift. The ship worked better when it had a "real" night and day; and in consideration of the crewmen who were diurnal, the night shift was largely run by people who had minimal difficulty with being awake at night, especially members of naturally nocturnal species—a surprising 30 percent or so of hominids.

Vehau was one of these. The Delasi were quite humanoid, and gave no other indication of their nocturnal status than particularly large, sensitive, and (McCoy thought) beautiful-looking dark eyes. When McCoy came into the Bridge, he found Vehau looking with mild annoyance at her station. "Here, Doctor," she said. "It's already queried me twice."

"Where do I look?" he said.

"Here, this scanner, sir."

McCoy bent over it and kept his eyes wide, waiting for the ruby flash of the retinal-scan laser. It came, and immediately the console began to chatter softly to itself. "There you go," Vehau said, and touched a stud. "Do you want to take it in your cabin, or would you rather have vision and sound here?"

McCoy sighed and sat himself down in the center seat. "I'll take it here, I suppose," he said. "Nobody here but us chickens, anyway. Who's on call for Weapons and Navigation, by the way?"

"Navigation is shut down for the moment," she said. "The ship's orbit is on automaintenance . . . might as well be: she doesn't need anyone here to handle a standard orbit. Sulu volunteered to take an extra shift on Weapons. He's on his break; he'll be back up in a while. Just us chickens, as you say." She wrinkled her nose a bit. "What *is* a chicken?"

"An Earth beast famous for crossing roads," McCoy said. "All right, Vehau. Let it rip."

The screen showed the usual Starfleet time-and-date-stamp trailer. Then McCoy found himself looking at a man sitting at a desk. "Oh hell," he said, for the man was Admiral Delacroix, a name that he had heard Jim mutter about more than once. "Superannuated," Jim had said, and there was truth in it; Delacroix looked as if he had been around since the Ice Age—the earlier one. He was white-haired and tall, with chiseled features, and the kind of stance and bearing that says a person prides himself on being better, or at least older, than you are.

"Delacroix," he said. He sat there with his hands folded on the desk, looking like a man who was about to give some schoolboy a serious scolding. "To Leonard McCoy, presently in command, USS *Enterprise.* Commander McCoy, we are in receipt of your report and find it a rather disturbing collection of documents.

"First of all, our concerns regarding the divergent evolution of the planet's three species are not being dealt with in the approved manner. Much pertinent data is missing regarding the third species, the ;At." He didn't pronounce it any better than anyone else, McCoy thought; there was that small consolation. "We expect better performance in data gathering from a starship of *Enterprise*'s reputation. We assume the fall-off in efficiency is due to the missing status of Captain Kirk, which we will deal with in a moment. At any rate, we expect the information shortfall to be dealt with immediately. Please take the necessary steps."

"Oh, sure," McCoy said bitterly. "What am I supposed to do? You can't find a species that doesn't want to be found, dammit all—"

But the recording was continuing. "Second. Surveys concerning planet-exploitable resources are not proceeding at the speed we would wish. No informed decisions can be made regarding diplomacy without full data on planetary resources. Your crew rosters as submitted show too much concentration on sciences and linguistics at this point. Please reassign personnel from linguistics work to planet survey and report soonest on mineral and other resources."

McCoy sat there tight-lipped. *He's saying that all of a sudden they don't want to talk to these people until they find out whether they've got anything worth having! Dammit, that wasn't our original brief from Starfleet! Who put this turkey on the job all of a sudden? Where the hell are Llewellyn and Tai Hao, who backed this mission in the first place, on scientific grounds?*

"Third. We regard with grave concern the disappearance of Captain Kirk. From your report we must assume that the Captain was not in breach of his orders when he transported down to the planet, since at that point the situation seemed to be stable." McCoy frowned; the man sounded as if he were faintly disappointed by this fact. "It becomes apparent that there has been some deterioration in your exploratory group's relations with one or more of the indigenous species, possibly the ;At. This breakdown is almost certainly due to inadequate data gathering regarding this species, and you are required to rectify this situation immediately. We note your attempts to locate the Captain. We confirm your brief to take all appropriate action to recover the Captain, including the military option if you find it prudent or necessary. We will expect a report with your next transmission as to what steps are being taken and what results are forthcoming. If no results are forthcoming within one standard day, orders will be issued regarding possible action to be taken against the planet. Until then, matters are left to your discretion, within our guidelines."

Delacroix stopped and cleared his throat a bit, as if he were about to say something distasteful. "Last: regarding your present position in command. Despite the fact that your service record indicates no previous experience with starship command, other aspects of your record indicate that this is a duty you should be adequately equipped to undertake; and Captain Kirk is an officer of sufficient skill to have had some good reason, under the circumstances, to leave you in command. We are reluctant to countermand Captain Kirk's orders in his absence and relieve you of duty. We expect that your conduct will justify this judgment. However, in light of the past day's occurrences, there will of course need to be some kind of inquiry into the management of this mission on your return to Earth. You are advised to bear this in mind.

"Reply is required within one hour of receipt of this message, already verified to us. Starfleet out."

"And what about the goddam Klingons??!" McCoy shouted at the screen. It ignored him, going blank and showing him the serene face of Flyspeck turning beneath the ship as she orbited.

Vehau said, "Shall I save you a copy of the message, Doctor?"

McCoy was very tempted to make several creative suggestions as to what Vehau might do with the report; one of them, involving the report, Delacroix, a can of surgical lubricant, and a protoplaser, struck him as particularly attractive, but he pushed the thought aside as unworthy of him. "Yes, please. I'll want Spock to see it in the morning. Meanwhile, would you record a reply for me?"

"Do you want to make it now?"

"Certainly. Just voice. I don't want that old prune seeing me without a shave and my boots polished; he'd probably order me tied to a gun carriage and left out in the rain, if I know his type."

He sat thinking for a moment. *Maybe I should call Spock and ask his advice,* he thought. *He's probably not sleeping anyway.* But after a long moment, he pushed that idea away. *Hell no . . . I've got to do my best to manage this myself. Even if it drives me crazy, and scares me to death. Have to wonder, though. Who else at Starfleet is going to see this report when I send it back?*

And who leaked the first one? . . .

He thought for a moment about who might hear what, and what might be done with the information. Then, "Ready?" he said to Vehau.

"Go, Doctor."

"From Leonard McCoy, commanding USS *Enterprise,*" he said. "Your message received and understood. Will comply in all parts." *But not the way you think, you old fool.* "Search for Captain Kirk continues. Other conditions continue normal." He paused

131

for a moment, then added, "Klingon situation stable. McCoy out."

Vehau chuckled softly as she completed the reply. "Anything else, Doctor?"

"Nope. Send it. That should give them something to think about," McCoy said. *I dearly hope.* "And now I'm going to go back to my downy couch. You have a good shift, dear, and don't call me for anything less imperative than an invasion."

"Will do, Doctor."

"Bureaucrats," McCoy muttered softly, and staggered off to bed.

In the morning he was in the center seat bright and early, having managed to work in a little stress reduction before breakfast, and was feeling rather more alert and ready for things. Also, he had had some time to think. "Spock," he said, when he had settled in and Spock had given him the morning report, "have you seen the wonderful message from Starfleet that we had last night?"

"Doctor," said Spock, "you exercise your usual talent for choosing unique and perhaps unexpected words to describe a situation."

"Yes, indeed, you saw it too. Spock, I think we should do everything they suggest."

Spock looked at him in mild astonishment.

"Yes, indeed," McCoy said. "I want you to make some reassignments from linguistics to survey. Take, oh, Nuara and Meier—Wes, not Wilma—and give them one of the shuttlecraft for the next day or so. I want a mineral survey. Particular concentration on iron ore deposits, the usual."

"Doctor," Spock said, "we have already done that

scan from the ship. It came up broadly negative, as you know. The planet is very metal-poor, and rare earths are in a much lower-than-usual concentration. Nor are there any deposits of dilithium or other useful energy-managing elements."

"Yes, you're absolutely right. Well, evidently Starfleet wants more information, and they want some people reassigned to that duty, so let's give them what they want. Full shuttlecraft survey, with sensors on high-density."

"That will result in a massive data load," Spock said, "on the order of—"

"It's Starfleet's nickel," McCoy said. "Let them worry about it. And won't someone there be pleased when they see so much detailed data? They'll be hours going through it. Days, if we're lucky."

"Analysis will of course show them that there is nothing here worth pursuing as far as minerals are concerned."

"And that'll be exactly right. Though I have a feeling there are some people at Starfleet who may not want to believe that. Not people working *just* for Starfleet, you understand."

Spock turned an expression on McCoy that was covertly approving. "Your orders will be carried out," he said. "Meanwhile, as regards the personnel reassignments—I think the Admiral will have had rather more people in mind."

"He didn't say," McCoy said regretfully. "Can't go second-guessing the man if he won't make himself clear."

That covert approval got more overt. "Doctor," Spock said, "while I understand your intent, there are some at Starfleet who could construe it as insubordination. *That* would give them an excuse to relieve you, and whatever the results as regards finding the Captain, the damage to your career could be extreme."

"At the moment," he said, "I'll take my chances. But thanks for your concern, Spock."

Spock nodded and went to his station, preparatory to going back down to the planet. McCoy sat in his chair and gazed at the screen, looking at the tiny dot of the Klingon vessel tailing them, far back, at a respectful distance.

"No news from them, I take it."

"No. They have been busy on the planet all night, doing mineral surveys and so forth, if I am correctly reading our recordings of their activities. The action seems to have stopped for the moment."

"It's their night, perhaps?"

"Difficult to tell. Power levels on their ship have not changed much since they arrived."

"Hmm. Rude to make noise and wake the neighbors. I'll say hello to them later. Meanwhile, have you got any ideas about Jim?"

Spock came down from his station and stood by McCoy, gazing at the screen. "Doctor," he said slowly, "I have tried every kind of analysis of the presently available data that I can think of. The Captain does not seem to be on the planet at the moment. Certainly he *was* there. Less certainly," Spock said, "there is no evidence of him leaving it."

"Huh? You saw that disappearance trace."

"Yes. Doctor, think for a moment. Even if a transporter of some kind unknown to us had taken hold of the captain and pulled him off the surface of the planet, it could not have done so undetected. The universe does not work that way. There would have been energy residue of at least one of several hundred kinds—some indication of the source of the instrumentality that removed the Captain, leading off-planet. I have spent the night in careful analysis of all the ship's sensor data for the past two days. No indication of any such outside interference occurs; all background radiation is exactly as it should be. Faced with this data—or lack of data that would disprove it—I am forced to conclude that Captain Kirk is still on the planet."

McCoy raised his eyebrows, then lowered them. "The Ornae and the Lahit *have* been saying that the Captain's right there, and he's fine."

"So they have. At first I did not consider it evidence to be taken at all seriously, not with the Translator algorithms still so uncertain. But their certainty is increasing hour by hour, as Uhura and Kerasus do their work, and the translation of that piece of information does not change."

"And," McCoy said, "there's that odd radiation you picked up. The Cerenkov radiation, and those Z-particle decays."

"Yes. I cannot understand what they mean as yet, but I am still working on our scan data. There have been more occurrences of the radiation over the past day, but not associated with any consistent event or set of events that I can correlate."

McCoy looked thoughtful. *Now how do I phrase this so as not to bother him?* "Spock," he said, lowering his voice, "you occasionally have a knack for, uh, feeling what's going on with Jim, at a distance. You haven't had any 'bad feelings,' have you?"

Spock was silent for a moment. *Uh-oh,* McCoy thought. But then Spock said, very quietly, "Doctor, I

135

have not. I can frequently 'hear,' from humans, what is best expressed as a sort of mental white noise. I cannot detect the Captain's. But there is no sense of his ideation having stopped; it simply feels as if it is *elsewhere.*" He looked at McCoy a bit quizzically. "Not evidence admissible in court, certainly. But in its way, reassuring."

"Well, let me know if you find out anything interesting, or anything you think I can help with. High-energy physics is way over my head, but I'm good at some other things."

Spock raised an eyebrow. "I had occasionally noticed," he said, and went back to his station.

McCoy sat back and gazed at the screen. "I wish I could get down there," he said softly. "Oh, well."

They were coming out from over the night side of Flyspeck. The terminator fell away beneath them in a sudden sunrise; or a backward sunset—McCoy wasn't sure whether they were orbiting the same way the planet rotated. *I should start paying attention to that kind of thing,* he thought. *Not that I really want to . . .*

"Hmm," said Chekov from the helm. "Some activity over there, Doctor."

"Who? The Klingons?"

"Affirmative. Transporters running." Chekov watched his scanners for a moment, then said, "They're beaming down a party near where three of our groups are working, near the First Clearing."

"Uhura, give our people a shout and let them know that company's coming," McCoy said. "It's morning where our group is, isn't it?"

"Yes, Doctor," Spock said. "About three hours after local sunrise."

136

McCoy nodded. "Chekov," he said, "you just scan that new landing party and see if they're carrying anything antisocial-looking."

Chekov peered at his screens for a moment. "Nothing, Doctor," he said. "Standard sidearms, and some light digging equipment—core samplers and so forth."

"Such as you might use when looking for minerals?" McCoy said idly.

"That's right," Chekov said. "A small ground wehicle, too. Not armed."

"Hmm," said McCoy. "Well, I wish them luck. At least they'll be getting some fresh air and exercise."

Chekov chuckled. "Setting off away from our landing party, Doctor. At a pretty good rate, too."

"Message from the landing party, Doctor," Uhura said. "They say the Klingons passed through their camp like—" She chuckled. "They passed through very fast, heading for the hills to the north."

McCoy nodded and sat back. "Keep our people posted on that party's movements," he said.

Uhura nodded. "Will do, Doctor."

It got quiet. People moved around the Bridge, all doing their business; everybody but McCoy, who sat in the middle of things and began to feel the boredom nibbling at the edges of his mind. *There's nothing for me to do here,* he thought, *except wait. I hate waiting. Maybe I could just go down to Sickbay and do a couple of routine exams . . . No, Jim ordered me not to . . . and I accepted the order. Dammit. I should have just defied him right there and let him throw me in the brig. It's quiet down in the brig. Insulting people from Starfleet don't send you rude messages in the middle of the night when you're in the brig . . .*

Uhura's station made a querulous little queeping noise. McCoy glanced over at her as she fitted her transdator to her ear. Her eyes widened. McCoy didn't like the way they widened at *all*.

"The Klingon vessel is hailing us, Doctor," she said. "It's Commander Kaiev."

Uh-oh. "Put him on," he said.

The screen changed to show Kaiev's face. It was not a happy face, not at *all*. The Klingon seemed to be torn between rage and a cold sweat, and McCoy didn't like the look of either. *Hmm. Atypical petechiae on the face and brow ridges. Now what was that syndrome again*—"Good morning, Commander," McCoy said, to put his oar in first. "Or good evening, whichever it is. To what do I owe—"

"MakKhoi, you are responsible for this!" Kaiev shouted. *"My people were engaged in a peaceful exploration of the planet and you disintegrated them! This act of hostility will not go unpunished!"*

McCoy stared at him. "Pardon?" he said. "We've just been sitting here. We saw your party go down there, all right, but we—"

"It is useless to try to deceive me! They vanished from our scans without trace, in a matter of a second or so! What other explanation could there possibly be?!"

Uh, McCoy thought, and looked over at Spock. Spock raised one eyebrow, and shook his head.

McCoy turned back to the screen and looked carefully at the man. "Commander," he said, "you want to calm yourself a bit. Klingon blood pressure's high enough; you keep on like this and you're going to blow a fuse. And you just getting over that bout of arthasomiasis and all. Sure way to bring on a liver spasm."

Kaiev's mouth fell open for a fraction of a second. *"You—How do you know I have had arthasomiasis?"* His expression suddenly grew crafty. *"Your intelligence network is as far-flung as I have heard, then. Which of my crew is your spy? I will kill them all until I find the traitor!!"* He half rose from his chair, then sat down suddenly, with a look of surprise and pain on his face.

What are they doing, sending people like this out into space? McCoy thought, disapproving. *Their stress screening program must not be worth much.* "See now," he said, "what did I tell you? You go have a word with your medic and tell him or her to raise your regulation dosage of Tacrin. It's not high enough yet." He waited until the Klingon's color improved a little and the secondary muscle tics associated with the spasm began to taper off.

And then his temper flared. "And as for your landing party, son," and he began to rise out of his seat as he got louder, "let me tell you that if I felt like killing them, I'd just haul off and *do* it, and I wouldn't bother lying to *you* about it afterward, so don't flatter yourself!" He sat down again, ignoring the shocked looks from all around the Bridge. McCoy had always been a good shouter, and he had had a good shout coming for about two days now. It was a pleasure to be able to use one appropriately.

The Klingon looked at him with a mixture of somewhat abated fury and half-concealed admiration. He opened his mouth. "Now you just get hold of yourself," McCoy said immediately, "so we can talk like reasonable beings here, and if you use that tone with me again, my boy, I'll open your ship up like a sardine tin, and later on I'll fish your corpse out of space and thaw it out and stitch it back together the old-fashioned way, with a needle and thread, and then I'll use your guts for garters. Now go see your medic, and then get yourself back here and we'll talk. Out."

He jerked a thumb at Uhura in the gesture that he had seen Kirk use so many times before. She killed the connection, and McCoy sat back in the center seat and began to sweat.

"Doctor," Spock said into the silence, "I think I know what has happened to the Klingon landing party."

"So do I, Spock," McCoy said, and got up so that he could go spend a few moments in the turbolift before Kaiev called back. "So do I."

Chapter Six

"ALL RIGHT," KIRK SAID. "What can I tell you about us?"

The ;At stood silently for a long while, considering that. Kirk was in no hurry. He sat down in the warm sunshine and said, "I'll wait this way, if you don't mind."

"Of course not," said the ;At.

Kirk sat crosslegged on the short, fine turf, looking down at it, touching it. The stuff was less like grass than clover; its small round leaves, fat with moisture like some Earth succulents, were springy and tough. The leaves were the same brilliant blue-green as most other kinds of plant life on Flyspeck. That faint spicy scent that Kirk had noticed earlier rose from it when Kirk pressed it with his hand. He breathed the smell in gratefully. Much as he loved the *Enterprise,* and for all the efficiency of its air-scrubbers and ionizers, the ship's air never quite had this smell of atmosphere scrubbed only by sunlight and wind.

"Can you show me where you come from?" said the ;At.

Kirk put aside the seeming oddness of the question. He was aware that, though Linguistics might have managed to iron out his Translator's problems with the language proper, there would still be conceptual problems that would be weeks in the ironing, and many questions about things that the ;At would take for granted, but humans would find strange. Their sensorium in particular, which seemed adequate for identifying the *Enterprise* from the surface of the planet, in daylight, and perceiving details about her, was phenomenal; Kirk would have a few questions of his own to ask about that. In any case, McCoy had been certain that this species was somehow the key to this planet, and Bones's hunches were never barren; they always paid off, though sometimes not in the way you expected. Kirk was determined to spend as much time as he could with this creature, and to make it "quality time." Sooner or later somebody from the ship would call him, and he would have to go back and lever poor Bones out of the center seat and get back to work. But for the time being, he was going to relax and enjoy himself.

He squinted up at the sky, looking for the planet's moon to give him some orientation; but it had set. He had paid insufficient attention to the coordinate system his people had set up. He knew that the planet's north pole pointed more or less toward the Galactic ecliptic, but that was little help as far as this question went. "I would need to wait for nightfall," he said. "Aboard my ship, I could identify it for you fairly quickly. Out this way, I would need to see a star I recognize, and I can't do that in daylight."

The ;At didn't move or speak, but there was a feeling as of it nodding, in confirmation of something it had expected. "What is your home system like?"

Kirk chuckled a little. "Very small," he said. "Very, very small." In his mind's eye he could see the splendor of Earth at night, all the lights shining on the night side, the golden glitter of the cities alive with billions of people, the glint of moonlight or sunlight on orbital facilities and satellites as they swung by, the cold clear brilliance of the cities on the Moon. Many an *Enterprise* passenger had seen the huge shining orbital facilities of Starfleet that serviced the ship when she came home; everything was sleek, huge, modern, impressive, and quite a few of Kirk's various passengers had fallen silent, or grown voluble, over the achievement of human beings, alone and jointly with their alien companions of the other humanities. For a lot of them, Earth was the bit of the Solar System that mattered; all the other planets were just colonies. But for Kirk, the home system was more than its hearth-planet. He had come coasting in from far intergalactic space enough times to be more im-pressed and moved by crossing what he privately called "the doormat"—the radiopause, the place far out beyond Pluto's orbit where the Sun's gravity and wind could first be felt on the *Enterprise*'s hull. That was where the Solar System began for *him,* out there in the dark. It was a long ride in on impulse engines, and gave you time to look around and think. What stuck with him were the long cold silences of the outer fringes, the vast emptiness; the little yellow G-type star, a yellow dwarf really, nothing particularly spe-cial, just a pinprick of light for the longest time; and at the end of the ride, the pretty, tiny world, dwarfed and insignificant against the robust ruthlessness of the gas giants of the outer reaches—a delicate thing, an accident, a miracle almost thrown away a time or two.

He tried to tell the ;At about that. He wasn't sure how much of it got across, less due to problems with the Translator than with his own difficulty expressing himself. But the ;At listened patiently, and said at last, "You seem fond of the place."

"Well, it *is* my home," Kirk said. "Or, to be honest, it was. The *Enterprise* is my home these days. I may visit Earth for longer or shorter periods, but I always want to be back aboard."

He smiled to himself, amused that he should be discussing with an alien what he had been mulling over on the Bridge days ago. *Not settled down* with *her after all,* he thought; *settled down* in *her. Very different. And that answer will do for the moment.*

"You've come a long way to see us," said the ;At.

"We were sent," Kirk said, "yes."

"And you came willingly?"

"Always. Well," Kirk said, reconsidering, "almost always. There are occasionally missions we don't care to undertake, but do, to keep the peace. There are other species who take a less, uh, easygoing approach to life in the Universe than we do. Not that we're always perfect, either."

This is a dangerous line to be walking for a man who's trying to get the species of this world into the Federation, Kirk thought. But he had a feeling that the comforting vagueness of diplomatic jargon would not suit this situation. The ;At might seem wise, and somehow dangerous, but there was a sense of innocence about it that he had no wish to abuse. It was one of the things about an alien race that he had always most treasured—its own way of being—and damned if he was going to take the aggressive-colonizer mode and try to force another being into the mold of his own expectations. That was not why he and the ship had come.

"Let me ask you something, sir, if I may," Kirk said. "You are the only one of your people that we've seen so far. There have been plenty of Ornae and Lahit, but only one ;At. Do you speak to me as representative for your people?"

There was a silence. Kirk could physically feel the ;At looking at the question. "I think you could say," it said finally, "that I am the only one of us you need to see. One is adequate to speak for all. We are very like-minded."

Kirk was quiet for a moment. There had been planets where he had been handed similar lines, and the reality had turned out to be laughably different. But here he knew the truth on sight. This, then, was the chief ;At, or what would pass for it.

"Very well," he said. "What about the other species? Do they have anyone who speaks for them?"

"Not of their own species," said the ;At. "They feel no need. In matters where their welfare is concerned, we speak for them."

The rumble of the ;At's voice acquired, for the first time, a slightly threatening note. Or, not specifically threatening, but there was an implication within it that anything that would adversely affect the other two species would have *it* to answer to, and the answering would not be pleasant.

Kirk said, "Good enough. That's what I was trying to find out."

"Why?"

Kirk stretched his legs out. "You will have gathered, I think, that we didn't come here simply because we felt like it."

"Correct," said the ;At.

"Well then. We are the representatives of a large number of species who associate with one another for the sake of mutual benefit in trade and exploration. And," Kirk added, "to tell the truth, for company. Life in a universe with other species is much more interesting than in a universe where there *are* no others."

"That is certainly one way to put it," the ;At said. Once again Kirk got that feeling of pressure, as if the creature were considering him so closely that the whole weight of its thought was bent on him, and the weight was as tangible as its stone. He sat still, and bore up under it the best he could.

It eased off after a few moments. "Are there many of you?" it said.

"Many billions," Kirk said, "scattered across thousands of worlds. Not all of us travel the worlds, by any means. But many do."

"And you 'trade,'" the ;At said.

Kirk nodded. "We have many different kinds of needs. Some of our worlds are rich in things that other species need, or desire—goods, or knowledge. We find ways to fulfill one another's needs, so that all have what they require for their lives to be worthwhile." *At least,* he thought, *that's the way it's supposed to work.*

"And do all these species never do one another harm?"

Kirk sweated, and said, "Yes, I'm afraid sometimes they do. We have a long way to go yet before we can walk through the Universe merely smelling the flowers. Some of us step on them. Sometimes accidentally, sometimes on purpose."

There was a silence. "Show me a flower," said the ;At.

Kirk looked up at it, bemused, then said, "Certainly." He got up, looked around the clearing. It was not all the fine turf he had been examining earlier; there was some low shrubby growth dotted about it here and there, and bright spots of color showed among the branches. "Shall I bring one over for you?" he said to the ;At.

"No need," said the creature. "Show me one."

Kirk got up and started walking over to the shrubbery. That was when he got another surprise, because the ;At went with him. It didn't move. But at the same time, it was next to him with every step he took, without disturbing a single leaf of that springy blue-green ground cover, or so much as a crumb of dirt. It was a very impressive trick, and Kirk wondered how in the world it did it.

Then again, they said the ;At's physicality was 'occasional.' Is it voluntary, I wonder? Do they turn it on and off at will? And how does it affect their metabolism? He smiled to himself again. *Now I understand why it made Bones so crazy when I called him back up to the ship. I've got to find a way to make it up to him later.*

"Here," he said, pausing and kneeling down. The bright bits of red in the bushes turned out to be berries; but the turf had more than one kind of plant in it, and Kirk reached down to touch a small broad-leaved plant, like a miniature primrose, with delicate white orchid-like petals. "That's what we would normally call a flower. I'm not sure it's strictly analogous

147

to flowers on Earth; you'd have to check with my Biology people."

The ;At leaned over him—rather, it didn't move, but its shadow fell over him and the flower both. "Yes," it said then. "I understand the idiom, I think. To interfere with natural processes already in place."

"Yes," Kirk said.

The ;At straightened—or rather, its shadow shortened, and it was suddenly standing straight in the ground again. "I thank you," it said. "Now let me show you something."

And immediately, night fell.

It was a night full of fire, and screaming. The screams were like nothing that Kirk had ever heard before, but it took only a moment for him to recognize the scratchy noises of Ornae, suddenly pitched terribly high, and the rustlings of Lahit whipped to a terrible speed. Phaser and disruptor bolts were lancing down through the utter darkness, kindling fires where they struck. There was the occasional crash of explosive in the middle distance. Kirk held still, because he couldn't see to run. Somehow he knew that the ;At was still beside him, with terrible emotions rumbling in it, but leashed for the moment.

A phaser bolt hit nearby. Lahit screamed; a grove of them went struggling away through the darkness, their branches flailing in agony, all afire. Another bolt illuminated the Ornaet structure it destroyed; iridescent flesh exploded, protoplasm melted and hissed into steam. The air reeked of burning resin and alien flesh. After a few seconds, the attack stopped. But silence did not fall; the screams of the Lahit lasted a long time. From the Ornae there was no sound at all anymore.

Something passed overhead, silhouetted silver-edged by the light of the one small moon—a blunt, sleek shape, that went over with a roar of ion-drivers and was lost against the moonhaze at the horizon.

Kirk cursed, and found that he was standing in daylight again, the ;At beside him, looking down at a flower.

He looked around at the bright sunlight, breathing hard with shock. Beside him the ;At stood silent and stolid, as if it had been rooted in that spot since the morning of the world; and it cast no shadow.

"Do you know that vessel?" said the ;At.

"From what I saw of it," Kirk said, "it looked like an Orion pirate lander. The mothership would have been up in orbit somewhere."

"Yes," said the ;At.

Kirk shook his head. "How did you do that?" he said.

For the first time, he got an impression from the ;At that felt like uncertainty. It was very strange, from something that until now had seemed solider than some mountains Kirk had climbed. "I shall have difficulty telling you," it said. "Tell me; where will you be tomorrow?"

Kirk shrugged. "Back aboard my ship, I suppose. I may be able to get down here again if I can finish my other work." He looked around at the sunny woods and said, "I'd like that, if I could. This is a nice place."

"Yes," said the ;At. But there was something faintly troubled about its voice. "Can you not make a picture for me of where you will be tomorrow, as you have been doing of where you were at other times?"

"A picture—?" *Oh Lord,* Kirk thought, *the creature's a concept telepath. It's been in my head all this*

149

time, seeing every image that's occurred to me. Heaven only knows what I've shown it! This thing could destroy us with a thought if it wanted to—

Then he shook his head. He could hear McCoy saying very annoyed, *Why does it always have to be a thing? The creature shows no sign of destroying anything . . . and it's had enough destruction visited on it.* "Sir," he said, "I can't do what you're asking me. You're asking me to predict the future. Visualize it, yes, I can do that. I can approximate future events in my mind. But not one of all our peoples can truly tell, reliably, as an act of will, what will happen tomorrow. Or five minutes from now."

The ;At was quiet for a moment. "This will be our difficulty," it said, more to itself, Kirk thought, than to him. "Captain, I must try to make you understand us a little now."

"Be my guest," Kirk said.

"So we shall be. I think that you perceive—the past—and now—but not the future. Am I right?"

Kirk sat down in the grass again—gratefully, for he was feeling slightly weak-kneed after that sudden episode in the dark—and said, "You mean you *can* perceive the future."

"Exist in it. Yes. To a limited degree."

"Holy cow," Kirk said softly.

"Pardon?" said the ;At.

Kirk laughed. "Sorry, the image must have looked strange. And what about the past?"

"You saw for yourself," said the ;At.

"So I did." Kirk shook his head again. "This ought to be impossible," he said, bemused. "Spock will have a field day with you. The future shouldn't be accessible, by any rules we know. Even the Guardian of Forever can't get at it."

The ;At paused a moment, perhaps looking at the image in Kirk's mind. "That instrumentality is operating on different principles," it said. "It is only capable of managing one time-branch at a time; its programming forbids more, if I read correctly the way it described itself to you. We are living in a way the Guardian is not. All time-branches are accessible, though the past ones are simpler to access."

"Oh jeez, time," Kirk said, for in the midst of all the excitement he had forgotten to check in with the ship. "Sir, would you pardon me for a moment? I won't go anywhere. I just need to talk to my people."

"Of course, Captain."

He pulled out his communicator and flipped it open. "Kirk to *Enterprise*."

"Enterprise," Uhura's cheerful voice said. *"How are you doing down there, Captain?"*

"No problems. How's the ship?"

"No problems up here either, sir."

"Fine. Kirk out."

He put the communicator away, and leaned back a little to gaze up again at the ;At. "Now then . . . where were we?" Kirk rubbed his head for a moment. "You were telling me that you people can visit the future."

"We live in it," said the ;At. "To a limited extent, as I said. Also the past and the present, as you perceive them."

"We were actually there, just then, weren't we? That was the last time the Orion pirates attacked your planet."

"Yes."

"How often has this been happening?"

"At irregular intervals for some six rounds of our sun, now."

"That's more or less eight of our years. Sir—" Kirk paused a moment. "I really do wish you had a name," he said. "I may not use it much, but it would help to have something to think of you by."

The ;At looked at him, and suddenly had a shadow again, which fell over Kirk. "We have little use for them," it said. "The others, the Ornae and the Lahit, sometimes call me by words that mean the one who manages things, having understood them."

"Chief," Kirk said. No, too nonspecific. "Boss." No, too informal. "Hmmm . . . Master." As in teacher, or skilled proponent of some art. That sounded more like it.

"Master," said the ;At, "says it well."

"Fine. So these people have been raiding you for eight years now—" Kirk tried to fit that together with reports he had heard concerning their depredations in other parts of space. "They've come a long way from their usual hunting grounds if they're all the way out here. Then again," he said, "it's possibly our more widespread presence, and the Klingons', that has driven them away from the more populated parts of the Galaxy." He thought for a moment. "What are they after? Can you tell?"

"Every time they come here, they dig," said the Master. It sounded rather bemused by that. "What for, I could not say."

"It's not minable minerals," Kirk said. "Your world is poor in those. Then again, McCoy was getting rather excited about the dirt earlier. And Spock mentioned that the plant life here seemed rich in

152

medical alkaloids." That rang an unfortunate bell. "It could be drugs," Kirk said. "There are substances on some worlds that are innocent enough in their own environment, but when used on an alien species, are psychoactives of greatly varying strengths. Such things bring huge prices . . . and those who obtain and sell them don't hesitate to kill." He shook his head. "But it's just a guess."

"What I do not understand," said the Master, "is why these Orion beings feel it necessary to kill our people as they have been doing. Surely they could take what they desire and depart unharmed. There are many parts of this world with the same plants, the same earth, but where none of us lives."

"Sir, sometimes people like that just like killing. It's a game to them. Or else they see it as fumigation . . . cleaning an inconvenient infestation off a world so they can more easily exploit it." Kirk's mouth set in a straight hard line. "The Orion pirates have done that often enough before. Early on in their history, they sometimes destroyed whole inhabited planets simply because they weren't economically viable . . . then used the fragments to build Dyson spheres and populate the increased areas with slave labor. In a way, they did us a favor . . . their behavior so disgusted a lot of worlds that the profit motive went out of style. There are a few holdouts, here and there. But the pirates . . . I think they just like to kill."

The Master rumbled, a low slow sound that would have made Kirk very nervous if he had thought it was being directed at him. "I would tend to agree with you," it said.

Kirk stood up and started to pace slowly back and forth among the flowers. "But you've told me that you can exist in other times. That's a tremendous advantage, or it should be. If you can exist in the future, why can't you perceive the pirates coming, and act to keep your people away from them? Or find some way to stop them?"

Kirk got a sense of profound regret from the Master. "Don't you think we would if we could?" it said. "We can exist in the future, but we cannot *act* on it or in it without withdrawing our presence from present and past. We would have to live permanently in the future, our own future, so that we might warn ourselves in the present of any danger. To do so would be to give up life in the present, forever."

Kirk thought about that for a moment. "I guess living in the future wouldn't be any more healthy than living in the past," he said. "You're right. There must be some other way."

"It is hard for us," the Master said. "We are prepared to do that if we must. We are, in our way, the guardians of the Ornae and Lahit. They share our perception of time, but not the wider view; they can live in past and present and future, but in only one at a time . . . not all at once. They are innocents, with their own concerns—mostly one another, discovering their differences and likenesses. There are many."

"There certainly are," Kirk said. "That's partly what brought us here—we know of no other place where three species so different all evolved together."

The Master seemed gently amused by that. "Yes," it said, "we enjoy it—this discovering how different others can be, while still being alike at root. Life is a joy because of it."

"I think I understand you," Kirk said. "Though it's possible I'm deluding myself." He shook his head.

"Your ability to coexist among times alone is going to raise a lot of questions. Especially since you seem able to extend the effects to others. You may find yourselves having a lot of visitors . . . not just Orion pirates." He clasped his hands behind him as he paced. "There must be some way to put a stop to *that,* though."

"We should be glad to hear of it," said the Master.

McCoy sat in the center seat, holding onto his temper with both hands. "Kaiev," he said, "I'll tell you again. I have better things to do with my time than go killing your crewpeople. *I* don't care how they go running all over the planet with their little toy diggers and I don't know what all. If they've vanished, that doesn't surprise me. I *told* you that strange things were happening down there, but you wouldn't listen to me—oh no. We've had people vanish too, and we don't know where they are."

"How many?" Kaiev demanded. *"When?"*

"Classified information," McCoy said. "You should know better than to ask. And I don't care if it means taking our statement on trust. You'll just have to deal with it. If you don't believe me, and you want to make something of it, you just go right ahead."

McCoy looked at Sulu and Chekov meaningfully, and threw a glance over at Scotty. He could see that the screens were already up, and Sulu brought up the little firing sight on his console. Kaiev could see all this, and was having a hard time keeping his face still.

"Now son," McCoy said, "I'm an easygoing man, but you have an attitude problem. If you force me to, I'll be glad to adjust it for you, permanently. Make up your mind."

He was very glad Kaiev couldn't see how his hands were sweating.

It was very quiet over on the Klingon bridge. *"About what?"* Kaiev finally said.

McCoy smiled. "About whether you're going to cooperate with us. We'll send down some extra search parties and help you look for your people. We have this place a lot more completely mapped than you can have just yet; that may be an advantage. Also, we'll do some analysis on their sensor traces and see if we can't find out where they went. We haven't had much luck with finding our own missing yet, but we'll share what we've discovered with you. Spock," McCoy said, looking over his shoulder, "make up a data packet about that odd radiation and see to it that the Science Officer over there gets it, will you? Thanks."

He turned to the screen again and smiled. "Anything else you need, Kaiev?"

The Klingon commander looked at McCoy with an expression that was difficult to decipher completely, but there was a lot of perplexity in it. *"Before,"* he said, *"you mentioned that some of your people had been—eaten by trees—"*

McCoy raised an eyebrow. "Tell your people to leave their chain saws home, Kaiev," he said. "McCoy out."

Uhura ended the transmission. Spock came down to stand by McCoy, and favored him with a look of mild annoyance. "Doctor," he said, "have you any idea of the weapons ability of a Klingon battle cruiser?"

"Enough to know that he can't take us one to one," McCoy said, "not with our screens up and with our fingers on the button. Which is where we will stay,

156

until this situation has become calmer. It may take a while. Yellow alert until I say otherwise."

"Noted, Doctor." But Spock had not finished being admonitory yet. "I must ask, however, why you are being so provocative."

"I'm being nothing of the sort," McCoy said. "Spock, it's pure Klingon psychology, or as close to it as an Earthman is going to get at the moment. Snarl first, and louder, and never let up. Out-aggress the aggressor, and he falls over and shows you his throat. It works for wolves. And there are aspects of Klingon behavior that suggest that 'pack' psychology is most effective with them."

Spock still looked dubious. "You were showing dangerous signs of enjoyment, Doctor," he said. "Would you care to comment on the chance that you are taking out your own anger at this situation on the Klingons?"

McCoy laughed. "Why, of course I am, Spock. That's one of the things emotion is best for: to use as a tool, consciously, to achieve a goal. One's own emotions, of course. In your case, I speak theoretically." He smiled; Spock looked at the ceiling. McCoy was satisfied by this result. It would be a poor day for him, even under these horrendous circumstances, if he couldn't manage to tease Spock a little.

"Meantime," he said, "I have to start putting together some more information for Starfleet; they're going to be wanting my log extracts, damn them. Have you found out anything else about that radiation?"

"There continue to be minor incidences here and there on the planet surface," Spock said, "but again, none of them seems attributable to any specific event that I can identify. I shall continue working on the problem. But you should know," he said, "that I have had a look at the heat and radiation scans for the area in which the Klingons disappeared, and the traces are identical in nature to the remnants left by the Captain. Whatever the instrumentality is that is operating here, it is the same in both cases."

"Wonderful," McCoy said. "So something now has both Kirk and a batch of Klingons in the same playpen. I needed something like this to put my mind at ease."

"There is of course no evidence that any such thing has happened—"

"Spock," McCoy said, "I will bet you a nickel."

Spock raised his eyebrows. "Do you mean to indicate an actual coin?"

"Just so happens that in my quarters, carefully secreted from prying eyes, I have a genuine buffalo-head nickel, dated 1938 old date. I bet you that nickel that the Captain and the Klingons are going to wind up in the same place. And," McCoy said, "I bet you that Jim is going to run rings around them."

"If I lose this bet," Spock said, "I will be unable to redeem the amount in question. I am afraid I do not have any nickels."

"That'll do," McCoy said. "Here, give me that padd. I've got to think of something that'll sound good enough to keep Starfleet off my neck for the next few hours."

"Are you expecting something to happen in that time?" Spock said.

"Spock, with my luck, something will. You just watch."

* * *

Katur was a young officer, but experienced in many landings in her time. She prided herself on her ability to cope with the unexpected. She had seen many things that had been the deaths of those less prepared than she, those less ready to react in a second, to kill quickly and without undue consideration of the consequences. Too much thinking, Katur felt, was bad for the pulse rate. Reaction, reflex, swift and merciless, that was the secret of survival . . . and advancement in rank.

But she had not been prepared for anything like *this*.

The briefing with Commander Kaiev had been brief and simple. "The place is full of aliens," he had said. "There are indications that some of them may be dangerous. Use due care, but do not hesitate to make examples of them if you find it necessary. Our intelligence indicates that this planet is most likely a rich source of *tabekh*. You are to search out the necessary raw materials, and once identified, bring as much back to the ship as possible. At all costs, stay away from the Federation personnel. We do not desire them to have any idea what we are after in this area, lest they attempt to co-opt the resource. Understood?"

Katur had understood all too well. There would be precious little glory on this landing. *My mother did not raise me to dig in the dirt like a menial,* she had thought, as she went to the Transporter room with the others. *But one must suffer in silence sometimes to gain greater goals.*

Katur frequently thought like that, in axioms and wise sayings. It was a bad habit she had acquired from her brother, who had died suddenly in midaxiom on some world south of the Galactic Rift, when a creature with too many teeth and no appreciation of wise sayings had leapt on him from a tree and bitten his head off. Katur had never cared much for her brother, so she had been little moved by this, except to take the occurrence as an omen that wisdom was best left to others, and that thinking too hard tended to distract one from what was going on in the immediate vicinity. The wise sayings continued to rattle about in her head, but she kept them to herself, and did her best to ignore them.

Now she sat in the back of the all-terrain vehicle and muttered to herself over Kesaio's driving, which was certainly suitable for a muck-cart, but nothing much better than that. The transporter had put them down practically in the middle of the Federation camp, and they had had to endure a great deal of staring and interest as they made their way out of the clearing. That was another problem—the lack of proper roads. The Commander had forbidden them a flyer, apparently thinking that the Federation commander, not the famous smooth-talking Kirk but some other officer, was too easily antagonized, and might misconstrue the flyer as being rather too handy should they decide to attack the Federation landing parties.

That statement alone had made Katur's liver twist in her. She despised Kaiev, even when he was being prudent; perhaps more than usual, then, for he so rarely seemed to exercise good judgment at other times. He was capable enough of being reckless when the foe was small and helpless, which annoyed Katur. No honor in such pretenses; enslave them and be done with it. But this sudden careful courtesy being exhibited by Kaiev in the face of *Enterprise*'s puny guns annoyed Katur considerably. It was a great pity that the ship had been prepared for them. All it would have taken was a moment's surprise to add glory to all their names. Glory, and an early end to this tour of duty in the middle of nowhere at all.

Instead, they were forced to act meekly, and drive out through the Federation people. And even worse, through the aliens. "I would shoot them all," Katur muttered to herself. "Look at these disgusting things."

"I am trying not to," said Helef, who was sitting beside her and glowering. And it was understandable, for they *were* revolting. Half of them were like fat bags of sickly colored jelly; the other half were dumb plants, except they had little cold eyes that made it plain they were watching you, and thinking no one knew what.

"I will take an axe to one of them yet," Katur said under her breath. "Why is it that everywhere we go, we keep finding these *things?* Does the idiot Universe have nothing better to do than to keep creating more and more life? And most of it not worth conquering." She shuddered. "All simple life, no sophistication about it, no elegance, no grand passions. The Universe is hopelessly pedestrian, Helef."

Helef shrugged and looked away. He was no philosopher at the best of times.

Kesaio took them out of the clearing along a narrow, bumpy path. Tree branches whipped at their faces; they ducked, and Kesaio and Tak in the front seat all swore. Katur longed to see the day over with. *Digging* tabekh *like any servant,* she thought. *Someone ought to call challenge on Kaiev for this, and cut his liver out. Except we need the stuff, I suppose.* It had

161

indeed been three weeks now since any of them had had *tabekh,* and there had already been several murders aboard ship as one crewmember or another ran out and killed another for his or her supply. To happen on a planet that was a source was incredible luck, and had to be exploited. But Katur was intensely annoyed at having been sent to do the exploiting.

They came out into another clearing and went roaring across it. And then something happened. Katur was not sure of the details even later, when she had time to think about matters, but it seemed as if suddenly there was a stone in the middle of the clearing, where previously there had been none. She had little more time to consider the problem, as she was pitched out of the vehicle over the windshield.

She was well-taught enough to hit the ground rolling, and a moment later she was on her feet, sidearm out, looking for the others. They were all lying about in various states of disrepair. Kesaio was sitting up groaning, with the blood coming down from a good long scrape on his head. Katur went and helped him up roughly by one arm. "A pity you weren't killed," she said, "but that's all right; the Commander will do that for you when he sees what you've done to the vehicle."

Kesaio wasn't up to much but groaning yet. Katur went over to Helef, pausing along the way to kick at one of the pulse-diggers, which had come down and broken rather neatly in two pieces. "Fine," she said. "We're going to have to do all this by hand now." She helped Helef up; he was stunned, that was all. "Tak?" she said.

"I'm all right," he said. "Katur, did you see that? The stone got in front of us."

162

She stared at him. "You're addled. Here, pick up your gun."

He picked up his sidearm, but at the same time he was looking suspiciously at the rock. "Katur, I mean it. It was somewhere else first, and it moved."

"Nothing moved," she said scornfully. "Don't be a fool. How should a rock move? Do you see any marks in the grass, anything of the kind?"

"No, but—"

"Idiot," she said, and stalked away. Another disappointment. She usually rather liked Tak, but if he was going to start hallucinating on her, there was no point in him.

Katur stared at the vehicle. A ruin. How quickly everything could go to pieces in the world. She had gone out with hopes of a commendation for a task well done; now there would be discipline for all of them. And still no *tabekh*.

The windshield of the vehicle was quite shattered. Katur looked at it, rubbing her slightly sore neck, and wondered how she had managed to go flying over it and not hit the rock.

Unless the rock *had* moved—

No, ridiculous. She went over to the other digger and picked it up. It was still in one piece, but whether it would function was another question. "Come on, the lot of you," she said. "At least we still have one of these left. We'll get the damn *tabekh* anyway, more than enough for everybody."

"What about the vehicle?"

"We'll tell the Commander that one of the wretched tree-things got in front of it," Katur said. "Rocks we can't explain except by people's clumsiness." She glowered at Kesaio. "But we can catch one of the trees

163

and make it look as if the alien got clumsy. Nothing easier. Here, take this," she said, and handed the surviving pulse-digger to Helef.

He took it with ill grace, but he had no choice; she *was* most senior. "Here," she said, "give me your scanner." He handed that over reluctantly as well. He had spent time making special alterations in it, and disliked having his settings fiddled with. She knew it, and delighted in discomfiting him. Katur changed the reading-slides until they suited her, then did an all-around scan.

"There," she said. "There's a positive trace. North-northwest, no more than four thousand paces away. We can make it in an hour or so, I should think. Come on, let's get this over with."

They set off north-northwest, up toward the blue-green hills. A long soft afternoon, blue with haze and the planet's idiosyncratic chlorophyll, was settling over everything. Katur, uncaring, was blind to it.

Another thing she also did not see, that she might have cared rather more about, was the rock, which was following them.

Chapter Seven

KIRK WAS SITTING in the shadow of the Master of the ;At, thinking hard. Afternoon was setting in; the light was changing from the odd cool/warm mixture of the morning to earlier day to something almost wholly warm, though blues and greens were still predominant. The brassy light of Flyspeck's sun was shading down to old gold through the still air. In the trees leading up to the hills northward, birds were beginning to sing, or something that would have passed for birds. The song was muted, abstract, and slightly melancholy. It reminded Kirk of nightingale bats, or chickadees in winter, and it suited his mood, and the feeling of the place, exactly.

The Master had not spoken for some time. Kirk leaned back against its bulk—it had told him it didn't mind—and waited. One feeling he had been getting steadily, ever since he had beamed down, was that there was no point in rushing this process. This was exactly what the *Enterprise* had come for—the diplomacy, taking place in a rather different manner than he had originally imagined, but taking place nonetheless, and requiring the same care and attention as if the usual forms were being observed. *Pity more diplomacy can't take place like this, though,* Kirk thought. *Sitting out in the fresh air and the sunshine is a lot more pleasant than being stuck in stuffy meeting rooms and bureaucratic cocktail parties.*

He kept finding himself looking around, though, as if to reassure himself that the day would not suddenly give way again to a night full of bombs and phasers. There was no question in his mind that he had *been* there, physically. It begged an interesting question: could the ;At affect others' physicality, as well as their own? It seemed likely. But he would need Spock later to help him work on answers to that question, and many others. There was no doubt that the Federation would be very, very keen to get Flyspeck in.

He could not allow that to concern him, however. His business was to discover whether membership in the Federation would be as good for the ;At—and the Ornae and the Lahit—as it would be from the Federation's point of view. If it wasn't, he was going to tell the Federation to go take a flying leap. Theoretically, if that was his decision, they would support him.

Theoretically.

He sighed and thought again of that horrible night full of carnage. "I think I can understand," he said after a while, "why you're in the mood to be a little cautious of aliens."

There was a silence. Then the Master said, "Can you? Can you indeed?"

Its tone of voice was curious, and made him wonder if he had been missing something. Kirk said, "You're implying that there may be reasons for your caution that I *don't* understand as yet. Nothing is more likely. But I don't know what questions to ask as yet, sir, to get the right answers."

"Nor do I," said the Master. "I suppose we'll just have to play Galactic Twenty Questions until we both discover what we need to know."

Kirk chuckled. As they had been talking, the ;At's idiom was becoming more and more fluent, even witty. Kirk supposed it was picking this up from his mind somehow, catching snatches of other people's conversation as he remembered them in the course of his own talking and thinking. "That's as good a name for this as any," he said.

He stretched. "It's a pleasure to have the time to ask the questions today," he said. "I feel a lot less pressured than usual." He cocked an eye up at the ;At. "That wouldn't be your doing, would it?"

The ;At hesitated—Kirk was growing able to hear its hesitations now—and said, "I couldn't answer that until I was certain I knew what you meant by *doing*. I would have to tell you everything I *do*, I suppose."

Kirk was amused. "And what *do* you do?"

"Watch the world, mostly."

"No different from most of us. Except we have to do things about what we see happening. Not always the right things, I'm afraid."

The ;At made a long slow rumble that Kirk was coming to recognize as agreement. "You do a lot of *doing*," it said.

"Yes."

"It must be strange," said the Master, "to spend so much of your time in the present."

Kirk laughed outright at that. "We're kind of stuck with it. The future is a closed book . . . the past is frozen. The present is all we've got to work with."

"Very strange," said the Master. *"Time* as you conceive it is a little place, it seems. A box. You sit in the present moment, with everything outside the box inaccessible to you."

"We get out," Kirk said slowly. "But only occasionally. Dreams . . . there's no time there. A hundred things happen in an eyeblink."

"Yes," the Master said, "that is the way it is."

"There was a saying on Earth, among some of the early philosophers, that time was Nature's way of keeping everything from happening at once."

The Master rumbled with amusement again. "What a quiet context you must exist in," it said. "A simple place."

"Simple!"

"But do you see," said the Master, "what our caution is founded in? Here our people have this perception of time as a whole thing, unbreakable; a field that we live in, and move through at will; sky, sun, trees, wind. Now comes a species that tells us that all other species, nearly, live in boxes, and let in the sun only a blink at a time, glance at a star only once in a while. Should that not seem unutterably strange to us? Frightening? And should we not fear that the species we live with, and care for—the Ornae and the Lahit—might somehow catch this view from contact with these other beings, be contaminated by it? Might we not fear that our friends, who see the world mostly as we do, might themselves crawl into the boxes, and come to ration their perception of the world to the occasional breath of air, a glimpse of sunlight through the cracks?" It sounded grave. "I think that would be a mistake in our caretakership."

"You would be right there," Kirk said. "But you have no guarantee it would happen. You might as easily become enriched as impoverished. Think of the other side of the question. People from a hundred worlds coming here—as many new, strange ways of thinking as you can imagine; more than that. For strangeness doesn't always have to be terrible. We got over that fear, though it took us a long time. Some of the most different of us are the best friends. Maybe there's something to what people say where I come from, that opposites attract, that people as unlike as they can be have nothing to argue about, and get along the best of all, much better than people who are more alike."

"Like your friends the Klingons."

Kirk laughed. "We may be a little too alike for our own good. We were both bred from predator species. Are there any predator species on this planet?" he said, for he could feel the Master's momentary confusion. "Creatures that live off other creatures, by actual ingestion of their tissue, or by taking something belonging to the other creatures from them?"

The ;At shuddered. Kirk did too, in sympathy; perhaps the Master was leaking emotion a little, for its wave of shock and revulsion went straight through him. *What was the image in my mind?* he wondered, for he had never even noticed. *Lions on the veldt? Or something worse?*

"We have nothing of the kind here," said the Master, and there was an undertone of unhappiness in its voice, "though I have heard of the concept. This, then, would also go far to explain the behavior of your

Orion pirates, if they are descended from predators too."

"Hominid stock," Kirk said. "I'm afraid so. Most hominids had ancestor-creatures that hunted and killed to live. The habit is in our genes. It's hard to break. Some of us choose to break it. Some delight in the killing, and see no problem in that. We try not to judge them by our standards." Kirk sighed. "We have trouble enough living by our own."

"You can see," said the Master, "the difficulty I would have in justifying contact with such kinds of creatures."

"Justifying to whom?" said Kirk.

There was another of those long pauses. "I will have difficulty explaining that," it said, though there was an undertone to its rumbling that sounded almost cheerful.

Kirk shook his head. "Never mind, then. It can wait till later. I'm more concerned about the pirates. They're bound to come back again. They'll keep coming back until they've drained your planet of whatever resource they started coming here for. And they'll kill more of your people, and the Ornae and Lahit, in the process."

"Oh, they haven't killed any of my people. We are hard to kill," said the Master.

"I just *bet!*" Kirk said. You could drop a planetcracker bomb on a creature that could put its physicality in abeyance; and when it came back, not a vein of its stone would be out of place. "But the others . . . yes. I would prevent that, if it could be prevented."

Kirk weighed his next words for a few seconds. "This might be one advantage that being in the

Federation could offer you," he said. "One of the things we cooperate in is protection. If it became known that your world was affiliated with our Federation, odds are that the pirates would avoid you. We have had run-ins with them before." Kirk smiled, and the smile was grim. "Generally not to their advantage."

"You were telling me," said the Master, "that you thought perhaps the reason they were coming here was because they had been driven out of other spaces —by you and the Klingons. Should you come here, then perhaps they would be driven farther out—to some other world even less able to defend itself. Some world that your people would see no advantage in defending. For clearly you see advantage in us."

"I can't deny that," Kirk said.

"I would find it hard," said the Master, "to take on my conscience the burden of deaths on another world. This one is problem enough."

Kirk had to see the logic in that. *So much for the diplomatic initiative,* he thought unhappily. *I have a feeling these people are going to say no to us at the end of the day. Regardless, something has to be done to help them.*

"This predation," the Master said, thoughtful, "seems unusually widespread. One wonders if something could be done about it."

Kirk smiled slowly. "I'm sitting here trying to think of ways to help your people," he said, "and you're trying to think of ways to help mine."

"Well, who wouldn't?"

"The Klingons, for one."

"Yes," the Master said, still thoughtful. "But that's their problem. They cannot help their genes any more

171

than you can. One must transcend such things, not try to deal with them by simple removal. Removal never turns out to be permanent, or effective."

"So we found out, sometime back in our history," Kirk said. "Mastery is better than change, as a rule. And usually more satisfying."

"*Yes,*" said the ;At, and the earth round about shook with its agreement.

Kirk steadied himself until the bouncing stopped. *I have the feeling I've just missed something significant,* he thought. *I wish I knew what it was.* "In any case," Kirk said, "the Klingons don't seem particularly interested in transcending their heredity. They appear to be very fond of it." He shrugged. "Their choice."

"Yes."

"At any rate, I thank you for trying to think of ways to help us. But I think that we would probably not benefit unless we implemented the help ourselves."

"I was going to say something similar to you," said the Master, and Kirk could feel it smiling, though there was not the slightest change in the contours or terrible weight of that great tall stone. "And you see, if we had to depend on others for our protection, our—sufficiency—would be impaired. Never again would we, or the other species, be quite whole. It might be better to die, than to lose that wholeness. It is all we have, really."

"Live free, or die," Kirk murmured.

"Yes," said the Master of the ;At. "That is the choice to be made, I think."

"And you will be making it," said Kirk.

"Oh, I *have* made it, eventually," the Master said. "I just don't know what it is yet."

Kirk sighed. Every now and then the Master's

172

tenses became confused, but it had something to do with the ;At's odd perception of time, rather than a glitch in the Translator. "Well, let me know when you find out," he said.

"You will be the first to know," said the ;At. "And possibly the last. Tell me something, if you would."

"Certainly," Kirk said, thoroughly confused.

"The other ship—tell me about that."

"Oh, our initial survey vessel," Kirk said. "They were under orders not to reveal where they came from or what they were doing here. I have regrets about that, in retrospect," he said. "It seems a childish way to treat another intelligent species. Unfortunately, I don't make the policies; my job is to carry them out."

"Not that ship," the ;At said. "The *other* ship in orbit, the one with the name *Ekkava* on its hull. There are not as many people aboard it as there are aboard your vessel, but the ship seems to be carrying many more of the energy-directing devices than yours does."

Kirk broke right out in a cold sweat. *Bones!! And my ship, with a green officer in the helm, one that no one else will be able to relieve because of my orders.* "*Ekkava*—that sounds uncomfortably like a Klingon ship," he said. "Sir, I need to contact my ship." He pulled out his communicator and flipped it open. "Kirk to *Enterprise.*"

The result was a horrendous electronic squeal that he had heard before, and it raised the hair on the back of his neck—not with delight, either. "Jammed," he muttered. "What the devil are they up to?"

"They appear to simply be orbiting at the moment," said the Master. "I can tell you this in certainty: your ship is in no danger from the Klingons."

"If you don't mind," said Kirk, "I'd rather be the judge of that."

"A moment only. We have been discussing the Klingons mostly in the abstract," said the Master. "Do you consider them as bad as Orion pirates?"

Kirk had to think about that for a moment. "There are more of them," he said, "and they're less cautious, and more violent, in more straightforward ways. Usually they're better armed. But they're usually more predictable. We know each other moderately well," Kirk said.

"So it seems. Well, they are here, and I suppose they must be entertained as well." The Master sounded to Kirk more like a host who's worried about the hors d'oeuvres running out than a creature with what might be the beginning of an invasion force sitting on its doorstep. "What would you recommend we do?"

Kirk frowned furiously at the nonfunctional communicator, and put it away. "Probably," he said, "get ready for a fight."

Captain's Log, Supplemental. Commander Leonard McCoy recording in the absence of Captain James T. Kirk:

(Oh Lord, Jim, where the hell are you?)

Conditions remain largely unchanged since our last log entry. We are keeping a channel open to the Klingon vessel to keep them reassured that we harbor no ill will against them, and continue to check in with them regularly regarding their missing crewmen. No sign has been found of their people as yet, or of Captain Kirk, though our searches have extended to include three of the other continents and the waters off the continent on which most of our researches have been done. Mr. Spock continues to investigate odd radiation readings and other slightly unnatural phenomena that he feels may shed some light on the method used to remove the Captain. The Ornae and Lahit on the planet continue to insist that the Captain is present and unhurt, though they are unable to prove this, or to tell us how they know.

Meanwhile, datagathering continues on the planet, though many personnel have been diverted to searching for the Captain. We have rediscovered penicillin eighteen times, streptomycin and hemomycetin three times, and have isolated several very promising antifungal and antibacterial agents. The planet also seems to harbor some plant life that occurs on planets a good ways away, such as snortweed, which as far as we knew only grew on Delta Orionis Eight. Other specimens have also been found and identified, leading some members of Botany to suggest that the Preservers may indeed have been out this way, but may have transplanted vegetative plant species rather than the usual intelligent animal-descended ones, and may have used the planet as a greenhouse rather than a zoo breeding program. The interest of this planet continues to increase. My only wish is that the Captain were experiencing it from up here, rather than wherever he is.

McCoy handed the recorder to Uhura. "Did that sound all right?" he said.

"You're getting the hang of it," she said. "Thanks, Doctor. This will go out with the next transmission in a little while."

"Good." He frowned a little. "Aren't we due for another love letter from Starfleet pretty soon?"

"Yes."

"Oh, wonderful." He was feeling the dread in the pit of his stomach, a feeling he hadn't experienced since he was in grammar school, sitting and waiting for what he knew would be a failing report card to be put into his hands to take home.

"Don't panic yet," Uhura said. "They'll have your last reply at this point, but it's going to take five hours for them to get this one and figure out what you've been doing with what they told you. Maybe something will happen between now and then."

"Maybe," he said, not wanting to rain on Uhura's parade. But he had a feeling that if anything was going to happen, it was on that little spark of light that was trailing them two hundred klicks back in orbit. It made his back itch. Several times now he had considered telling Sulu to slow their orbit so that the Klingons would slip in front of them. But he had restrained himself. The *Enterprise* could fire just as well backward as forward, and as for the Klingons, any sudden move on *Enterprise*'s part might make them nervous. No use doing anything that might alter the delicate balance that presently prevailed.

"Spock," he said, looking over his shoulder, "anything new?"

Spock was bent over his station's viewer, intent. He straightened up slowly and said, "I am . . . uncertain, Doctor."

"How uncertain?"

Spock came down to stand beside the center seat. "Doctor," he said, "you said that high-energy physics was a little 'over your head.' How far over?"

McCoy shrugged. "I understand the basics; you have to, to understand most of the diagnostic imaging systems we use in Sickbay. I can fix our little cyclotron when it breaks down, but that's about the size of it."

Spock nodded thoughtfully. "I have been doing some time-lapse scanning of the planet surface," he said, "concentrating on the area where the Captain went missing. I keep locating Z-particle decay of a certain kind, the kind associated with tachyon incursion in atmosphere."

That surprised McCoy a bit. Tachyons were the

heralds of particles that had been traveling at more than the speed of light, and had slowed down and so become perceptible in the "real" timeframe; their high red shift always gave them away. "That's curious," he said. "What do you make of it?"

"I have no theories as yet," Spock said. "But we have come across these particular kinds of decay before."

"Where?"

"On the planet of the Guardian of Forever."

McCoy raised his eyebrows. "The characteristic decay patterns are all there," Spock said. "Typically they were found when the Guardian had just been active in engineering a timeshift."

"You think there's another Guardian down there?" He swallowed. No question but that the Klingons would be interested in *that*. "Is it buried somewhere? Is that why our friends down there were out with their digging gear? Maybe we were wrong in thinking they were hunting mineral resources."

"Insufficient data," Spock said. "All I have been able to determine is that the radiation decay is the same. I must say that I doubt the Klingons have had time to come to my conclusions."

That struck McCoy as small consolation, at the moment. "Has something grabbed Kirk and thrown him into some other timeline?" he said. "Is that why the Ornae keep insisting he's there . . . but can't produce him?"

"I cannot say. But I will continue my investigations."

McCoy brooded a moment, then said, "Have our people down there been asking the Ornae if they know where the Klingons are?"

"Yes, but the answers have not been conclusive. They are still trying to get replies that make sense."

Spock turned away. "Still no sign of the ;At?" McCoy said.

"None, Doctor." And Spock went back to his station.

McCoy sat back, watching the screen, which at the moment was showing the main clearing down on the planet. In the background of the picture Lt. Kerasus was sitting with an Ornaet half in her lap, talking a mile a minute to her tricorder, and herself now using the scratchy noises the Ornae used. Lia was off at one side, peering among the branches of a grove of Lahit, using an ophthalmoscope on their holly-berry eyes. The eyes were following her as she moved around, and goggling at her. He smiled a bit through his annoyance and concern.

The ;At are at the heart of this, somehow, he thought. *If Jim hadn't called me up just then, I would have found out something about what's going on here . . . I know it. Maybe I would have been the one to disappear, but who cares about that? I'd have found out.*

I hope.

Uhura glanced over at him. "Doctor," she said, "we've got a transmission coming in. I'm afraid it's Starfleet."

McCoy moaned. "I guess there's no use in trying to avoid it. Let me have it live."

Uhura smiled demurely and said, "Yes, sir." She touched a button.

The pleasant scene on the screen went away and was replaced by, oh Lord, Delacroix. And puns aside, he looked cross. He was sitting in exactly the same position as he had been for the previous message.

Does the man ever get out of that chair, I wonder? But this time his face looked as if he had been sucking lemons. McCoy tried to be inconspicuous about gripping the arms of the center seat.

"Starfleet Command, Delacroix," he said. *"To Leonard McCoy, commanding* Enterprise. *Commander, we confirm receipt of your last set of log extracts and data. As of this stardate, you are re—"*

The picture broke up in a howl of noise and a blizzard of static. Very slowly, McCoy turned around and smiled at Uhura.

"Nice job," he said. "Oh, Uhura, that was *nice.*"

"I didn't do it, Doctor," she said. "Much as any of us might dislike the contents of the message, I can't interfere with reception. Ethics."

McCoy sighed. "Yes, well then . . . what did?"

And the horrible suspicion hit him. "Or who?"

"Checking," Uhura said. She turned her attention to her board for a moment, touched a couple of controls, and said, "I thought so. It's a jamming signal, Doctor."

"Klingon?" he said.

She nodded.

"Never thought I'd be thanking them for something, but by Heaven, if I see Kaiev, I'll buy him a jelly pastry," McCoy said.

Spock looked over at McCoy with a bemused expression. "I am uncertain why you're celebrating, Doctor," he said. "From the syntactical construction we heard, the probability is high that the Admiral was about to relieve you."

McCoy stopped right where he was. He had been so delighted not to have to take a scolding from Delacroix that that hadn't occurred to him. His mouth dropped open, and he said, "Damn. Damn, damn, *damn!*

Then he stopped. "Wait a second," he said to Spock, and advanced on him with glee. "If you're so sure that that's what he said, then you have to relieve me!"

"Doctor, I only said the probability was high. One officer cannot relieve another on a probability. The order must be heard. We did not hear him finish."

McCoy's scowl came back. "I'll kill him," he said, turning to Uhura. "Uhura, get Kaiev on the horn. I'm going to give him such an ache in that bumpy head of his—!"

"I take it the jelly pastry is off, then," Uhura said softly, and reached out to her console. Before she could touch it, it beeped at her.

"Put it on screen," McCoy said angrily, and swung to face it. It lit up with Kaiev's face a moment later.

"Commander," McCoy said to him, "do you know that it's not polite to interfere with people's communications with home?"

Kaiev looked both annoyed and upset, and for a moment McCoy found himself wondering whether he was running up to another liver relapse; he was pale. Kaiev said, *"Commander, I have just received a number of orders from our High Command—"*

Oh boy, McCoy thought. *It never occurred to me that* he *would have his own bureaucracy breathing down his neck. I should have thought of that long ago. I am really not cut out for this job—*

"We have decided that you and the indigenous peoples of this planet have conspired in the kidnapping of our personnel. We are also convinced that your stories of missing personnel are a blind to allow you to

180

stay in the area for reasons of your own, probably treacherous. Therefore, if our crewpeople are not returned to us within one of your standard days," Kaiev said, *"I am ordered to destroy your ship. Reinforcements are being diverted to this area. If you attempt to leave without returning our people, we will hunt you down wherever you run, and blow you out of space. We have jammed your communications to prevent your calling for help. Since we are a peace-loving species, and wish to give you a chance to rethink the consequences of your aggression against us, for the present we will take no action against your landing parties on the planet, and will allow you to recover them. But any Federation personnel found on the planet after the one-standard-day time limit will be considered a casualty of the security action that will be mounted to recover our own people. You may also wish to warn the planet's inhabitants that should they repent their collusion with you, and assist in the return of our personnel to us, we will spare them. Otherwise we will kill one thousand of them for every one of our missing people, and will continue to do so every standard hour until our people are returned. Long live the Empire."* And the screen went black before McCoy could get in a single word.

McCoy sat down and swiveled around to face Uhura. "Are we jammed as he says?"

"Yes, Doctor, we are. Subspace is full of artificially generated black noise. Not a thing we can do about it without leaving the area. At the strength they're using, not even a signal buoy would do us any good within the time limit."

"Wonderful." A moment later he said, "Wait a minute! They can't do this. The Organians—"

Spock shook his head. "Doctor, test cases of whether or not the Organians will or will not intervene, this far away from their home space, are very thin on the ground. I should not care to rely on their intervention. Would you?"

"Mmf," McCoy said. "Yes. Well, I suppose the Universe helps those who help themselves, eh, Spock?"

"The body of statistical data does indicate something of the sort."

McCoy folded his hands and thought. "Look, Spock," he said after a little, "will it help you if we take some of the people who're doing general survey work and get them looking for more of those tachyon-Z particles?"

"I doubt it," Spock said, "but the decision is yours."

McCoy could hear Spock's private thought: if it made McCoy feel better, it would do no harm. "No," he said, "let them keep doing what they're doing, then. Uhura, put together a buoy anyway, and get it ready to take last batches of information that the landing parties will be bringing up tomorrow at this time. The DNA-analog analyses will be done by then, and that information in particular mustn't be lost, if this whole mission isn't to be wasted."

"Yes, Doctor," Uhura said.

McCoy sighed. "Spock," he said, "opinions?"

"I should say that we are in a difficult position," said Spock.

"Thank you ever so much. Analysis."

Spock looked thoughtful. "Kaiev's ship by itself is not capable of taking on the *Enterprise* successfully," he said. "But three or more ships would be; and three

182

is the usual number of ships sent along on an intervention of this kind. With four-to-one odds against us, our ability to leave the encounter without serious damage becomes seriously impaired."

"Spock," McCoy said gently, "your bedside manner is flawless. You mean, we're all going to be blown to hell."

Spock hesitated, then nodded.

"Right. And if we run, they'll run after us . . . with the same odds."

"They would. Tactically, our advantage increases slightly if we remain in orbit. Space battles in the close neighborhood of a planet are a complex business, but the opportunities for mistakes involving the planet's gravity increase exponentially, and that is to our advantage."

"If an experienced officer is directing the fight," McCoy said softly.

Spock simply looked at him.

"Right," McCoy said. "Well, we can't do anything else at the moment, so we'll sit tight, and prepare ourselves the best we can. If any suggestions occur to you, let me know. Uhura, make sure a complete recording of that last little lovenote goes in the buoy. Spock, department heads' meeting this evening. We'll want to make sure everybody is as ready as they can be for this gymkhana."

"Acknowledged."

McCoy got up. "I'm going to go off and have my lunch," he said. "Call me if anything interesting develops."

"Yes, sir," Uhura said.

McCoy got into the turbolift; the doors shut, and he waited for his shaking fit to start. It declined. "Oh hell," he said. "Don't tell me I'm getting used to this *now*."

As far as he was concerned, this was a bad, bad sign.

Katur tossed the digger to the ground and said words that would probably have astonished her mother. "We must have come half a kalikam," she said, "and there's nothing to be found. What do they mean, sending us on a mad chase like this?"

The sentiments were treacherous, but none of the other members of the party seemed inclined to disagree with her. She sat down on a big rock and looked around her. This was a wretched planet. Ugly colors, hot dry atmosphere, dim little sun—a waste of time. And they were stuck down here, and the ship hadn't answered their last call. Katur supposed there was something wrong with the ship's transmitter again. It wouldn't be the first time, or the last.

"Never mind that," she said to Tak, who was slogging on up the hill as if he still meant to obey orders. "Come back down, Tak. There's no point."

"I think I see something up here," he said. "It looks like the right color of leaves."

"Oh, go ahead," she said. "Let us know if it's *tabekh* after all." *I hope it's not, you miserable little sycophant . . .*

"I wonder why all these rocks look so much alike," Helef said. He was leaning against one, mopping at his face. Helef was soaked with sweat; typical of him, Katur thought. He had not been in shape since he was first assigned to the ship, knowing that no one cared about his physical condition as long as he completed his duties and did not bother the ship's physician by becoming ill. Helef was soft. But this had its advantages as well. One who knew his weakness could exploit it when necessary.

"What about the rocks?" Katur said, looking back down the valley, the way they had come.

"They all look alike. See this one—" He squinted up at the one he was leaning against. "It looks almost exactly like the one that Kesaio hit."

She glanced at it and away . . . then looked back. Odd, but it did bear a resemblance to that other standing stone. And there was another one farther up the hill that looked similar—several of them, in fact.

"Someone else must have lived here once," she said. "None of those jellybag things, or the trees, could put up anything like that. They haven't enough technology to crack nuts."

"Foul things," Helef muttered.

She nodded, wondering why the Federation people were so eager to bother with aliens at all. She had heard a theory that the Feds had such an inferiority complex that they had to consort with animals to make themselves feel like real people. That made a kind of sense. All she knew for sure was that she would rather die than so lower herself.

Tak was running down the slope, waving his arms and shouting something. Katur looked up in surprise.

"It's *tabekh,* it's *tabekh!* Not where I thought it was; farther up. There's not much of it, just a little patch—"

Well, that's something. We won't be whipped when we get back for completely failing in what we were sent to do. But I for one will be sure that Kesaio has to account for the vehicle. Katur sighed, picked up the digger, and began to walk up toward Tak.

Then she turned around, blinking. For a moment

she had been sure something had moved behind her. There was nothing, though.

She turned again . . . and found another rock in front of her.

—except it was gone—

Katur blinked several times, hard. Her eyes were all right. True, it had been a while since she had eaten, but she was hardly faint with hunger just yet.

Afterimage, she thought. She had been staring at Helef's miserable rock, and had seen an afterimage of it when she turned. After all, the shape had been exactly the same.

Tak came down to her. "Definitely *tabekh,*" he said. "There are some of the tree-things up there, but we can get rid of them. Come on!"

"Helef, Kesaio," she called, and led the way up the slope, with Tak scrambling after her, hurring to keep up, and panting. Truly he was in terrible shape.

Though it was astonishing, Katur thought, how steep some of these slopes could turn out to be; much steeper than they looked. She didn't mind, of course. The stoniness of them was a bit of a problem, though. And each time they turned a curve in the gully they were following, there were more of the tall stones to be seen. There must have been a civilization of some other kind here at one point. *Probably,* she thought, *these jellybags and the trees are their degenerate pets. Probably a mercy to put the things out of their misery.*

"Here," Tak said at last, leading them over the brow of a little wooded ridge. On the other side was a sort of dell, surrounded by the ubiquitous blue-green trees; and in the middle of the dell, among the scrub and turf that floored it, were the unmistakable leaves of *tabekh.* It was of course the roots they wanted, and

Katur wearily unhooked the digger from its strap and started to set it up on its legs. "All right," she said to the others. "Let's take this. Don't miss the taproot. It will be somewhere near the center, and if we can keep it alive, the Hydroponics crew can clone enough of the young plants so that none of us will run out for the rest of the tour. Come on, then. We don't want to be all day about this."

It was then that they heard the odd rustling noises, and something stranger, a tearing sound that Katur could not identify. She whipped around to see a whole little herd of the tree-things coming at them, all their nasty little eyes glinting, all their branches waving about. The trees were hissing, the kind of noise you hear from trees in stormy weather, just before the storm breaks. And they were actually wading through the ground, their roots breaking it, tearing it. In a moment they would be into the patch of *tabekh,* and tearing *that* up—and there would go any hope of cloning it.

Katur pulled out her sidearm and shouted, "Stop!" and fired into the ground in front of the aliens. They paid no mind, but kept moving.

"Very well then," she said, and fired into the branches.

Or should have. Something struck her hand from one side, hard, and sent her sidearm flying. She must have tottered off balance, because immediately thereafter she stumbled into one of the large rocks, hitting it hard with the length of her body, right up from leg to side to cheek and temple. Stunned, she caromed back, rubbing at her eyes to try to clear her vision.

But that wasn't there before—she thought.

"Drop those," she heard a voice say in Federation

talk. She scrubbed at her eyes again, opened them, and managed to see something through the tears of pain—a hominid figure, an Earth-human, in Starfleet uniform, standing with drawn phaser. Behind him was a very large rock, the one that Katur had rammed into; the one that occupied a spot that had been empty air a second before.

"Back off," the man said. Katur looked and saw with disgust that Tak and Kesaio and Helef had already dropped their sidearms. Helef was shaking his hand as if to get rid of the violent pins-and-needles of a stun-level graze.

The man was looking them over with an expression somewhere between amusement and annoyance. Katur flushed with anger, but that was all she could do; her own sidearm was somehow or other half-buried underneath the foot of the tall stone.

"You are interfering with a mission team of the Klingon Empire, Earther," she said angrily. "The penalty for such interference is death."

"Yes," the man said, grinning amiably at her, "I just bet it is. Whom have I the pleasure of interfering with?"

"I am First Specialist Katur of the Imperial Vessel *Ekkava*," she said, furious at being mocked.

"That's nice. I'm Captain James T. Kirk of the Starship *Enterprise,* and you were in the act of attacking a harmless indigenous and intelligent inhabitant of this planet without provocation and in a breach of the Organian Treaty." He made a disparaging tsk-tsk noise at them. "Shame on you," he added.

Katur's mind whirled. *James Kirk!!* "You lie," she cried. "All know that Kirk was killed in a duel, and another took his place and commands his ship."

The man's face started out blank . . . then an odd smile began very, very slowly to spread across it. "Ah," he said. "And by any chance . . . would the new commander's name be McCoy?"

Katur's face gave everything away, against her desire.

The man nodded slowly, then turned and looked up at the rock, as if sharing a joke with it. "Well," he said, "as usual, the reports of my death have been greatly exaggerated."

The confusion in Katur's mind quieted to one thought. If this *was* Kirk, then someone must get word to the Commander . . . and quickly. Things aboard the *Enterprise* were not as they had seemed.

The look in the man's eyes hardened suddenly. "Yes indeed," he said. "So for the meantime, my dear, you just sit down right where you are, you and all your friends. I want a moment to think."

Katur sat down, thinking too.

Chapter Eight

Captain's log, Supplemental. Leonard McCoy recording in the absence of James Kirk:

It is now twenty hours since the issuance of Commander Kaiev's ultimatum to us, with four hours remaining. We have scant hope of finding the Captain within that time. Mr. Spock continues his researches, but has so far found nothing that would enable him to find the Captain, much less retrieve him.

It can, however, be said that there is no sign yet of the other Klingon vessels we have been expecting. Mr. Sulu's best estimate of their arrival was within eighteen hours of the ultimatum—such ultimata are rarely issued without the issuers being fairly certain of the reinforcements turning up early, and thus putting added pressure on the ultimatees, or perhaps even catching them incompletely prepared for battle, and forcing an engagement before they're ready, which usually concludes in the ultimatees becoming plasma shortly thereafter. This is a conclusion that we are eager to avoid, so I have had the ship on red alert for some time previous to the eighteen-hour point. This makes certain unavoidable changes in the ship's shift structure, and adversely affects the number of people we have gathering

190

data—but I also have a responsibility to see that those people and those data get home safely.

A buoy has been prepared to take all the data we have so far gathered out of the system. It will make its way eventually back to Federation space if we are lost. A copy of all log entries since the Klingon jamming began will also be sent out. If there is time to manage it, a second buoy will go out with the same information. A duplicate never hurts.

IT WAS LATE. McCoy was sitting up in the center seat, gazing at the sedately turning shape of Flyspeck underneath them. As he watched, it passed out of its day side, into night, and the light of its one little moon glinted silvery-blue on the wide empty spaces of the planet's largest ocean.

I never did get to go down by the water, McCoy thought. *Usually that's such a priority for me. Joanna got me hooked on the water, all those times ago when we used to go out to Montauk Point and try to see across to England.* He found himself smiling a bit as he looked around the night Bridge crew. *A long time ago,* he thought.

"Ensign Devlin," he said, "you lived on the East Coast once. Ever go out to Montauk Point?"

"Oh, yes, sir," she said, looking up from the Engineering console. "My sister and I used to go out there and watch for sharks. Sharks were a hobby of hers."

"You see any?"

"Yes, we did! One was the biggest one we ever saw. It was a real Great White, the Point biologist said. At least eighty feet long, but I think it was more like a hundred."

McCoy visualized that. "That could have eaten a shuttlecraft," he said. "Or at least it could've taken a good bite out of it."

Devlin nodded and stretched her legs out in front of her. After a moment, she said, "Nervous, sir?"

McCoy was aware of other eyes on him, around the Bridge, not obtrusive, but interested. Lawson and Tee Thov sitting at the helm, minding Weapons and Navigation, didn't quite turn around, but he could see from the muscle tone of their backs that they were listening. Parker and North, at Science and Communications, glanced at one another. McCoy laughed, just a bare breath of laughter. "Well," he said, "I'm half ready to bite my nails down to the elbows. But there's no point in it, and I might want my elbows for something later."

"No sign of them yet," Tee Thov said, looking over his shoulder at McCoy.

"None yet," McCoy said, "but they're not scheduled onstage just yet anyway. Doesn't matter. We'll be ready."

He leaned back and tried to look as confident as he wanted them to feel. Usually, there was no problem with this . . . when he was in Sickbay. His bedside manner had always been the envy of his classmates. It was a simple thing, really, once he discovered it: *never* lie to your patients, but find the best truth to tell them that you can, and keep reminding them that the Universe does strange things, and that health can overcome the worst diseases if given half a chance and a little faith.

Faith was always the problem. People were so used to certainties, most of their lives—death, taxes, pain —that the occasional need to believe in something without evidence tended to be beyond them. It was the ones who could have faith, and not care whether anyone thought they were stupid, who always got

192

better the fastest, and survived what were usually the most fatal maladies. Bodies were, after all, just educated meat—and not that educated. Before the certainty that lived at the heart of faith, very few bodies had any defense.

The question was: Was his faith about the *Enterprise*'s continued survival going to be strong enough? Or was it caught at the stage where you insisted, "I believe, I believe!" and you didn't, and the Universe wasn't fooled?

He snorted at himself a little, then. There were, after all, other wills, other faiths, involved. It was entirely likely that theirs would carry his, this time out—that the crew of the *Enterprise*, so used to not dying in horrible situations, would go on as always, and he would survive with them.

Then again, there was always a first time . . .

"Doctor," Devlin said, "are you okay?"

He laughed softly. "Fine. I just wish the Captain would walk in here. You know the trouble with this chair?"

"Wish I did," Devlin said with undisguised envy.

"You're nuts," McCoy said. "Well, each to his own insanity. This thing has *no* back support to speak of." He got up and pointed at the very insufficient lower back padding. "Now just look at that. Any one of you has a better chair. But if you have to sit in this thing for more than an hour, it makes you want to get up and pace around. *Now* I know why Jim was always all over the Bridge half the time. The damn chair was driving him crazy."

There were chuckles here and there from the Bridge crew. "If some one of you wanted to make me really comfortable," McCoy said, "you'd go get me a nice pillow."

"Does it have to be an embroidered one?" said Parker in his dry Earth-British voice.

McCoy snickered. "No, one of the fat-substitute pillows from Sickbay would do all right." He reached down to the arm of the center seat, punched the button. "Sickbay."

"Sickbay, Aiello," said the cheerful voice. Pat Aiello was the night nurse, a big cheerful dark-haired woman with a round happy face. *"What do you want this time of night? Why aren't you in bed?"*

"Pat," McCoy said, "have you got a spare weight-dist pillow down there?"

"A few of them."

Have someone send me up one when you have a chance. This center seat was designed by Torquemada."

"Will do. Must be nice for some *people,"* Pat said in an offended tone, *"sitting on their bottoms all day, while honest crewmen work their fingers to the bone—"*

McCoy had to laugh. "Spare me the philosophy and send up the pillow."

A couple of minutes later, the turbolift doors hissed open. Spock was standing in the turbolift. He had the air of a man who had been in an extreme hurry, but who had been stopped in midrush and given something he didn't understand. He was holding a small flat cushion. "Doctor," he said, "I think possibly this is meant for you."

"Thanks." McCoy got up and went to take it from him.

"Your night nurse," Spock said, moving quickly to

his station, "is a woman of few words, but forceful ones."

"Have you got something?" McCoy said.

"That we shall see," Spock said. "Certainly I have something to show you."

Parker had slid hurriedly out of the way as Spock sat down. "Doctor," Spock said, touching the console here and there to bring up some data from the computer in his quarters, "you will remember we were talking about those radiation decays that were more typical of tachyon artifact than anything else?"

"That's right." McCoy looked over Spock's shoulder.

"Searching along those lines, I have found a great deal more artifact of the same kind," Spock said. "Again, it seems not to attach itself to any specific thing going on on the planet below. But if one plots all incidences of such decays against time and location—"

He paused for a moment, waiting for the computer to finish a calculation. At the screen above his station it brought up a schematic of the smaller clearing, as seen from above, where McCoy had earlier seen the ;At. "Now watch, Doctor," he said. "By good chance we have earlier scans of that area, before you or the Captain entered it. Fortunately we were on the correct side of the planet for enough scan time. Look."

A faint fog of light became visible in the clearing, strengthening to patches that became thick, vague lines. "Those look like deer trails," McCoy said.

"They are areas of probability," Spock said, "where such particle decays as I have been investigating are most likely to occur. Now look at the same area after the Captain vanishes."

Suddenly there were more sets of tracks—smaller ones, that intersected with the larger set. McCoy began to smile slowly. "Jim," he said.

"The data is not absolutely conclusive," Spock said. "But see here. We are now looking at time-lapse readings. The Klingon landing party—"

Their traces were suddenly added to the already existing tracks of tachyon artifact. Those traces began at the point where they had disappeared, and then went off northward, toward the hills. Shortly thereafter, the previous traces seemed to follow them away and out of the scanned area.

"All right," McCoy said, still smiling. "There they are, then. What now?"

Spock straightened and looked dissatisfied. "Doctor, it is not quite so simple. Their traces are obviously there in 'real time'—but *they* are not. These particles are decaying in a way that indicates a fairly substantial timeslip, but whether into the past or future, I cannot tell. And even if I could, I am still without an inkling of how to come *at* the Captain. It is certainly something of a relief to discover that he is apparently alive—or was. However—"

"*Something* of a relief? Why, you green-blooded—"

"Doctor, please. Your blood pressure."

"Mmf . . . never mind that now. Spock, wait a minute. You said the past *or* the future. No one can travel to the future!—I thought."

Spock looked more dissatisfied than ever. "You are correct . . . at least, according to present received opinion. Unfortunately, the particle decays have a characteristic that sheds some doubt on the question.

A significant percentage of them show a quality that has some relation to the 'red shift' that happens in light when it is slowed up in the interstellar medium; though this quality is actually associated with the 'up' and 'down' characteristics of so-called 'plain vanilla' quarks. It illustrates entry into the present time-stream from a 'faster' one—that is to say, the time that has not occurred yet. The compression factor—"

McCoy's head began to hurt. "Spock, time's a-wastin' here, no matter what else it may be doing. Let's cut to the chase. We know where Jim is . . . more or less. We know *when* he is . . . more or less."

"If he were more than a week in the past, or the future," said Spock, "I would be very surprised."

"Great." McCoy smiled, but it was not a cheerful expression. "So if we had been here a week early—or if we hung around for a week more—Jim would turn up."

"So I believe."

"Well, then, all we have to do is survive the next week. And then after all the dust settles, if he doesn't turn up in the future—the *present* future—oh, you know what I mean—then we use the 'slingshot' technique to go back in time a week or so and pick Jim up."

"Time travel is not to be taken lightly, Doctor," Spock said. "You should not assume that—"

"Spock," McCoy said, "you worry too much. Look, I'll bet you a nickel that the ;At will be with him . . . and I'm going to ask it some questions."

"I daresay the Klingons will want to as well," Spock said, "should they still be here."

McCoy sighed and made his way down to the center

seat. "A little less than two hours now," he said. "Keep working on it, Spock. Unless you feel you're needed elsewhere."

"I will do so," Spock said.

The first hour, the next half hour, went by too quickly. Nothing happened. McCoy thought he would get more and more nervous as the time went by, but bizarrely, he found himself getting calmer and calmer. That was assisted, he thought, by the fact that the three or four Klingon vessels they were expecting had not yet arrived.

At about minus half an hour, Sulu and Chekov took the helm, and Uhura took the communications board. Spock had been working quietly at the Science station for a long time, saying nothing to anyone. McCoy busied himself chatting with his returning officers, keeping calm, keeping them calm. It was one of the things he best knew how to do. Just because he might be dead in half an hour was no reason to stop doing it now.

"Minus fifteen minutes," Sulu said.

"Scanning?" said McCoy.

"Nothing in range," Chekov said. "And nothing out of range, either, as far as I can tell."

"It might be a trick," McCoy said. "Keep alert." But his brain was simmering with surmises.

"Negative scan," Sulu confirmed. "No sign of anything in subspace at this point, at least not in the neighborhood. Our range is limited on subspace scan."

"All right," McCoy said. He sighed. "Ladies and gentlemen and others, I would prefer nothing untoward to happen in the next fifteen minutes. But if it comes to that, I intend to fight this ship the best it can be fought with our resources."—*with an untried innocent in the helm, and its Captain missing!* "And if I have anything to say about it, they won't get to paint *our* silhouette on their sides."

"We're with you, Doctor," Sulu said. There was a murmur of agreement around the Bridge.

"Good enough," McCoy said. "Then let's take the adventure that comes to us. Uhura? All secure?"

She nodded. "The last landing parties are aboard."

"All right. Is *Ekkava* moving, Mr. Chekov?"

"Not an inch, sir," Chekov said. "Maintaining standard orbit."

McCoy's smile got grim. "Playing it coy, are they? Fascinating."

Spock quirked an eyebrow, but said nothing.

They waited. Five minutes passed. People whistled softly, twitched, fiddled with controls. McCoy held himself still, very still, at the center of it all.

"Two minutes," said Sulu, almost cheerfully.

"Noted," McCoy said.

And a minute went by, and took a year.

"One minute."

McCoy nodded, and concentrated on breathing— slowly. In, and out. In, and out.

"Zero time," Sulu said then.

And nothing happened.

Nothing.

More nothing.

"Status of the Klingons," McCoy said.

Sulu looked down his scanner and shook his head. "No change, Doctor. Weapons are powered up, but not activating."

"Shields?"

"His shields are up," Chekov said, "not that that would help him should we fire. I would approximate five seconds of resistance at full barrage."

McCoy sat still. "Wait," he said.

For two, three more minutes, five, ten more minutes, they waited. The Bridge got very quiet, but the tenor of the quiet had changed. At the end of ten minutes, McCoy began to smile. "All right," he said. "Either something's happened to their cavalry, or our friend here has been bluffing from a busted flush. Either way, I've goddam well had enough of it. Mr. Sulu, tip us over nice and easy. Bring all forward batteries to bear, and reduce orbital speed. A nice easy drift. I think you know what I have in mind."

"Aye aye, sir," Sulu said, his voice full of relish.

McCoy did not need the screen to show him what was happening. He could see it as if from the Klingons' viewpoint. A challenged enemy waits the time of battle. Waits past it, waiting for the challenger to make good his boast. The challenger, out of countenance, looks at his enemy. Sees the silver-white shape, all this while facing away from him, now tilting slowly forward in its orbit, the great forward disc pitching downward, the nacelles tipping up; watches the pitch continue, a leisurely, massive, graceful pinwheeling on the central lateral axis; sees that disc, upside down now, come swinging up into line, revealing the opening throats of the great main phaser batteries, and the yawning photon torpedo ports. Then just as slowly, the ship begins to turn on its longitudinal axis, righting herself, and at the same time drops off orbital speed. Your speed is not changed yet, and so in your forward screens this silvery monster swells, grows huge, overshadows you—coasts to a delicate halt, relative to your speed, and hangs there, looming, staring down your throat, orbiting backward, not even concerned about the virtuosity this requires of the helm officer. And what further virtuosities will the weapons officer show you shortly, out of the open jaws of death? . . .

"Shall I open a channel, Doctor?" Uhura said softly.

He opened his eyes. "Not yet," he said. "Let them think. Sulu, Chekov, arm us. Full spread on photon torpedoes, maximum-damage harmonization on all phaser banks. Take your time, be deliberate about it. I want their scan officer to see. Arm everything we've got, every last firecracker."

"Yes, sir."

He was aware of Spock's eyes on him from behind. "Psychological warfare, Doctor?" the Vulcan said softly.

"I know, Spock. Violence is violence. But this will be a hell of a lot less violent than what they were planning to do to *us*."

He waited for a minute or so more, just to be sure. "Uhura," he said at last, "open a channel, if you would. Hail them."

"Yes, sir."

Silence for a moment. Everyone watched the screen. "Incoming message, Doctor," Uhura said.

"Put it on screen."

The screen shimmered, showed them the bridge of *Ekkava,* and Commander Kaiev sitting there, visibly sweating and pale. "Well, Commander," McCoy said.

"Commander MakKhoi," said Kaiev, and stopped. He was trying to keep his face passive, and it wasn't working.

For the moment, McCoy refused to react to this. "Commander," he said, in a slow drawl, "I thought I told you to go get your Tacrin dosage regulated. What's the matter with you? Don't you realize what's going to happen if you have to have that liver regenerated? You'll be on your back for weeks."

"I will be dead," Kaiev said, looking slightly surprised. *"I cannot afford the procedure."*

"Can't afford—!" McCoy was outraged, but he put that aside too, after a moment of wrestling with the emotion. "We'll discuss this later. Always assuming we jointly decide there is to *be* a later."

Kaiev held very still.

"You have made certain threats against us," McCoy said, "which I assure you I do not take lightly. Especially since we are innocent of your accusations. But part of the equation is missing. Someone at your High Command have a change of heart?"

Kaiev said nothing. McCoy leaned back in the center seat. "I know well enough what one of your people would do to us, were the positions reversed," he said. "And I have to admit, I'm strongly tempted to knock you around a little to teach you the error of your ways."

"We will fight to the last—"

"Yes, of course you will, what a waste of time," McCoy said, waving a hand in disgust. "Sorry, Kaiev. I don't mean to impugn your worldview. But you know perfectly well that this ship can walk all over yours with cleats."

Kaiev looked bemused for a second. *"Pardon? This is some new kind of weapon?"*

McCoy's mouth quirked up at one side. "Never mind that. We can destroy you in what—about ten minutes, Sulu? Five? Thank you. About five minutes, Commander. If that long. My people are a little annoyed over your attitude."

Perhaps what Kaiev saw on the screen confirmed this. McCoy didn't look around to see. At any rate, the man looked righteously nervous . . . as he had a right to. *"Commander,"* Kaiev said, *"you know I cannot ask you for terms. You know that."*

"Of course I know that. Believe it or not," McCoy said, "I approve. Never you mind why at the moment. Commander, we have other fish to fry at the moment. But first, I want to hear you say that your planned attack is called off."

Kaiev looked even more uncomfortable. *"Commander, my orders—"*

"You have some latitude," McCoy said. "You have enough of it so that you don't have to commit suicide . . . *just* that much. Believe me, Commander, you'd better use it. I am in no mood for this at the moment. You make a move I don't like the look of, and I'll take your ship to pieces and sell it as souvenirs . . . because there won't be enough left to sell for scrap." He smiled a bit. "And besides, even if you promise not to attack us now, you don't have to make any promises about later. I know Klingons better than to expect *that*. A truce, until the situation changes."

Kaiev thought about it. McCoy smiled. Klingons were not really treacherous—that was a judgmental concept born of the human mindset. However, they *were* vigorously opportunist. They would promise you anything, and keep the promise until the situation changed in their favor. Then all promises and bets were off. McCoy didn't mind that; at least he knew what was going to happen, and until it did, there would be that much time when he wouldn't have to worry. The time might make a difference.

"Well?" he said. "Come on, Kaiev, don't sit there dithering. We have things to discuss. Do we have a truce? Or do I blow you up now, collect the souvenir material, and go back to looking for our missing people?"

"Very well," Kaiev said. *"I promise. I have not much choice, for you have us at a disadvantage."* He frowned. *"I still cannot understand why you people are always behaving this way. I* would *have destroyed you."*

McCoy shrugged. "Let's just say we're crippled by our own worldview," he said, "and go on from there. Kaiev, I think we may know where your people are."

At that, the man's eyes positively lit up with relief. *Interesting,* he thought. *A relative in the landing party? A close friend? "Where?"* Kaiev said.

"This is going to sound strange—"

"Commander," Sulu said. *Strange not to be called Doctor,* McCoy thought, glancing at him. "Sir, ripples in subspace. Getting stronger. I think we're about to have company."

"Noted. Get ready. Kaiev, we think they've been shunted a short distance away in time, no more than seven to ten standard days in one direction or another. I *told* you it was going to sound strange," he added, as the Klingon's face went from eagerness, through bewilderment, toward anger. "Just deal with it. Do what you can with the data, because things are about to change. But they *were* on the planet—or they will be shortly. We need to—"

"Incursion," Sulu said. "Splitting the screen. Three

vessels, out of warp, incoming. Two light-minutes out. Decelerating, ETA to orbit two point nine minutes."

"Kaiev," McCoy said, "we need to survive this. Keep your wits about you, because if we don't live through this encounter, you have no hope of getting your people back. Believe me."

Kaiev looked stricken. "Believe me," McCoy said again. "The odds of your duplicating our data and results are very, very slim. I have no ill will against you, and I want my people back as much as you want yours. Don't blow both our chances."

"Positive IDs," Chekov said. "Klingon vessels *Sakkhur, Irik,* and *Kalash.* All fully armed, all weapons systems ready."

McCoy nodded, glanced around the various stations. "Noted. Ladies and gentlemen, stand ready." *Dear God, I wish I were in Sickbay, where I belong!* But he had to smile. *And may this not be the last time I think that, either . . .*

The screen showed the three Klingon vessels sweeping in toward Flyspeck, braking down from lightspeed They were all sister-ships to *Ekkava*—no bigger, but four of them together would be able to do what one alone hadn't a prayer of pulling off. McCoy shifted a bit in the center seat.

"Uhura," he said, "a moment of quiet, if you would." She nodded and silenced the connection, while leaving the visual signal alone. "Spock, how long do you reckon we could hold out against a concerted attack by these four?"

Spock thought about that. "Some minutes. Less, if we were unlucky, or were maneuvered into an unfavorable position."

I don't want to break orbit. But there seems no reason not to do it. It's not as if Jim is down there physically . . . He sighed. There were other considerations than just Jim. There were the Ornae and the Lahit to think about: innocents—at least relatively—and undefended against any attempts the Klingons might make to attempt to "frighten" them into giving their crewpeople back. "Let's not be, then," he said. "We need to stay close and protect this planet as best we can. Sound on again, Uhura. Kaiev," he said, "this is it, then." He held the other's eyes for a moment. "Take care of your liver."

Kaiev looked down and said nothing.

"Commander," Uhura said, "hails coming in from the other three ships. They require us to surrender."

"Later, Commander," McCoy said. "Uhura, kill it." Kaiev's face faded from the screen, to be replaced by the images of the incoming ships. "And as for those others, tell them 'nuts.'" As the Bridge crew looked at him in a mixture of astonishment and approval, he said, "Well, it's traditional, isn't it?"

"Doctor," Spock said, "I had not thought to find you so expert in militaria."

McCoy looked over his shoulder at the Vulcan, who had come down to the center seat to stand beside him. "You know how it is, Spock," he said. "Those who don't know the mistakes of the past won't be able to enjoy it when they make them again in the future."

Spock raised both eyebrows, then glanced up at the screen.

The Klingon ships had come to rest in a standard surround formation around the *Enterprise,* a diamond shape—*Ekkava* in front making the fourth corner."

"Uhura, any answer from them?"

"Nothing yet, Doctor. They must be running semantic analysis."

"What? Hasn't *anybody* ever told them 'nuts' before?" McCoy was amazed.

"Perhaps," Spock said, "everyone else was thinking that it had been used before."

"Thanks so much, Spock. Go sharpen your wits or something."

"Messages passing back and forth between the *Ekkava* and the other vessels, Commander," Uhura said. "Can't get the content for you just now, though. They're using a new scramble."

"Oh well."

"No, it's all right," Uhura said. "Give me fifteen minutes or so."

"You think you can crack it?"

Uhura smiled. "Let's see," she said.

There was quiet for a few minutes. Then Uhura said, "Message coming in for us from *Irik,* Doctor."

"Let's have it."

The screen resolved into the image of the bridge of another Klingon battle cruiser, but this time the forward position was occupied by a young woman—very intense, and with a fierce expression and very striking reddish-gold hair, which McCoy had never heard of on a Klingon before. *Not dye, surely. Maybe just a genetic hiccup?*

"You are Commander McCoy?" she demanded, in a voice that sounded not at all like a fierce officer's. It was one of those tiny, soft voices that make the owner sound about thirty years younger than she really is.

"Ma'am," McCoy said, bowing slightly from the waist where he sat. "You have the advantage of me."

"Indeed. But we will come to that shortly. I am Com-

207

mander Aklein, senior commander in charge of this task force."

"Pleased."

"I rather doubt that." She peered at him suspiciously. *"I must say it is hard to believe that you have killed the mighty Kirk in a duel. You do not look like the dueling type."*

McCoy just smiled. "There are arts of killing that require more than mere muscles," he said. "Cunning will do nearly as well . . . or the knife in the back, in the dark."

He didn't dare move to look around at his people's faces. Aklein frowned a bit. *"That sounds like a page from our book, Commander,"* she said. *"Perhaps we have a few more likenesses than we have thought."*

McCoy shrugged. "Commander, forgive me, but you haven't come all this way to do a sociology study. What are your people thinking of doing?"

Aklein settled a bit in her own chair. *"Sir,"* she said, *"the kidnapping of our personnel on the planet is a hostile action that cannot be permitted, whoever perpetrated it—"*

McCoy rolled his eyes. "There's no evidence of kidnapping, Commander. Not of our people, *or* of yours. Planetary scans show perfectly clearly that none of our people was anywhere near yours when yours went missing. There was no Transporter usage at that time, as our records and yours will confirm—"

"We know all that. That leaves us with the conclusion that one of the alien species here is responsible. Though our suspicion is that you somehow put them up to it—"

McCoy began to laugh. "Commander," he said, "I

will be delighted to furnish you with records of our dealings with the people down there over the past few days. Putting them up to *anything,* including giving straight answers to straight questions, seems to be damn near impossible."

Aklein looked a little put out by that. *"No matter. We will conduct our own search of the planet surface, to confirm* Ekkava's *findings, and then begin punitive operations against the natives until they—"*

"I will not permit that," McCoy said.

"You will be hard put to stop us," Aklein said, smiling a bit.

McCoy did not smile. "Think again, Commander. This is *Enterprise.* She is more than one man, though that one man might have made her famous—or, among you, infamous. She is four hundred thirty-eight people—to whom you're an interesting enough problem . . . but one that we're long used to solving."

"You do not frighten me, Commander."

"Good," McCoy said. "Fear is much overrated as a deterrent. Death works much better."

She blinked. "Commander," Sulu said softly, "more subspace ripples. Two more vessels incoming."

"Really?" McCoy said. He glanced up at the screen. "I thought you said you were in command of this task force, Commander. Can it be that someone at home was second-guessing you?" And a happy thought occurred to him, impossible though it was, and he went on, "Or can it be that *our* reinforcements have arrived?"

Her eyes widened; she glanced down at her own command console, then up again. *"But Kaiev—"*

"I'm from the South, ma'am," McCoy said, "and

even down there, where we're friendly people, we don't tell even our friends *everything*. Much less so for people we're less friendly with."

"Not two vessels, Commander," Sulu said suddenly.

"More?"

"No. One."

"One?" McCoy got up to peer over Sulu's shoulder at the scanner. "Good Lord, what *is* that? Am I reading it right? It looks huge!"

"It is huge, Commander," Spock said, coming down from the Science station to look over Sulu's shoulder as well. "I too thought it was two vessels at first. But it is a single trace. Incoming at warp 6, decelerating, about to go sublight."

"How about it, Commander?" McCoy said to Aklein. "A bit of a surprise? That's nothing of yours that *I* know of. I wonder whose it is?"

"Back to Alert status," Aklein said hurriedly to one of the officers behind her.

"Aklein, you've hurt my feelings," McCoy said. "You mean you came *off* Alert at the sight of us? We're going to have to discuss this later. Are we all set?" McCoy said to Spock.

"We are ready," Spock said.

"Gone sublight now," Sulu said, alarm in his voice. "Massive vessel, Commander. Braking down hard from point nine nine. Point eight nine, seven nine, seven, five nine—"

Spock had hurried back up to his station. "Unknown type," he said after a moment. "Greatly overengined for its size."

"Extremely well-armed," Chekov said, glancing at the weapons console. "Twenty phaser banks, all on

210

charge, all arming. Photon torpedoes, tractors, flash-plasma generators—what do you make of that?" he said to Sulu.

Sulu looked too. "Phased-packet particle-beam accelerator," he said. "Leaking leptons." He shook his head and looked at McCoy. "Very nasty," he said. "It's a screen-ripper. Fortunately, they can't fire while they're using it."

"What's the ID on that thing?" McCoy demanded.

"No ID, Commander," Spock said. "But configuration matches some intelligence I have seen recently."

"Who the hell is it?!"

"A high probability that this is an Orion pirate vessel," Spock said.

The weapons console began to make an unnerving beeping noise, which McCoy had not heard before, and fervently wished he wasn't hearing now. "Sulu," he said, "would you mind—"

"Aye, sir," Sulu said. He killed the audio alarm. "It's got a firing lock on us, whatever it is."

"Lock right back at it," McCoy said. "Prepare to fire if it fires. Get us a visual, for pity's sake! Damned if I'm going to shoot at something I can't see. Scotty, what about the shields?"

Scotty looked nervous. "That particle-beam accelerator, that's a nasty little weapon they've got there, Doc—Commander. Starfleet's engineering department is still working on countermeasures."

"Oh, come on, Scotty, don't tell me you haven't invented something already!"

"Well, to tell you the truth, the problem *has* been preyin' on my mind a bit—"

"Let it prey. What can we do in the meantime?"

"Shoot," Sulu said.

"Not yet," McCoy said. His Oath to preserve life, even pirates' lives, was ringing in his mind—but it was arguing with his oaths as a Starfleet officer, to protect and preserve the ship, and the argument was loud. "Wait for it. Spock, visual yet?"

"Now," Spock said, and the screen split to show the image of the thing that was coming at them. The ship *was* massive—more like four times the *Enterprise*'s size. "That's a whole city there, isn't it, Spock," McCoy said, as the great sleek oblong bulk, studded and lined with ports and drop-tubes and weapons apertures, came coasting along toward them. "They live in that—must be a couple thousand of them—and go from world to world, robbing what they like."

"That is the supposition," Spock said. "However, we have little data. They tend to attempt to destroy any ship they meet that is not already in association with them."

"Good luck to them," McCoy said. He looked over at the image of Commander Aklein. "Well, ma'am?" he said. "What now?"

"I must confer," she said hurriedly, and shut the connection down from her end.

"Hurry up about it," McCoy said, as the ship shuddered a bit. "Ranging shot, that was?"

"Yes. Phaser beams."

"They're too far away to hit us," McCoy said, very hopeful.

"No, they're not," Sulu said. "Those beams have been dilithium-augmented."

"Isn't that a little expensive?" McCoy said, sitting down again, rather hurriedly, as the ship shuddered once more.

"Not if you're an Orion pirate," Uhura said. "One

of the few things we know about their language is that the word we use for 'stealing,' they translate as 'getting paid.'"

"Shields holding," Scotty said. "But they won't for long if they open up with that particle-beam shredder."

"Hail them, Uhura."

"I've been trying. No response to hails."

"Dammit," McCoy said, feeling his options going away one by one. "What do they want?"

"Probably to scare away the poachers," Sulu said. "Someone horning in on what they see as their territory. They wouldn't just come in here firing unless they'd been here before and didn't want anyone else around."

"I must agree with Mr. Sulu that that hypothesis seems likely," Spock said.

"Wonderful," McCoy said, and gripped the arms of the center seat. "Prepare to fire."

"Ready," Sulu and Chekov said.

McCoy waited. One breath.

One more.

One more. The ship swelled in their screens.

One more—

—and everything went white—

Chapter Nine

"WELL," KIRK SAID, "aren't we all snug."

He was looking around at the rather disgusted Klingons. They were avoiding looking at him, now that he had relieved them of all their weapons and communicators, and they were sitting about on the ground of the glade having a truly massive sulk. He didn't mind; it was preferable to having them trying energetically to jump him.

He turned to the Master of the ;At. "Sir," he said, "I must get in touch with my ship. The presence of these people means that they're very likely in some kind of difficulty."

"You hear the way your device is behaving, however," said the Master. "I fear I can do nothing about that."

"Yes, but I had an idea—"

One of the Klingons, the young woman, looked at Kirk with undisguised disgust. "How can you pretend to understand that gibberish?" she said. "You are either mad or perverted."

"Sorry, First Specialist," Kirk said. "You don't know me well enough to accuse me of either." *Still,* he thought, *if they really can't understand what's being said, the situation is that much to my advantage. Of course, it might be a trick, too, to get me to feel free to discuss things with the ;At . . .*

"What sort of idea?" said the Master.

"A little while ago, we were discussing your ability to . . . inhabit . . . other parts of the time-space continuum."

"So we were."

"My communicator is presently jammed. But would there be anything to prevent you from moving to an, uh, different location in time-space—and informing one of my people of what's going on? Or *will* be going on?"

"Unfortunately," said the Master, "yes. We learned a long time ago not to tamper with the fabric of things in that way. It invariably produces more trouble than it solves."

Kirk sighed. "Well, I had to ask. Sir, forgive me, but my place is with my people at a time like this. I have to find a way to get to them."

"I am sorry for your discomfort," said the Master. "Correct me if I misunderstand your technology, but if your communications are not functioning, most likely your Transporter will not be either, since the carrier signals are interrelated."

"That's true," Kirk said, not surprised that the ;At knew it; he had been thinking about it earlier. "Well, at any rate, I should get back to my people down in the clearing; and I'll take this lot down with me and keep them out of your hair."

"What will be done with them?" said the Master.

"Oh, we'll send them home to their ship, no problem with that. Their Commander will probably be annoyed with me, but not as annoyed as I'm going to be with him or her for sneaking up on us without so much as a hello-how-are-you. I want to find out how they did that." Kirk was feeling a little grim; it was not like the *Enterprise* crew to let a ship come into system without letting him know about it. If this was McCoy's doing somehow, that might put a slightly different complexion on it. But not much. He could just hear Bones saying, "I didn't see any point in worrying you, there was nothing you could do about it, and they seemed harmless—"

No, he thought, *no use trying to judge the situation without really knowing what's going on. It's just as possible that our friends here found some clever new way to sneak up on us. A new cloaking device, perhaps?*

But what do they want *here, anyway?*

"You," Kirk said, glaring meaningfully at the young woman. "First Specialist Katur?" She tilted her head sideways for "yes." "What the devil were you people doing here?" He looked around at the digging devices, and the path that the Lahit had been making toward the plant growth in the center. Even now the Lahit stood around the glade, making vaguely upset hissing noises.

Katur glared at him. "I shall not tell you."

"Oh yes you shall," he said, advancing on her slowly, "or you'll find out the truth of all those horror stories you've heard about me." He reached down to pick up one of the Klingon sidearms, on which the Master of the ;At was more or less standing. "May I borrow this?" he said. "Thank you. Nasty thing,"

Kirk said. "No stun setting. But then you people have always been of a rather terminal turn of mind."

Katur stared at him. "Let's have it," he said, letting his anger show in his voice. "What is that stuff?"

"Tabekh," Katur said hurriedly.

"What's that?" She hesitated. "I mean, what do you do with it?"

"Don't tell him," said one of the others. "They'll take it for themselves."

"What's it for?" Kirk demanded, taking another step forward.

Katur gulped. "It's the raw material for making *tabekhte.*"

"And what does that do?" He had a horrible thought. "Is it a drug?"

She glowered scorn at him. "Idiot! We put it on our food," Katur said.

Kirk stared at her. "Just the plant?"

"No. We make a condiment out of it."

He was interested in spite of himself. *Heaven help us, this is the raw ingredient for Klingon Worcestershire sauce,* Kirk thought. And then he thought of Spock's occasional complaints about the freshness of the vegetables from Hydroponics, and McCoy going on about tasteless dehydrated reconstituted meat, and Scotty muttering about the lack of neeps and tatties—*I really have to find out what "neeps" are*—for Burns Day. He smiled a bit. "First Specialist, grousing about the food aboard a ship is one of the universal rights of crewpeople everywhere, and if someone's declared it treacherous, then almost everybody I know is a traitor. But you really can't do without this stuff?"

They glared at him and said nothing.

"Then you'll have to come to some kind of agreement with the people who live here as regards whether you may have it or not," Kirk said. "And I wonder what else you might be here for . . ." No one said anything. "Well, I suppose that's something I need to ask your Commander, not you." Kirk tossed the Klingon sidearm back to the ground, and took a moment to admire the way the Master of the ;At managed to stand on it again without moving from its original spot. Or at least that was the way it seemed. "Sir, I should take these people back down to my people at the clearing. They'll hold them until communications are restored and we can find out what's going on up there."

"As you like," said the Master of the ;At. "Also, if they wish some of the plant, they may take it. The Lahit grant them leave."

Kirk glanced over at the nervously jiggling Lahit. "Do they have a use for it?" Kirk said.

"They talk to it," said the Master.

Kirk nodded. "Get to it, then," he said to the Klingons. They hurriedly began picking leaves from the plant.

"And you, sir," Kirk said, "I look forward to talking to you again tomorrow, if I may. I think we still have some things to discuss."

"Probably not," said the Master of the ;At, but its voice sounded pleased. Kirk raised his eyebrows. "But in any case, meet we shall. At your convenience, Captain. I think you are probably rather busier than I am."

"Tomorrow morning, then," said Kirk.

"Very well so," said the Master.

"All right, that looks like as much as you can carry," Kirk said to the Klingons, drawing his phaser. "Ahead of me, please. A little farther ahead than that." They filed out of the glade ahead of him. "Good afternoon to you, sir," Kirk said to the Master. "And a very nice afternoon it's been. Things seem very quiet hereabouts . . . very relaxing."

"I am glad you found it so. A good day to you, Captain."

Kirk nodded amiably to the pillar of stone—if that was what it was; he would be very interested in Bones's tricorder readings—and followed his little party out of the glade, over the ridge and back down the hillside.

"Damn!!" McCoy shouted. *"Are we dead?"*

"No," Spock said, "but it is uncertain how long that condition will obtain."

McCoy gulped. The ship was still shuddering from that last bolt, whatever it was. "Scotty, report!"

"Shields holding," he said. "Just. Doctor, I advise you to move."

"Too damn right! Mr. Sulu, take your best evasive action. Get us out of here. Uhura, give me the Klingon vessels, all of them. Broadcast it."

"You're on, Doctor."

"Ladies and gentlemen of the Klingon Empire," he said, "This is Commander Leonard McCoy of the *Enterprise.* You will pardon me for breaking formation, but the vessel incoming doesn't seem to be interested in the formalities. After we've dealt with the visitor in whatever way seems best, we'll be

219

returning to orbit, and we'll handle any other matters then. Meanwhile, I suggest you watch your rear ends. McCoy out."

"Done, Doctor. Acknowledgments from the Klingons."

"They'd better do better than acknowledge," McCoy muttered, watching the planet dwindle away behind them. *Back soon, Jim,* he thought. *I hope!* "Is the Orion following?"

"Affirmative," Spock said.

"Dammit," McCoy said. "The price of fame. If I commanded this ship on a regular basis, I'd paint her numbers over. Uhura," he added, "what are the Orions using for scan?"

"Difficult to say, Doctor. Standard scan, the last I heard. Mr. Spock?"

"Standard scanners are usual, as I understand it. They are not too different from ours."

"Good. Can we block them? Or hide them?"

"To some extent, at deep-space distances."

"Good. Sulu, get us well out of orbit. Then turn back in—a nice, long, tight hyperbola. Chekov, plot it so that we can slingshot around the planet and go out again afterward, without any additional power. Spock, once the orbit is set, just before we turn, I want everything we can shut down, shut down. No emissions that we can help."

Spock blinked. "Doctor," he said, "this is a familiar-sounding strategy . . . and an effective one. If I did not know better, I would think you had been reading Jellicoe. Or possibly Smith."

McCoy smiled a little sheepishly. "Jim would keep giving me these books on strategy and telling me I should read them," he said. "Never saw the point, at the time. But he may have had something. I started getting caught up with my reading last night."

"Doctor, one Klingon vessel is leaving orbit," Chekov said. "It's *Kaiev*."

McCoy blinked at that. "Wonder what he's up to."

"Doctor," Sulu said, peering down his scanner, "he is firing at the pirate vessel from behind. Full spread of photon torpedoes.—Ineffective," he added a second later. "All clean misses."

"What's he at?" McCoy said softly. "He could cut and run."

"Hail from *Ekkava,* Doctor," Uhura said. "Not live. A squirt."

"Show me."

Abruptly they were looking at *Ekkava*'s bridge again, and Kaiev. He was still sweating. McCoy began to wonder whether the man's medication was ever going to take . . . or whether the sweat had to do with something else. "Enterprise," he said, *"you have dealt bravely with me. I would do the same with you, before we all die."* He paused a moment, then said, *"And I have had my Tacrin dosage increased.* Ekkava *out."*

McCoy smiled, the only thing he had *really* felt like smiling about for some time now. "Keep an eye on him, Sulu," he said.

"He's still firing, Doctor. Another spread of torpedoes.—One hit this time. But ineffective. The ship is too well shielded."

"It's reactive shielding," Chekov said. "Some of the newer Klingon vessels have it . . . not these, I don't think. The shield's forcefield is much more highly charged than the usual weapons shield; it doesn't just

221

absorb the force of the photon torpedo, it bounces it back. Very nasty, especially if you're following too closely."

"Noted," McCoy said. "Funny, though. The Klingons are usually hot for any new weapon that comes down the pike."

"Not these, Doctor," Spock said. "Reactive shielding, and the particle-beam weapon they're carrying, require massive power supplies . . . much more than a ship the size of the Klingons', or even the size of ours, can supply. There are probably not more than several hundred people on board the Orion vessel, despite its size; most of that space is given over to engine and weapons installations." He folded his arms and looked thoughtful. "This is a scenario that is sometimes played out in simulation at Starfleet . . . but more as an exercise in creative evasive action than anything else."

"Mr. Sulu is pretty creative," McCoy said, cracking his knuckles, and then chiding himself. It was a bad habit he had when he was nervous. "What's Kaiev doing?"

"Still firing," Chekov said. "The pirate vessel is ignoring him."

"He's either trying to distract it," McCoy said, "or—" He shrugged. "Maybe, as he says, he's just being brave. I wish he'd get out of there."

"Two of the other Klingon vessels are breaking orbit, Doctor," said Spock. "On tactical."

The computer supplied the front screen with a tactical view, looking down on Flyspeck's part of space from above its north pole. *Enterprise* was almost off the bottom of the screen, the tag-numbers in X and Z axes changing rapidly. Behind her, the pirate vessel was swinging out to the left, ascending out of the plane of the solar system after her. Close behind it, *Ekkava* was still firing. Closest to the planet, the Klingon vessels were swinging out of orbit, rightward and behind the planet.

"Now where are they going," McCoy wondered, "and what are they going to do?"

Spock said, "I can give you visual display if you prefer, Doctor."

"No, keep it like this," McCoy said hurriedly. When he saw ships, he saw people, and lives, and his Oath started having noisy arguments with other obligations in his head. But when he saw a clean, neat, computer picture like this, it reminded him more of readouts in Sickbay than anything else—diagrams, complex perhaps, but tidy and manageable. And tactics he understood. 4D chess, and Go, and gwyddbwyll, those he had been playing for a long time.

And there were other sources of good ideas as well.

"These people," he said, looking at the spark of light that represented the pirates, "they're not much on subtlety, are they? Come in shooting, that seems to be the favorite tactic."

"I would agree with you," Spock said, coming down from his station to stand beside the center seat for a moment. "Historically, they have preferred to overweapon themselves, and simply bludgeon any resistance into ineffectiveness. Surprise and treachery have always been favorite weapons."

McCoy nodded. "Good."

"Good?" Uhura said, slightly bemused.

"Yes. Uhura, did you manage to do anything with that Klingon code?"

"What? Oh, certainly. I cracked that a while ago."

"The new one?"

"I had a few minutes."

"Wonderful! Send this to *Ekkava:* 'Going to play hide and seek. Note orbit.'"

Spock looked concerned. "Doctor . . . is this wise?"

"I think so. Do it, Uhura. Code it and squirt it."

She worked at her console for a moment. "Done."

"May I inquire what strategy you are considering, Doctor?" said Spock.

McCoy leaned back. "Are you familiar with twentieth-century warfare? The idea was to run silently."

"The strategy has some virtues," Spock said. "But bear in mind that some aspects of our presence, such as residual radiation and heat, cannot be blocked or otherwise concealed."

"I know that. But Spock, isn't it true that this close to the system's star, space is still too 'hot' for us to be easily seen by *just* heat radiation?"

"That is true," Spock said, "but the closer we come to the system's heliopause, the less protection we will have from that sort of detection."

"I know," McCoy said. "I don't plan to go out that far. Though I hope our friend thinks I will. How's the orbit coming, Chekov?"

"Plotted, Doctor," Chekov said, and touched a button. It appeared on the tactical display: a very tight hyperbola indeed, almost the shape of a comet itself, or of an old-fashioned hairpin. One leg of it was a tangent to the circle of the orbit *Enterprise* had been describing around Flyspeck. The other leg missed the planet by some fifty thousand miles, then began to fall in toward it again in the slingshot curve McCoy had asked for.

One part of the hairpin, near the turn at its top, was marked off in red against the white of the rest of the hyperbola. "We must use the engines *there,*" Chekov said, "to acquire that orbit, Doctor."

"Understood. Lay it in and execute it."

"Done, Doctor."

"Once we execute, shut everything down that can be shut down. Scotty," McCoy said, "that means the warp engines, too. If I remember what Jim used to say about scan, that's the major thing they'll be tracking us by."

"Aye," Scotty said, very unhappily.

"You don't need to shut down cold," McCoy said. "Hot restart would take you—how long?"

"In this fuel configuration, six minutes."

"All right."

"Message from Kaiev, Doctor," Uhura said. "He says, 'Acknowledged. Note ephemerides. Change to opposite.'"

"That's his orbit," Chekov said, his fingers dancing across his console. "I think he means he'll be inverting his own parabola. Tricky. He must be planning to use thrusters—"

There was quiet for a moment; then Chekov put *Ekkava*'s orbit up on the screen. It neatly swung out rightward from his present visible course away from the planet, and then back toward it again, slingshoting around as McCoy's did, but from another angle and from higher up. The two orbits came quite close near the planet, then diverged.

"All right," McCoy said softly. Any ship that chased

one of them, without knowing where the other was, would eventually find one or the other of them behind it, unsuspected. "Not much of an advantage," McCoy said, "but the best I can manage for the moment. We can't outgun this guy. And we can't outrun him. We can't do much of anything until we see what kind of scan he's got."

"We will be vulnerable while the impulse engines are running," Spock said.

"I know that. Can't be helped. How are those people's computers, Spock?"

Spock looked thoughtful. "There are rumors that they have been buying them secondhand from the Romulans. That would be both fortunate and unfortunate. If the computers are an old model, so much the better. But the Romulans make very good computers, ones that are not only flexible, but easily upgraded. Are you concerned about their ability to process their scan data quickly?"

"Yes."

"I would say they are not as fast as, say, the Klingons," Spock said judiciously, "but there are always unpredictable factors in any such assessment. As you say, Doctor, subtlety is not usually their style. Most people who deal with Orion pirates are destroyed, or run away to keep from being destroyed. They will not be used to a protracted engagement . . . certainly not with a combined Starfleet-Klingon force. We might last quite a long time."

McCoy didn't care a great deal for the way Spock had phrased that, but he could understand why he had. "All right. Kill everything nonessential, from the shields out. I don't like losing shields, but they stand out like a lightbulb in the dark, and if they can't see us, they can't shoot at us. At least not very successfully. Douse the lights, shut down the warp engines, you all know what to do. Get on with it."

Everyone at the various Bridge stations got on with it. The lighting faded to evening mode. "Uhura," McCoy said, "let the whole ship hear me, will you?"

She nodded.

"This is Dr. McCoy," he said, and for the first time in all this silliness, his voice cracked. "Ahem. Sorry. Ladies and gentlemen, we are about to be very small and quiet for a while, in hopes that the extremely large vessel presently hunting us will lose us long enough for us to do something useful that will get it to stop. You don't have to be quiet—" he glanced at Spock for confirmation; Spock nodded—"but positive thinking is always a help. Meanwhile, please avoid using any equipment that you can possibly do without, remembering that our shields are down, and we will leak electrons quite nicely, and visibly, if we're not careful. There will be a short run of impulse engines in about—" he glanced at Chekov—"twenty minutes. After that we will be coasting back in toward Flyspeck, and considering our other options for getting this nasty situation handled. Everyone keep your calm, and think good thoughts. McCoy out."

He sat back in the center seat and waited. Spock said, "Doctor, this may not work out . . . you are aware of that?"

"I thought I could depend on you to point that out," McCoy said. "Spock, you just trust me this once. Besides," he added, "can you think of anything more likely to keep us alive at this point?"

227

Spock hesitated a moment. "I would not want to give you false hopes," he said, "but . . . no. The strategy has much to commend it."

"Good enough, then. The worst that can happen," he said, leaning back in the center seat, "is that we'll all be horribly blown up, and Jim will still be alive on the planet surface . . . so this situation," he dropped his voice a bit, "won't be a total loss. Very unfortunate . . . yes. But the Orions won't have killed all of us."

Spock nodded; a thoughtful look. He went slowly up to his station.

McCoy sat there thinking, *And now comes the worst part; the waiting. How does Jim stand it?—just sitting here—when he wants to be out kicking someone's tail, or just wants to get out entirely, not fight at all?—for there are enough times that he'd rather not.* It was a state of mind that, at the moment, he found curiously difficult to sympathize with. McCoy himself, at the moment, desperately wanted to see the pirate ship blown out of space, just to reduce the tension a little.

But the lives . . .

"How many people," he said to Spock, "did you say were on that ship?"

"It is difficult to estimate," Spock said, "but I would estimate somewhere on the close order of seven hundred."

"Thank you, Mr. Spock," McCoy said, sitting back again, saying nothing. He had seen about seven hundred people die in the first year of medical school, what with one thing and another. Everything you could think of—infectious, traumatic, chronic, every kind of syndrome, pathology, and disorder. Memory dulled how many of them had died of something he had done to them, or not done. Not too many, he always hoped. That was all anyone could do, in that situation. Hope.

It was good practice for this.

"Eighteen minutes to impulse engines," Sulu said.

"How extended a visual can you give us at this range?" McCoy said.

"Not very," said Sulu. "With all the power shut down, we can't exactly probe the area the way we'd like to; it would give us away. You'll have to make do with augmented tactical, Doctor."

"Good enough." It would have to be.

He watched the tactical, and tried to maintain the calm. It took such a long time. One got used to the *Enterprise* going where she wanted to in a crack of thunder and a cloud of dust, as it were. This creeping through the dark was agonizing. *But it'll save Jim . . . and the rest of us. I hope.*

"Sulu," McCoy said, "did you get a decent visual of that pirate ship?"

"I was wondering when you were going to ask," said Sulu, and worked over his console for a moment. "Here."

Tactical split off to one side; the other side of the screen became occupied by the huge thing that had come blasting out of nowhere at them. In the relatively bright light near Flyspeck, all its superstructures and external additions stood out very clearly. "What's that?" McCoy said, pointing to one feature. "Looks like a greenhouse."

"I think it's probably a targeting bubble," Sulu said. "External shielded sensor arrays and so forth."

"Thing looks like it was built out of bits and

229

pieces," McCoy said. He was used to the tidiness and grace of the *Enterprise*'s design; this thing looked clumsy and ineffective beside her. But that was a dangerous fallacy.

"Probably it was," Sulu said idly, leaning back and stretching while he kept one eye on the course. "They would have bought the pieces here and there—and then when they've got everything together, they have it all shipped out to some backwater shipyard down in the bottom of the Sag Arm, or maybe tucked away in the Coalsack—we hear rumors about places like that. Put it all together out in open space. A lot of people die—more die when the building is finished, to make sure no one spreads the word around about what that particular ship has, who bought it, what they paid, what it's armed with . . ." Sulu looked disgusted.

McCoy said, "Funny . . . I thought you were interested in the swashbuckling life. Piracy on the high seas and other delights."

Sulu chuckled. "Aye, wi' a wanion! A sword, and the wind in your hair—fight a ship gun to gun and sword to sword, take her doubloons and bury them on some pretty Caribbean island . . ." He looked thoughtful. "Even now, they haven't found the wreck of the *Maria Rea,* or the *Estevan . . ."* He smiled. "But that was a different time. A ship or two here or there, a little redistribution of the wealth, on that scale they didn't do much harm. But this kind of thing, where if a planet's not profitable enough, you destroy it—" He shook his head. "Not for me, Doctor."

"I didn't think so." McCoy looked thoughtful, then said, "What's a wanion?"

"I think it's a curse," Sulu said, not sounding very

certain. "Or a little fish that runs when the moon's full."

"I had to ask. And how is our own private wanion at the moment?"

"Following on impulse," Chekov said. "Accelerating to full power."

"My, he does mean business, doesn't he," McCoy murmured. Generally speaking, a good starship captain tried to avoid near-relativistic velocities; they tended to do odd things to one's engines . . . and crew. But this pursuer obviously thought that the prize was worth a little wear and tear. "How is our own velocity?"

"Eighty percent of that, at the moment. Borderline. Running without shields, it's not too healthy . . . but the computers are all right for the moment, not showing any timing problems. Mr. Spock?"

At his station, Spock nodded. "For the time being, at least. But if we increase velocity much without any protection, the computers will eventually begin to suffer. I should not like to take her much above three-quarter impulse."

"All right," McCoy said. "Shout out if you come across anything else I should know about."

"Of course."

That was the best part of it, McCoy thought. No one *minded* his being in command—there was no competitiveness, no strain; they all *wanted* him to succeed. But then, they all had the same thought; he needed to hang on until Jim could get back in the center seat. They wanted Kirk there as much as McCoy did—if that was possible. Fond as he was of the crew, as well as he knew their loyalty, McCoy had his doubts.

"The Orion vessel continues accelerating," Sulu said. "Gaining on us slightly. Ten minutes to impulse."

"How likely is he to see our engine trace?" McCoy said.

Spock shook his head. "That will depend on the direction his main scan installation is looking at at the beginning of that period. There is a fair chance, if we accelerate slowly enough, that he may miss the ionization trace for some seconds, perhaps a minute or so. If that is the case, then he will have that much less data from which to predict what course we are intending to make."

"The less he sees of us, the better," Chekov said. "We just have to hope he's looking farther out than where we really are."

"Too much luck required in this operation," McCoy grumbled. "Not the best odds for a first-timer."

"On the contrary, Doctor," Spock said, looking up from his work, "a first-time commander actually has a much better chance of survival in a situation of this sort than a seasoned one. The new commander does not know which mistakes to make—and so his antagonist has more difficulty judging those mistakes, and the reasons for them. His tactical choices are likely to be most unpredictable, and when they succeed, most effective. And there is also a slight, strictly statistical advantage, in that he has not been in a battle recently, and the laws of averages combine with chaos theory to—"

"—give me a headache, mostly," McCoy said. "Thank you, Mr. Spock . . . Chekov, what are the other Klingons doing?"

"They're all in long cometary orbits, like ours, but plotted in a way to let them either exit the system quickly or cut in warp drive and fall back in quickly," said Chekov. "All very cautious. I think they know the Orions have us outgunned, but they want to see whether we have some trick up our sleeve about which they ought to inform the Empire."

"Once again our reputation goes before us," McCoy said softly. "I'm not sure I like this fame business. It doesn't make for a very quiet life."

At that the ship shuddered—a very sharp, very noticeable shake, unlike the usual rather softened one. But they had no shields—so every jostle was going to feel three times as acute as usual. McCoy said, "Another ranging shot?"

"I think so, Doctor," Sulu said. "They're not sure where we are, so they're trying the occasional shot in the dark. But I saw where that bolt was aimed. They have our position pretty wrong."

"Thank heaven for small miracles. And when we turn, it should get wronger, right?"

"That's right."

"I'll drink to that," McCoy said, "later."

He sighed and thought about Kaiev, somewhere out there in the dark, with his liver syndrome and his nervous looks. You could never tell who was going to come in handy in a pinch. *There is someone I'll look forward to buying a drink when all this is over,* he thought, *if the fates are kind, and we have a few minutes to rub together after these problems are all solved.*

If we survive—

On the screen, he watched the point creep closer where they would go back on impulse. No more than a few minutes now. McCoy stared at the little point of light that represented the Orion ship, and wondered, *What makes them do it? Do they feel that this is just a job, something they have to do? Do any of them ever think about the people they kill and enslave, the planets they've terrorized over the years? Some of them must. Certainly some of them on that ship have, over time, regretted things they've done. Some of them surely want out.*

And they're likely to get out, too, because we're going to have to kill them—or try to. They won't let us go; we're too rich a prize, and we're threatening their livelihood. No way to talk your way out of this one, Leonard my boy. Out here, the only recourse is good astrogation, and the good cold dark to hide in . . .

"Two minutes," Sulu said. "Doctor, they're continuing on their earlier course. If they keep going that way, when we turn, we'll definitely lose them. They're far enough away from us to miss an impulse burn if they're looking the wrong way."

"Hold that thought," McCoy said.

Another minute slipped by slowly, slowly. McCoy watched the diagram, considering his options. What was he going to do if that monster *didn't* turn? "We must be more maneuverable than that thing on impulse," he said.

"I would think so," Spock said from his station. "It is well enough provided with impulse engines, but at the same time there is so much raw mass to move that it is perilously close to its point of diminishing returns."

McCoy nodded. "Under the circumstances, it sounds like a mistake to let it scare us into warp."

"Unquestionably. That ship is certainly better

armed than we are. It would have a considerable advantage in warp; I would certainly resist the temptation." Spock sounded unusually vehement.

"Spock, if our advantage rests with impulse, then that's where we stay. You don't have to convince me." But the problem was that they couldn't stay in impulse forever. There was going to have to be a resolution to this problem . . . and McCoy couldn't see where it was.

"Thirty seconds," Sulu said. McCoy watched the screen, watched the little white dot that was *Enterprise* inch toward the marked part of the parabola. "Check course."

"Confirmed," Chekov said, and read out a string of numbers. Sulu nodded. "I check you," he said. "Doctor? Last chance to countermand."

"Go," McCoy said.

The impulse engines came on, all at once, as they tended to—no slow build of sound vibrating in the ship's bones, but a *whoomf!* of loud power. McCoy sat upright in the helm, astonished. "Are those engines all right?" he said.

"It's that everything was shut down," Sulu said over the noise . . . which truly wasn't so loud, once you had heard it for a second. "It sounds louder by comparison."

"Does it ever," McCoy said. The "burn" went on. Normally the impulse engines' functioning was almost unnoticeable. But now McCoy wanted to call Engineering and find out whether there wasn't some way they could make the things run more quietly. It was absurd; there was no way the pirates could hear them in space. But all the same, McCoy twitched.

The noise went on and on. It seemed to have gone

on forever—certainly long enough for anyone not completely blind to not miss seeing their ion trace—

The noise stopped. He breathed out in relief. "Well?" he said to Sulu and Chekov.

Chekov was looking at his computer readout; Sulu didn't wait—he was busy studying their orbit, and the Orions. The pirate *seemed* to be heading farther and farther away from them—

"That's a good burn," Sulu said. "We have our tight hyperbola, as planned, and the slingshot will work. And our friend doesn't seem to have seen us—"

I hope Kaiev did. "Well done, gentlemen," he said. "Report on the Klingons."

"Kaiev has dropped off scan, Doctor," said Spock. "I would project him to be about here." On the forward screen, a small red pinpoint of light marked his spot, still swinging away from the planet, and into the orbit that would eventually intersect with theirs. "He will also be about to make an impulse burn, and so has taken the same precautions not to be seen as we have." Spock looked satisfied. "I would not care to speculate on whether this is a tactic he was already considering, or whether he borrowed it from you. But it was a wise choice, I think."

McCoy thought for a moment. "Now, then. Uhura, have we got another of those data buoys left over?"

She looked unhappy. "We have one, Doctor, but I haven't had time to load it as yet."

"That's all right. I don't want you to load it. Except maybe with a little garbage. Look—" He got up and went up to the screen, looking closely at the spot where the *Enterprise*'s orbit would more or less intersect with *Ekkava*'s. "What I was thinking of," he said, "was putting a buoy right about here—" He pointed to a spot a bit closer to the planet than the intersection point. "—and having it start broadcasting just before we get to that spot. Make it look like a data fault. Or no. Better—" He grinned. "Read our ID, and a distress call, into it. Make it sound like *us.*"

Uhura smiled too, a wicked look. "I could fake an answer, too, if you like," she said. "Starfleet saying that the task force was going to be a little late, and we should hold on—or I can imply that in the leaked message."

"Do that. I think it's a little smoother."

Spock was looking at the screen with interest. "You are thinking," he said, "of trying to lure the pirate between us and *Ekkava.*"

"That's right. Suggestions?"

Spock considered for a moment, then said, "I would suggest this spot instead—" and he indicated a point slightly closer to the intersecting orbits. "Postulating worst case, which is always wise in situations of this sort, one would desire to keep the maximum distance between your vessels and the pirate as small as possible. Your superior maneuverability—and here the Klingons also will do well—will enable you to react much more quickly to the bigger vessel's moves, and it in turn will have difficulty reacting quickly to you, because of your proximity."

"There has to be a catch."

"Naturally there are drawbacks as well. If the Orion vessel sees you, and fires at you, the odds of it missing are very low indeed. But I judge that danger to be roughly offset by our advantage."

McCoy smiled ironically. "Roughly?"

"Doctor, as you yourself know from your experience at chess, tactical situations of this sort are rarely expressible in percentile terms, or in terms of statistical averages. There are too many variables, including the onset of sudden unexpected insight, and the intervention of variables not taken into account." Spock looked as if he considered such intervention a breach of good taste. "But the balance of effects in the present situation is simply the best we can hope for. Your plan regarding the buoy is well reasoned. The Orions will certainly feel sure that the ship is doing exactly what it is doing now—running 'silent and deep'—and will eagerly attack the spot where the sudden leakage of signal reveals it to be. That is, if all goes well. The question then becomes, what to do next."

"Too right," McCoy muttered. His mind's eye was full of the image of *Ekkava* firing at the rear of the Orion vessel, and the pirate paying no more attention than if the Klingon ship were a fly. "I'm just hoping two of us will be enough."

"I have been screening the scan of the Orion vessel for possible vulnerable areas," Spock said. "That is probably our best line of investigation. It is not logical to attempt to make such a large ship completely 'bulletproof'; there will always be some areas that are considered less of a priority for protection, or too well protected by other 'active' defenses to need any. Mr. Sulu, I would welcome your input in this regard, and Mr. Chekov's."

"Certainly, Mr. Spock. Put it down on my screen, and we'll have a look."

The three of them got busy. McCoy watched the little white dot on the screen curve around and around the tightest part of its orbit, the hairpin. The Orion vessel was continuing away from the planet, its own orbit curving a little away from theirs, and upward, out of the plane of the system. *You just do that,* McCoy thought. *You just head right on out of the system, and good riddance.* But it was not very likely, and he knew it.

Two of us may not be enough, either . . .

"Uhura," he said, "how long will it take to get that buoy ready?"

"Not very long," she said. "I'm working on the programming now."

"Good," McCoy said, and yawned.

Uhura looked at him with a quirky expression. "Doctor, when did you last eat?"

"Huh?"

"I thought so," she said. "Shouldn't you go off and get something?"

"What?" he said, shocked. "In the middle of a battle?"

"Doctor, nothing is going to happen for at least the next ten minutes or so. Go get yourself a sandwich or something."

"I could have it brought up here," he said, starting to sit down in the center seat again.

"Doctor," Spock said, from where he had come to look over Sulu's shoulder, "if you are going to command, you must learn to delegate. You have not had a rest break for some time. And this is not a warp-speed battle, where conditions can change in a matter of seconds. You have a short time to refresh yourself, and

239

I strongly suggest you do so. I will call you if anything requires your attention, or your presence here."

"Well, if you're sure—"

Spock looked at him with that particular expression that always reminded McCoy of a kindly teacher gently instructing an acephalic. "I'm going, I'm going," McCoy said finally, and headed for the turbolift.

Chapter Ten

HE WENT TO SICKBAY, finally having been given an excuse. As he walked down the familiar hallway, a feeling of great relief washed over him, as if once he stepped through that door, everything would be all right. He knew it was an illusion. But it was a pleasant one.

When he walked through the door, the place was in chaos—the kind of chaos he knew how to deal with. The diagnostic beds were full of people having routine physicals done, and there were four or five people sitting around in the front room waiting to be seen— nothing serious. Lia herself was putting a pressure splint on Ensign Blundell's leg, and lecturing him about high-impact zero-gee sports. McCoy breathed the air of his favorite place with relief, and strolled on through.

There was general delight at seeing him, though Lia looked up, half teasing, and said, "What are *you* doing here?"

He glared at her and said, "Can't check out my own department? I've come to investigate the shoddy way you're running this place. Wasting a perfectly good splint on *him*. Mark, how many times have we told you about the way you throw yourself around the squash court?"

"She won't use the quick-fixer on me," Mark Blundell complained.

"And why should she, when you ignore everything we tell you? No, you just sit and suffer a bit, my lad. Besides, Taka over there needs the protoplaser more than you do, and anyway, you've had that bone regenerated four times this year already. You're over your threshold—don't want the cells forgetting how to heal themselves. You just sit out the next four weeks, and think about the error of your ways."

"It's torture, that's what it is. I'm complaining to Starfleet."

"You do and I'll put you on bread and water. And vitamins," McCoy added as he headed through into his office.

Quiet fell momentarily as the door closed. He went to his desk, opened the locked drawer, and rummaged around for a moment until he came to the large lump that lived at the back of it. It had been too long. He withdrew the object in question, looked lovingly at the white wrapper with its elegant black copperplate printing, and undid it.

"You shouldn't eat that," Lia said. "You know it's bad for your skin."

"Next you'll be telling me it'll give me heart disease," he said scornfully. "Sit down and be quiet, or I won't give you any."

He sat munching the chocolate, a present from

Dieter the last time he had visited—a giant bar of best bittersweet, glossy as a thoroughbred's coat, and a lot tastier. "Here," he said, breaking off a square and handing it to Lia. "Don't say I never gave you anything."

"Now how could I, after that last cold?"

"Don't tell anyone about that," he said. "You'll ruin my rep."

She smiled at him. "How're you doing up there?"

"Lia, it's sheer hell. But worse. In Hell you can complain that you were framed. I got myself into this. Teasing Jim all those times."

She shook her head. "I'll bet he'll be kicking himself when he finds out what's happened."

McCoy nodded, had one more bite of the chocolate, then started to put it away. "Want one more piece?" he said.

"Not me. Somebody out there will smell it on my breath and start demanding it too."

McCoy chuckled. "Right. I'd better get out of here. I'm not even really supposed to be here. I promised Jim."

"I won't tell on you," she said. "By the way, those bone marrow results are in for you."

"Later," McCoy said, heading out. He looked at the faces of his patients as he went out—all calm, all pleased to see him—and said to the group at large, "All of you get better and get the hell out of here!"

Laughter followed him out into the hall and back up toward the turbolift. That feeling of impending doom, held away for such a little time, came crashing in on him again.

The hell with that, he thought, and pushed it back by force. He had been doing too little mood control on

243

himself lately, letting himself react to things as they happened, instead of creatively altering his mood to use a situation to the best advantage. *I am the master of all I survey,* he told himself sternly as he got into the lift. *I am the master of my fate; I am the captain of my soul!*

Now do the Orions know that?

He laughed softly as the lift got going. The doubts were completely understandable (said one of his psychiatric departments, in the back of his head). Suddenly stuck with a strange new job, the fine points of which he knew only by hearsay—if at all—and with the lives of others dependent on him, he was bound to feel out of his depth, out of control, incompetent. But at the same time, he had the advantage of having listened often to one of the most successful practitioners of the starship commander's craft, as over a drink or a dinner he had analyzed his own performance— what had worked, and what hadn't, and why. McCoy was a good listener, and had internalized a lot of what Jim had discussed, without even really thinking about it at the time. And they had played chess—which was better than even Jim's endgame analyses, for it had given McCoy firsthand evidence and experience of the ways and means of a master of the unpredictable in strategy and tactics. McCoy held chess high as a powerful diagnostic tool, and in this case it was going to be more useful even than that. It might save all their lives.

If I can keep my wits about me. I am the captain of my soul. Unfortunately I'm also the commander of this goddam ship. A little more dangerous, and affecting a lot more people . . .

So *stay calm, and let's jump in there and do our best.*

The Bridge doors opened for him. No one even looked up. They were all watching their screens and monitoring the ship's status, and that of the other vessels in the area.

McCoy went and sat down. On the front screen, the *Enterprise* was well along the second leg of her parabola. The telltale for the pirate vessel was missing, though. "Where've they gone?" McCoy said.

"Uncertain," Spock said. McCoy's stomach began to twist again. "I believe they may have instituted electronic countermeasures."

"What? A cloak?"

"Possibly."

"Oh, wonderful. Just what we needed. Where would they have gotten it?"

"Possibly they bought it secondhand from the Romulans," Sulu said. "They've been dumping some of their older technology. But if it *is* the old cloak, that's all right. We know the manifestation signature for that, and as soon as our scanners come back up to power, we can find it without any trouble."

"Back up to power?"

"We have suffered a slight fault, Doctor," Spock said, tapping busily at his console. "One of our particle scanners has burned out. A group from Engineering is replacing it at the moment, but the work will take at least a half-hour, and we are going to have to proceed cautiously when the new one is in place. We cannot run the usual full-power test sequences while we are trying to conceal our presence."

McCoy sighed. "How far along are they?"

"About half done," Scotty said. "I would go down

245

there mysel', but there's no point; it's nae a creative job, just a straight replacement. I couldna do it any faster."

His Glaswegian is showing, McCoy thought. It was never the best of signs. The Aberdeen accent of Scotty's upbringing was what one usually heard from day to day, but at times of stress it got more pronounced, and began to shade into the rougher, more glottal sounds of Glasgow and its spacedocks.

"Right you are, then," he said to Scotty, and looked around to Uhura. "How's our buoy doing?"

"Almost ready," she said. "Do you want to talk to Mr. Spock about the course?"

McCoy shook his head. "Spock, I defer to your better judgment."

The expression Spock turned on him was bantering. "Possibly a historic decision," he said. "Certainly a first."

McCoy grinned. "Don't expect me to return the favor at your next physical. You go ahead, give Uhura what she needs. I want to get that thing out there. We can alter the course after it's gone, can't we?"

"I would prefer not to," Spock said. "The transmission would probably be noticed, and could very well betray the fact that we are using a decoy."

"All right . . . we'll burn that bridge when we come to it. Sulu, where are all our friends?"

"The three extra Klingon ships are still well out of range rightward on the screen," Sulu said, "orbitward. *Ekkava* is running quiet; we *think* she's about there—" and he indicated a point in *Ekkava*'s hyperbola that was a little farther along than the *Enterprise* was. "We should be making our closest rendezvous in about twenty more minutes."

McCoy rubbed his sweating hands together. "All right. Let's get that buoy out there. Uhura?"

"Ready."

"Launch it."

"Affirmative."

There was of course no sound or feeling of recoil, but a moment later there was another trace on the screen, a little green dot making its way hurriedly toward the point on which *Enterprise* and *Ekkava* were slowly converging.

"I'm going to let it get about thirty thousand miles from the spot where we're meeting," Uhura said, "before I start it hollering. That should be plenty of time for the Orion vessel to hear it and respond; they'll turn and make best speed—"

She glanced over at Spock. "Probably about ninety thousand kilometers per hour, at this point. They will have to drop some speed while maneuvering. It will take them, I estimate, six point four minutes to successfully change course, and another eight minutes to reach that spot."

"And blow the buoy up," McCoy said, "thinking they're aiming at us."

"Oh, close-range scan will tell them that it's not us. But they will fire anyway, to silence the buoy. Also, not seeing us, they may assume that we too are cloaked, and somewhere in the area. They may or may not know about the cloaking countermeasures we have devised, but whether they do or not, some bracketing fire in the area is desirable. If they *are* cloaked, or using other countermeasures, they will have to drop them while they fire. And while they are occupied with that—"

"We do a little firing of our own." McCoy got up

247

and went over to look at what Spock was up to. "How's that scan analysis going?"

"It proceeds." *Not as quickly as you'd like, though,* McCoy thought; he knew that phrasing. He looked at Spock's screen, which was showing a view of the pirate vessel. "Ugly big thing," McCoy murmured. "Looks like a brick covered with frozen spaghetti. Look at all those ducts and conduits."

"I would surmise that esthetics are not a major concern for Orion pirates," Spock said. He had the display rotate, then said, "Observe, Doctor. This surface—the narrower face of the oblong—appears to be not so heavily armored as some of the others, to judge by spectrography. That may possibly be a design flaw. It will be difficult to tell until the vessel begins firing."

"I can't tell you how happy that makes me," McCoy said. "I too am less than impressed with this situation," Spock said, "but there seems little point in complaining just now. From present evidence, that side of the vessel is our best chance. There are also doors on that side to the shuttle bays—their ships, like *Enterprise*, never land; they rely on large cargo shuttles for most of their acquisitions. Any one of those doors is a potential target; it must be fairly thin and light, or it would be impossible to move. But on the other hand, the ship's armorers will have known that perfectly well, and screen intensity over those spots will likely be higher than elsewhere. We will have to test our theories on the fly, I fear."

McCoy sighed. "The story of our lives. Well, let's get ready. Sulu?"

"Buoy is on track," he said. "No transmissions as yet, but it should be *there*—" He pointed at the screen, indicating its little green light, farther along than it had been. "The other Klingon vessels are beginning to turn."

That surprised him a bit. "Are they able to tell what's going on, do you think?"

Sulu shrugged. "No way of knowing. *Ekkava* hasn't broken silence. They may have looked at Kaiev's ephemerides and figured it out. But they're not showing any willingness to get too close. The turn is very gradual—they obviously want to remain uninvolved observers."

"They haven't hailed *Ekkava*, have they?" McCoy said to Uhura.

"No hails at all, Doctor. It's dead quiet out there."

"Let's find another way to phrase that," McCoy said.

For a little while more, there was nothing to do but wait.

Then, "Fifteen minutes to close approach to *Ekkava*, Doctor," Spock announced.

McCoy rubbed his hands. It really was astonishing how sweaty they got. *I could be a rich man if I worked out an anti-palm-sweat preparation to sell to starship captains. Hmm, aluminum hydroxide . . . no, too harsh—maybe restructuring the sweat glands; you could take a protoplaser and—No, then you'd only have to do it once, what's the point in that? How about—*

"Buoy's coming into position, Doctor," Uhura said. "About twenty minutes of optimum trans-mission-position time, starting now."

"Twist its tail," McCoy said.

Uhura touched a toggle. The Bridge filled with the soft chatter of the data transmission that the buoy was sending out. "An old code," Uhura said. "They'll have no trouble reading it."

"Good."

And they waited.

"Ten minutes to *Ekkava*, Doctor."

"Thank you."

There was no use doing breathing exercises anymore. All McCoy could do was sit there and sweat.

"Seven minutes, Doctor. There's *Ekkava*—positive trace, direct scan at reduced power." The telltale on the screen that had represented *Ekkava* realigned itself ever so slightly, drawing closer and closer to the one that showed *Enterprise*'s position.

"Noted."

It was amazing how much you could sweat in a matter of two or three minutes. McCoy thought about writing a paper on dehydration in personnel on battle stations.

"Five minutes. Doctor, *Ekkava* is showing faint traces of arming her weapons. The pirate has turned and is making good speed. Six minutes to the buoy."

"All weapons at standby, then. Don't arm yet. Scotty, stand by restart procedure. We may need it." McCoy gulped.

Dehydration, yes, it was fascinating how your mouth dried out and how your life started to pass before your eyes. No need to jump off a cliff at all. The regrets came marching up on you, each one demanding why you hadn't tasted that meal, watched that sunset, told that friend what was on your mind—

WHAM!! The whole ship wobbled as if some giant hand had grabbed it and rattled it to see if there was anything inside. "Pirates firing on the buoy, Doctor,"

Sulu said. "Making better time now. One minute out."

"Have they hit it?"

"No!" Uhura said.

"Good! Shut it up. Send to *Ekkava*: 'Now!' Just that. Sulu, tactical!"

The screen shimmered and changed views. There was a large oblong block in the middle of it, like a big ugly brick covered with frozen spaghetti. It blazed with a bright red halo, the computer representation of its screens. Phaser fire lanced out from it, off at one side, missing *Enterprise*, which was orbitward of the pirate. *Ekkava* was closer to the pirate, and fired at it, another full load of photon torpedoes. *Where do they get all those things?* McCoy thought. *Now I know why those ship have such small crews. The whole ship's as full of torpedoes as a chicken is with eggs—*

The Orion ship could not turn very quickly, certainly not quickly enough to immediately deal with the Klingons. *Ekkava* hurried off to one side, firing. The pirate began to decelerate, but it was going to take time. Slowly it turned, very slowly indeed—bringing that weak face toward *Enterprise*. "This is time for your best shot, Chekov, Sulu," said McCoy. "Spock, give them the coordinates—"

The tactical display narrowed in on the pirate. Circled crossbars centered on the vulnerable spots. "Everything at once, and we might overload their shields," McCoy said. "Might. Save us a little something in case we need it, gentlemen. Fire at will!"

They did. The pirate's screens lit up like the sun where they were hit, overloading—but not for long. Slowly they backed down into red light again.

Chekov wasn't done. He hit his console, and a spread of photon torpedoes leaped out.

From the other side, *Ekkava* was firing as well. Torpedoes as well as phasers struck the screens in all the vulnerable spots at the same time.

The screens flared and went down.

"Got him!" Sulu said, more in a whisper.

"Have we?" said Chekov. The pirate was turning more sharply, wallowing, but making better speed. Behind it, the Klingon vessel was falling away, not accelerating, not firing. Slowly the huge oblong shape turned toward them, chasing them on the hyperbolic course that was to slingshot them around the planet.

"Fire again, at will," McCoy said.

"Photon torpedoes recharging," Chekov said. "Phasers only."

He fired. The beams hit that massive shape—

—and it absorbed them.

"My God," McCoy whispered, horrified. He had miscalculated. "We're history." And the despair that he had been holding off came crashing down on him. No way to live, no way to save the ship and its people even though he himself should die—

The pirate bore down on them as they fired, uselessly, hopelessly—

And everything simply stopped. No light, no sound, nothing; everything went *out*.

Death— McCoy thought, despairing, before he went out too.

Kirk came down to the clearing with his Klingons marching before him, all ferociously angry but unable to do anything while he was holding the weapon. As they got close to the clearing, he was surprised to see through the blue-green trees that there were something like another ten Klingons there, of all ranks and types, standing around as if they were waiting for something. Some of them were talking with members of an *Enterprise* landing party. Kirk saw Lt. Janice Kerasus off at one side chatting with one of them, apparently a commander, in fluent and rapid Klingonese.

"Go on then, all of you," he said to his little crowd. "Katur, help your friend here back up to your ship."

The young Klingons noticed their commander's eyes on them, and vanished with some haste in the bright hum of the Klingon transporter beam. Kirk walked over to the man, who watched him come with something like pleasure in his face, and stepped away from Kerasus to greet him. Kirk kept his thoughts out of his face for the moment.

"Captain Kirk," said the Klingon, and actually sketched a little bow.

"Commander—"

"Kaiev, of *Ekkava*. At your service."

We'll see about that, Kirk thought. "Commander, would you tell me why you've been jamming communications?"

Kaiev twitched a bit. *Aha,* Kirk thought. "That was very unfortunate," Kaiev said. "We had a communications fault in one of our main boards—it shorted out in a test loop, and became stuck in jamming mode. Our comms were down too. But the problem's been handled now; communications are clear again."

"You'll excuse me if I check my equipment—" —*and your word!* Kirk pulled his communicator out, flipped it open. "*Enterprise,*" it said, in Uhura's voice.

"Kirk here. Just checking, Lieutenant."

"Yes, sir. Do you need anything down there?"

"No. I've had a very pleasant afternoon out, and tell Dr. McCoy I'll be beaming up shortly."

There was the briefest of pauses, then Uhura's voice came again, sounding faintly puzzled. "Aye, sir." Kirk frowned. *Now what was* that *all about? Had McCoy—*

"Captain," Kaiev asked, "is there a problem?"

"No," Kirk said quickly, "no problem. That's all, Lieutenant Uhura. Kirk out."

He put the communicator away and nodded to Kaiev. "So much for that, then. Commander, may I ask what your business is here?"

"None now," Kaiev said. His face had a relaxed look that was puzzling Kirk considerably. A thought occurred—that the man seemed to have no defenses up at all. Kirk had never met a Klingon before who wasn't on the defensive, and the experience was— intriguing—to say the least. "We were on survey," said the Klingon, "but there is nothing here of particular interest to us. Except," and he actually laughed, "some of the plant life."

"Yes," Kirk said, and at that he had to smile a little. "I understand you had a bit of a shortage. If we can be of any help as regards the cloning, please let us know."

"No need," said Kaiev. "But I thank you. Captain, not to be abrupt, but I have business elsewhere, and some disciplinary matters to attend to. We will be leaving orbit directly."

"Very well," Kirk said. "A good journey to you, Commander."

"And to you, Captain."

The Klingon took out his communicator. "Commander," Kirk said, feeling slightly confused, "— have we met somewhere before?"

"Oh, no," Kaiev said. "But MakKhoi has told me all about you."

The Klingon transporter effect took Kaiev, but not before he raised a hand in farewell. Kirk half-raised his own, totally confused; then let it fall as the man vanished.

Bones, he thought, *what have you been up to? I intend to find out.*

Ensign Brandt came along at this point, from the far clearing. "Captain," he said, "one of the ;At is over in the next glade. He says he'd like to speak to you before you leave, if that's possible."

"Certainly," Kirk said. He strode off through the soft grasslike plants of the clearing, looking up at the impressive building that about two hundred of the Ornae were busy building with themselves. It was a fantastic structure that looked half like an old Russian cathedral, with spires and onion domes, and half like a pillared *stoa* in the tradition of the Parthenon— with some Danish modern mixed in. It was certainly bigger than anything else he'd seen them build yet. There was a sort of triumphal arch off at one side of it. He walked through this, and was rewarded by several of the Ornae goggling their eyes down at him and making their soft scratchy laughter.

Kirk smiled too and headed into the next clearing. This had definitely been one of the more pleasant afternoons he'd had in a long time, if you discounted the momentary annoyance of having to deal with the overzealous Klingon landing party. The woods closed around him, cool and pleasant, with the long low golden light of the afternoon sun passing down through the branches in broad beams, gilding the leaves and even the floating dust motes. He took his time on the path, looking at the shapes of the leaves, the way the light fell. Heaven only knew when he would have time for this again. And on the other side of the little patch of woods, there was the second clearing; and in it stood the Master of the ;At.

Kirk walked over to the Master and greeted it amiably. "Sir, did you forget something?"

"Never yet, I fear," it said; but its voice didn't sound particularly fearful. "Captain, there are decisions to be made."

"So there are," he said. "I hadn't thought to hear any from you so soon."

"Nor had I thought to be ready to make them. But we must talk; and there is a thing I must say to you first."

"Is this going to take a while? I'll sit," Kirk said.

"Do. Captain, I have practiced a deception on you."

"You have?"

"Yes. And the consequences could be dire. You will probably be angry with me, and I will understand that. But it was utterly necessary."

Kirk couldn't imagine what it was talking about. Was this going to be another of those weird alien-viewpoint things? "Go ahead, sir. I may be angry, but I will try to be fair."

"So I see." There was a long pause, and Kirk became aware of that very long, slow rumbling, all around him, as if the earth were feeling the ;At's concern and trembling a bit with it. "Captain, when first we met, I desired to talk to you without interference."

"And so you did. I thought."

"Your Translator—" The ;At sounded a bit perplexed. "The word *talk,* I fear, says little of what I truly wanted to do. We are a deep-seeing species, Captain."

He thought he understood that. The Translator was doing its best to render some compound word, but what the ;At meant was that it was a concept telepath. "Sir, I have understood that for some time. I'm not troubled by it."

"That's well. What may trouble you, however, is how long you've been here."

Kirk looked around him, confused again. He was beginning to get used to the state. "It's only been a couple of—"

"Days," said the Master.

And immediately, without knowing how, Kirk knew it to be true. All afternoon he had been seeing things in more than the usual detail, feeling every passing second go by with much more than the usual acuity. The air had been like wine every minute, the light as rich as something in an old Dutch painting, every texture and sensation sharper than usual. He had assumed that it was just the effect of the leisure, of getting away for a few minutes. But now he knew the feeling of time being tampered with; it was impossible to mistake for anything else, now that he knew what it felt like. "You're saying," he said, "that though I've experienced only a few hours away from my ship, my crew has experienced two *days*—"

"A little less."

"My ship!!

He forced himself to calm down, for the effect was still working, and his fear was much sharper than usual. "The time has not been concurrent," the Master said. "I dislocated you slightly from your proper time-stream, into future time. A week, perhaps. I shall restore you immediately when we have finished talking here."

Kirk swallowed. "Sir," he said, "you're right. I am angry. But I want to hear what your reasons are for this."

"We needed to talk, as you know," said the Master of the ;At. "You are not the only one who has been deep-seeing, deep-feeling, this past while. I have as well. I had decisions to make—about you, and your people. I needed time in which to make them correctly—extra time. And to some extent, being able to exist briefly in the future, as I told you, I saw that this was the only way it was to be managed. For the Klingons were coming, and others with them, on their trail; and after that, all chances would be lost."

"Others—?"

"The Orion pirates."

Kirk's stomach curled up into a little ball and tied itself in a knot.

"I fear for your folk too," said the Master. "But my first fear is for my own people, whom I see suffering from that attack, and others. The help you hold out to us is very tempting. But I must balance it against the dangers of dealing with aliens. The pirates have not dealt very kindly with us. You came with fair words, but I had to be sure there was more beneath the words that was fair. I am certain of that now. Our three kinds will join your Federation, and learn to share what we have, and what we are. We will never be quite the same again; but I think that change must happen, and I think it will be worth it."

Kirk nodded, keeping himself calm by sheer force. "That said," he said, "and I thank you for it—what's to be done about my ship?"

"I think you should return to it," said the Master. "They are in the midst of a battle, and it goes hard with them."

"*Bones* is in a battle—?! He— They—How am I going to get up there?!" Kirk cried, jumping up. "They'll have their shields up, they can't use the Transporter—"

"This way," said the Master.

And everything stopped—

—and started again. He was on the Bridge, and red alert sirens were going off, and all Hell was breaking loose—

He felt, as he had felt it once or twice before, an actual flush like fire in his lower back, as a blast of adrenaline cut loose. "Tactical," he shouted, and all over the Bridge heads snapped around in astonishment and terror. McCoy alone didn't turn; he had his eyes on the screen, and said, "About time you got here, goddam it! Sulu, fire again—"

"Yes! And shields," Kirk said hurriedly, his eyes fixed on the tactical display, "and Sulu, cut hard right now! Chekov, give me weapons status readout—"

It came up on the screen. What a farrago! Ships everywhere, one of the big pirate vessels, mother of the shuttlecraft he had seen in the step back in time with the ;At—and four Klingon vessels, attacking it as well—

"We got some help," Bones said. "Kaiev there started it—in *Ekkava*—and the others pitched in after a while. I think they just couldn't resist a good fight."

Kirk nodded and stared at the screen. The pirate vessel was running on impulse, as everyone else was. Prudent. But this was no time for prudence. "I recognize this endgame," he said to McCoy. "Jellicoe, huh? Not sure it's working this time. Sulu, the hell with this, warp 4 and out of the system when ready."

"Restart is still in process, Captain," Scotty said from his station. "Four more minutes."

"Best evasive then, Mr. Sulu." Kirk looked at McCoy. "You were running quiet, I take it. Uhura, give me a padd and put the logs since I left on it." He looked at the screen. "One Klingon vessel I could understand. But four?"

"The first one misplaced a landing party," McCoy said. "The same way we did you. *Where the hell were you?*"

"On the planet," Kirk said. "With your friend the ;At."

McCoy blinked. "That's what the Ornae and Lahit kept saying."

"They have some connection with the ;At. They seem to know what they're doing. *It's* doing," Kirk corrected himself, as he took the padd Uhura gave him. "I only saw the one. Sulu, swing out a bit wider. I want some more room."

"Anyway, we couldn't find you," McCoy said. "You were gone from scan, and your communicator was missing."

"The ;At do something with time," Kirk said, scanning down the padd. "We'll get into the exact details later. Meanwhile, I understand the Master's reasons for doing it," he said, and he looked over his shoulder, "but it has created some problems for us all, and I am going to require some assistance by way of apology."

"The Master?" McCoy said, and looked where Kirk was looking. And froze, as did everyone else who looked that way; because there appeared to be a large, rough, brownish stone monolith standing near the turbolift doors. It was unquestionably too large to stand there—the ceiling was too low for its height. But the stone appeared to be sticking through the ceiling, without doing it any harm.

McCoy got up out of the center seat, which Kirk promptly sat down in, and said, "Sir—"

"Doctor," it said. "Your pardon that I had the Captain call you away. But it was he that I had to speak to, urgently; and time was short."

You had the Captain—"

"The Master is a talented being," Kirk said absently, still going through the contents of the padd. "This transmission from Starfleet, for example. This sudden loss of signal. Sir, there were times in the past when I would have very much liked to have had you around. Oh, well.—Sulu?"

"Gaining a little distance, Captain. The Klingons are making it difficult for the Orions. Its shields are back up, and they can't affect them much, but they're a lot faster than it is, and they're concentrating on its weak spots."

"Good. Keep running for a few minutes; buy me some room. I need to think a bit."

The ship shudded slightly. "Photon torpedoes,"

Spock said, coming down for a moment to stand beside the center seat. "Captain, may I say that it is good to see you back?"

"Amen to that," McCoy said, from the other side of the seat.

"Spock, I can tell you it's good from my side too. But it'll be better as soon as we can do something about this pirate." Kirk looked at the screen, and saw less of it than of some night down on Flyspeck, a night full of fire, and the screams of Ornae and burning Lahit. "Scotty, what about our restart?"

"Two minutes yet, Captain."

Kirk put the padd aside and drummed his fingers on the arms of the seat. "Bones," he said, "you don't have to stay. I've kept you away from Sickbay long enough."

"Uh-uh, Jim. I started this, and I'll see it finished."

"One way or another, you will. Anyway—you did a good job. That bit with Delacroix was priceless—couldn't have done better myself."

He looked with some admiration at the shape of the pirate behind them. "Some ship," Kirk said. "Starfleet really ought to look into who's selling them so much of our off-the-shelf technology. Not all the stuff welded onto that hull is Romulan."

"I was looking particularly at the sensor array near the close end," Spock said. "It appears to be Starfleet issue, with some modifications."

"So it does." Kirk frowned and considered that. "Hmm. Bones, are any of the Klingons cooperating with us directly?"

"*Ekkava* is. The others were just sent in by their High Command to try to intervene when that landing

262

party of *Ekkava*'s went missing, and we wouldn't tell them where we kidnapped them to."

Kirk snorted. "Typical. Uhura, ask Commander Kaiev to break off his attack and come up here to join us. Warn him that we're about to go into warp. That thing will certainly chase us—which is what I intend. We'll be looping around to come back through the system; I'm going to lead him through the other Klingons." He got up and leaned over Chekov's seat, programming in a course. "Read that from your console. See this point here? That's where we'll pop out of warp. Reaction time being what it is, the pirate will drop out a few seconds later, but we'll have flipped end for end and started dumping sublight velocity. We'll wind up behind him. Have the rest of them be there and ready to fire when that thing drops out. We'll collapse its shields—then finish this business. Uhura, see that they have Spock's list of vulnerable spots. Do all that now."

"Yes sir."

"Then in a moment we'll see about that sensor array." McCoy was staring at Kirk. "You know Kaiev?" he said.

"We've met," Kirk said. *And there are some interesting implications in that—but never mind that just now.* Kirk looked thoughtfully at the other side of the screen, now split and showing both the image of the pursuing pirate and the tactical display. "What's that little green trace there?"

"The communications buoy."

Kirk looked surprised for a moment. "Ah! Fake signal?"

"That's right," McCoy said.

263

Kirk smiled at him. "You were really getting into this, weren't you?"

"Not much choice," McCoy grumbled.

Kirk looked embarrassed. "No, I guess there wasn't. Still—" A bit of mischief came into his eyes. "Never turn down a learning experience, eh, Bones?"

"Jim, you can take your learning experience and—"

"Tell me later. Uhura? Are the other ships ready?"

"All set, Captain."

Kirk looked at McCoy with momentary interest. "Bones, would you mind telling me how you got all these people fighting *beside* us, instead of *with* us? Just curious. Starfleet will probably be interested."

McCoy looked a bit sheepish. "I can't take credit for the other three. As for *Ekkava*, I just shouted at him. Called him names."

"Hmm," Kirk said, thinking how many times he had wanted to do just that. Still, he had borne a fair amount of McCoy's name-calling in his own time, and it occurred to him that even a Klingon might be impressed by some of it. "Seems to have worked."

Again he bent over the helm console and touched a control here, another there. Sulu watched with increasing interest. "There," Kirk said. "Just hold that instruction in abeyance; we may get a chance to use it. Scotty?"

"She's ready, Captain."

"Good. Mr. Sulu, warp four, now. Keep an eye on the Z axis change. I want to go straight up like a turbolift on the fly."

"Yes, sir!"

She went. "Back to visual," Kirk said. The screen was empty for a moment—then filled again with the image of the Orion ship, a fair ways back at the moment, doing perhaps warp two.

"Won't take them long to catch up. Let them think we're making a run for it," Kirk said.

For about ten seconds, the situation did not change. Then slowly the pirate vessel began to creep closer. "Scotty," Kirk said, "you're using that new fuel configuration, are you?"

"For the moment." Scotty turned away from his station, looking a bit concerned. "There are problems with it; I wouldn't use it for very long, no more than an hour or so. After this we'll need to look for something else that will produce the same result. But at the moment, we're running at about 110 percent of normal engine efficiency. I can get you up to warp eight . . . for *very* brief periods."

"Noted. We may need that eight, though, so if you have to do anything special to the engines to get them ready, do it now. I intend to find out what our friend there has in the way of engines."

Scotty sighed and muttered something, and turned back to his console to begin making adjustments. Kirk smiled. Scotty always complained when you asked his machinery to stretch itself out; but then again, he complained when you *didn't*—so there was nothing to be done but to put up with the occasional mutter. "By the way, Bones," he said, "your Klingon landing party that went missing—you know what they were after?"

"I'm more interested in knowing whether they're back safe," Bones said.

"They are—I think. At least, I saw them go. Anyway, guess what they were after."

McCoy looked at him and shook his head. "Not a clue."

"The vegetable form of the anchovy."

"What?"

Kirk told him about the *tabekh* sauce. Bones nodded at that and said, "Yes, I've heard of it. I don't think you'd want to try it, though."

"Why not?"

"One of the other ingredients is arsenic."

Kirk blinked.

"Apparently they like the bitter taste," Bones said. "Also, the arsenides are pretty important in their diet. Klingons can get into horrible arsenide deficiencies if they're not careful, especially in stressful situations—"

"Bones, Kirk said, "thank you. Sulu, how's our friend doing?"

"Accelerating to warp four. No one else is in warp at the moment."

"Good. Warp five, Mr. Sulu. Accelerate as they do."

"Yes, sir."

Slowly they watched the Orions begin to catch up with them. "Not bad for off-the-shelf stuff," Kirk said thoughtfully, "but I still want to find out where they're getting it. We're not supposed to be selling material to anyone who will pass it on to the Orions—but then, I guess forging and falsifying end-use certificates is an old, old game."

"Warp six now, Captain."

"Noted. They *are* coming right along, aren't they?" He sat there and watched them, thinking. Some part of his mind noted how good he felt. It was always better to have space battles in the morning, if you had to have them at all. But no—this was almost evening, wasn't it?—for him, at least. Odd that his body *felt* as fresh and his mind as lively as if it were morning. He glanced at the ;At. He was going to have a lot of questions to ask, later . . .

"They're matching our warp six, Captain."

"Good. A nice, slow acceleration now, Mr. Sulu. Keep it regular. And mind the course. Turning too soon will throw the timing off."

"I've got an eye on it, sir."

They all watched the screen. The pirate vessel was creeping closer, all the time—and suddenly it was quite a bit closer, a swift rush forward, continuing. "Quick, Sulu, warp seven!"

"Done, sir—"

Enterprise surged ahead too. *Hang on,* Kirk thought. *Speed is what we need at the moment. Not for much longer. But show him your heels for just a little while—*

"Warp seven," Sulu said. "More, sir?" For the pirate was still gaining.

"Must be doing nine at least," Kirk thought. "Start the turn—we don't want to get too far out of the system. Go to warp eight."

"Ah me," Scotty said from his station.

"Not for long, Scotty, I promise," Kirk said. "Only a few moments. Then we'll drop out of warp and let things cool down. Though not for him." He looked grimly at the Orion ship.

Behind them, the pirate crept closer still. "He's doing eight-point-five, Captain," Sulu said.

"Go to nine-point-five, One minute. Then decelerate to warp four, hard, and drop out of warpspace. We need to match our old intrinsic velocity. Uhura, intership."

She nodded. "All hands, this is the Captain." Was that a slight sigh of relief going through the Bridge crew? Or just McCoy? Kirk said, "We're about to undertake high-speed braking maneuvers while in warp. You know that this will sometimes cause the artificial gravity system to fluctuate. If you're holding a cup of coffee, drink it. Maneuvers should take no more than one minute. We'll let you know when we're done. Kirk out."

He sat back in the center seat and watched the pirate draw closer and closer. *You do that,* he thought. *Right up our tail, the closer the better.* The vector-in-flight maneuver he was trying now had first been invented by vectored-thrust aircraft pilots in one of the old Earth wars; it was so effective, and along with others of their inventions had made them so deadly, that pilots on the other side often insisted that they had been shot down by viffers even when someone flying some other plane had done the deed.

We'll see if it still works—Kirk thought. So far it looked good. Maybe the pirate had never heard of viffing, for he was cheerfully running right up *Enterprise's* tail. "We should expect some fire shortly," Kirk said.

As if on cue, the white fire lanced out from the pirate. Sulu evaded before Kirk could say a word. Not much of an evasion, but at this speed, not much was needed; even the slightest drift to port or starboard could change your position by thousands of miles. The first shot was a clean miss, but the pirate kept firing, and the problem for Sulu was that he had a specific course to maintain, and couldn't deviate from it too much, lest they come out in the wrong place, far from their friends in realspace.

The pirate fired again, and again, and Sulu ducked and dodged, and Kirk clenched his hands on the arms of the center seat and tried not to show his nerves. One good shot at this velocity, and they would be so dead that they wouldn't know anything about it until God tapped them on the shoulder and asked them for identification. Behind him, Scotty was muttering unhappily at his station. "How about it, Mr. Scott?" he said.

"I'm keepin' things on an even keel for the moment," Scotty said, "but I canna say how long it'll last. She's not meant for this, not really—"

"Noted. Keep that keel even for just a few seconds more. I've heard about the screen-shredders those things come equipped with, and I don't want one used on us—the feedback alone would tear the ship apart at these velocities. Sulu—"

"Close to dropout point, Captain. It's in the helm."

"Keep an eye on it, and count it down."

"Fourteen," Chekov said, while the pirate got closer behind them, and more phaser beams lanced out. One was a graze, and *Enterprise* shuddered sidewise like a horse stung by a wasp. "Sulu—" Kirk said.

"Just lucky, Captain—"

"Them and us both!"

"—eleven, ten, nine—"

"Intership, Uhura. All hands, warp deceleration in eight seconds—brace yourselves! Out—"

"—six, five, four—"

The ship shuddered again, harder this time. "Lost number six screen," Spock said. "Covering with five and seven—"

"—two, one—"

Kirk's stomach flipped as the artificial gravity, true to form, went on the fritz. Even Scotty had never been able to do anything about that. At deceleration from such high speeds, the shields' priorities changed to favor maintaining the ship's structural integrity, and the gravity suffered as a result. The gravity came in again, went out again. People grabbed hold of their stations and hung on. McCoy, next to him, looked a bit strained; it was an expression Kirk had seen before, on people trying to keep their cardiac sphincters in line. His own was giving him a little trouble, but he had no time for it now. The screen showed the pirate vessel plunging past them at warp nine while they dug their heels into the fabric of space and slowed, slowed. The warp engines howled. Even Scotty couldn't make them like doing this—

"Warp eight, seven, five—four!"

"Now!" Kirk said. Sulu took control away from the helm and did the dropout himself, just to be sure. The whole ship rattled and boomed around them as she dropped out of warp, still decelerating. "Tactical—"

The screen showed four small red lights clustered together, ahead of them—seeming to rush closer, though it was *Enterprise* doing the rushing. "One," Kirk counted softly, "two, three—"

Ahead of them, the pirate dropped into realspace, and went plunging straight into the center of the waiting group of Klingons. "Mr. Sulu," Kirk said, "fire at will. Mr. Chekov, activate that intervention I put into the console."

Phaser beams hit the pirate vessel from five different directions. Its screens went down. "Close visual," Kirk said, hanging onto his seat as hard as he could. If the timing on this went wrong, the thing would merely drop back into warp, then come around for another pass—

The pirate filled the whole screen. Its screens flickered up for a moment, then went down again. Klingon phaser beams hit it hard from four sides, and *Enterprise*'s from the fifth. And something else hit it: a small shape that came streaking in out of nowhere, a little lump of metal no more than a ton or so in mass—but accelerated to almost half light-speed. The communications buoy struck the pirate amidships. No armor could have done anything to stop it, at such a velocity. It burrowed into the side of the pirate, and a great plume of fire and silvery atmosphere, freezing as it came in contact with space, billowed out of the side of the vessel.

"That sensor array, there," Kirk said, pointing. "Burn it out."

Without even bothering to wait for a lock from the targeting computer, Sulu took aim and fired. The glassy installation at the end of the pirate exploded in a cloud of plasma.

"Good enough," Kirk said. "Let him decelerate."

"Klingons are following him, Captain," Chekov said.

Kirk let out a long breath. Doubtless they had old scores to settle; the Orion pirates had preyed on their planets for as long as they could get away with it. Perhaps they thought that letting this one get away would be a mark of weakness on their part, an invitation to more destruction.

He looked over his shoulder at Uhura. "Send to Kaiev and the other commanders that this strategy was ours, and we require the right of disposal," Kirk said.

Uhura nodded. After a moment, she said, "They accept that, Captain. But Kaiev wants to talk to Commander McCoy."

Kirk turned to McCoy and smiled. "You want to take the call here, Bones? Or in Sickbay?"

"Sickbay, please," McCoy said. "But, Uhura, tell him I'm busy at the moment. I'll call him back later."

"Shall I follow, Captain?" Sulu said.

"No. Decelerate and stop."

Sulu said, "Yes, sir," in a slightly mystified voice. They all sat and watched the screen, watched the pirate slow, watched it begin to tumble.

"Major explosive decompression aboard the pirate, Captain," Chekov said. "Weapons and engine systems are down."

"Not as down as they will be," Kirk said, a touch grimly. On the screen, they saw the Klingons move in on the pirate, anchor to it with tractors, and begin to slow it to a stop.

Kirk watched and waited. When the Orion ship had come to a stop, some hundred thousand kilometers away, he turned around in his seat to glance at the massive block of stone seemingly sitting in front of the turbolift doors.

"Now, sir," he said.

And nothing changed except the screen—which suddenly showed them within five kilometers of the pirate and the Klingons tethering it.

Every head in the Bridge turned to look at the ;At, then at the Captain. Kirk smiled very slightly. *I don't know if the pirates could see that, but let the Klingons chew on it and wonder how we did it. I think things will be quieter on the borders of Federation and Klingon space for a while.*

He looked at the pirate vessel for a moment, then said, "Mr. Sulu, are the phasers ready?"

"Yes, Captain," he said, very quietly.

"Jim—"

He knew what McCoy was about to say before he even said it. "Bones," he said, "they're killers, many times over. They've murdered on this planet, and on ones that we protect, and on ones the Klingons do. I'm not sure they would understand a slap on the wrist at this point. *These* people are a hundred times more alien to me than the Ornae or the Lahit, or anyone else I know."

McCoy just looked at him, and let out a breath. "Your conn, Captain," he said.

Kirk looked at the ship to pick the best and quickest spot.

Hominid stock, his memory said to him, unusually clearly. *Most hominids had ancestor-creatures that hunted and killed to live. The habit is in our genes. It's hard to break.*

He sat quite still.

But with these? *They* need *killing, if anyone ever did!* That too vivid night of fire was with him again, the screams and the burning. *They're terrorists, pure and simple. They've earned their deaths.*

"Sulu—" he said.

"Sir."

Kirk took a long breath, and then let it out. "Burn all their engines out but one, the least powerful. No point in letting them all die of old age before they get back to the Coalsack with the news. And fuse all their weapons ports. Uhura, are their comms working?"

"I'm hearing some feeble intership," she said.

"Can you put a transmission into that?"

"Certainly."

"Starting now, then. Orion vessel, this is the USS *Enterprise.* We thank you for a pleasant chase, but as

273

you see from our last maneuver, we no longer need such chases. In cases of less importance, we now have the ability to move our vessels—and parts of them, including the weapon we used on your ship—without recourse to normal impulse or warp engines. The new instant-relocation devices will shortly be installed on all Federation vessels. We are allowing your ship to return to your home port so that you may carry this news to your people. Meanwhile, we strongly advise that you stay out of our spaces—including this area, which is now under protection of the Federation, by treaty newly agreed with its three species." Heads turned in the Bridge at *that,* but Kirk ignored them for the moment. "You may now leave. *Enterprise* out."

There was a small patter of applause on the Bridge. Sulu didn't join it; he was finishing the last of a number of delicate and skilled phaser blasts that destroyed exactly what they were intended to, nothing else.

"Query coming in from the Klingon task-force commander, sir," Uhura said. "They say they're disappointed in you."

Kirk smiled at that. "Tell them 'Sorry, I'm only human,'" he said. "And they should leave the pirate alone on his way home—unless they want us to pop out of nowhere on *them.*"

She nodded and turned to her station. Kirk looked around the Bridge. "Any damage from all that shaking around?" he said.

"No, sir," Scotty said. "All's well." He patted his station. "We build these lassies to *last.*"

Kirk looked at the ;At. "Sir," he said, "my thanks."

"And shall I see you tomorrow morning?" it said.

"Count on it."

"So I shall." And it was simply gone.

"I'd like to go with you," McCoy said.

"Sure, Bones. No problem. But don't you have a call to make?"

"As a matter of fact—" McCoy headed for the turbolift doors.

"Oh. And by the way, Bones?"

"Mmm?"

"You're relieved."

"Damn straight I am," he said, and the doors closed on him.

"What the hell are you all doing in here?" McCoy shouted happily as he bounced into Sickbay. "I told you all to get better and go away! Morrison, are you back *again*? We're feeding you too well."

"Doctor," Lia said, "I have these reports for you to sign—"

"Oh, lovely, bring them here—!" He grabbed the padd out of her hand, brought up the form screens, and signed each one, lovingly, artistically, with great relish. She took the padd from him, when he was done, and said suspiciously, "Are you all right? I can read your signature."

"What's the matter with you? I love forms. And if you want me to write a prescription, that'll be legible too," he said happily, heading into his office. "I have to make a call. Anybody wants me, I'll be right here."

For a minute or two he did nothing but sit and look at his office walls. They had no screens on them but the one that displayed pictures of people's insides, and there were no guns at all. No weapons, no shields, and only his own dear stupid computer terminal.

Bliss.

He reached out to his comm. "Bridge," he said. "Uhura, get me Commander Kaiev, if you would."

"No problem, Doctor. Visual?"

"Please."

After a moment, the screen lit up with Kaiev's face. The Klingon looked rather surprised—no shame to him. *"MakKhoi,"* he said. *"I had hoped you would speak with me before you left."*

"I don't think we're leaving right away," he said. "There's time for that. But, Kaiev, I wanted to apologize for lying to you."

"About killing your Captain?" The Klingon laughed at him. *"It was a good lie! A pity it wasn't true, though. But don't feel bad. Some day you will command a ship of your own. And you will do well!"*

"Oh no I won't!" McCoy said. "Kaiev, I'm a medic. I have no interest in command."

Kaiev stared at him.

McCoy shrugged. "It's the truth," he said. "Sorry if you're disappointed."

Kaiev said, *"If all medics are as skilled in command as you, I must remember to kill mine."*

"Might want to do that anyway," McCoy said, a bit drily. "After the way he hasn't been taking care of you. No, I didn't mean that. But it might do a little good if you threatened him some. He's not watching out for your health . . . possibly on purpose. And heaven knows what he's doing to your people."

Kaiev nodded thoughtfully. *"Perhaps. But Mak-Khoi—one question?"*

"Ask."

Kaiev looked around, as if checking to see if anyone was watching him. *"With this new weapon, surely you need not have feared even four more ships. You could have destroyed them all."*

McCoy just smiled.

"But you talked with us, as if you were the weaker. It makes no sense."

"Neither did not blowing you up when I could have," McCoy said. "Just part of being human . . . this week, anyway. You didn't always do the sensible thing either, Kaiev. Maybe people like you and I are the wave of the future. Our peoples may work together yet."

Kaiev looked at him thoughtfully.

Then, *"Impossible,"* he said with cheerful scorn.

"Well, at any rate," McCoy said, "perhaps you'll let me give you a physical before you go, so you have a proper baseline to compare your own medic's results against. As a gesture of respect . . . from one commander to another."

Kaiev nodded. *"I shall make time."* And the screen went blank.

McCoy sat back in his chair and smiled.

Chapter Eleven

Captain's log, Supplemental. James T. Kirk commanding—again:

The situation aboard *Enterprise* has quieted somewhat in the past day. Personnel who had been assigned on priority to Linguistics duty—or, alternately, to looking for me—have returned to the business of scientific research into the extremely strange evolutionary patterns and history of 1212 Muscae IV. Mr. Spock estimates that we might need to be here for as long as a month to complete a most basic survey, and give the people at Starfleet Sciences enough information to start asking the correct questions about this planet. Myself, I can't say I'll mind sitting still for a while.

I have been holding discussions with the Master of the ;At concerning the exact wording and workings of the treaty to be signed by us and the three species of Flyspeck. The Master has no problem with that being the name that goes on the treaty; since all three species have different names for the world, it will probably simplify matters. The Master does not wish the Federation to have a permanent base actually on the planet—he says that that would be "a breach of his jurisdiction," a phrase that I hope to have explained to me eventually.

The three Klingon ships that arrived to assist *Ekkava* during my—absence—have since left. *Ekkava* remains, at the request of the Master. Generally speaking, our relations with the Klingons here have been unusually warm and friendly, so much so that I sometimes feel tempted to pinch myself. Whether this can be ascribed to the effect of fighting on the same side as the Klingons, or to some other force, I can't say. Certainly the planet surface of Flyspeck is an unusually serene place, and both Klingons and *Enterprise* crew find it restful. Leave parties have been down for some time now, there being no rush, and no reason for quite a lot of the crew not to have a holiday.

The attached communications from Starfleet make it plain that there was some kind of organizational reshuffling going on at Starfleet, which resulted in Delacroix being put on our case. At any rate, the gentleman was thrown into handling our situation without the proper briefing. He has since been removed from it, and McCoy's record remains unsmirched, except for the time he stole the cadaver.

The Doctor himself seems to have survived a most difficult and painful experience, with difficulty but with gallantry. Recommending him for a decoration seems like the thing to do, though my suspicion is that Starfleet will refuse to give it on the grounds that so doing would encourage others to try to maneuver themselves into similar situations. But decoration or not, McCoy acquitted himself splendidly. I can't say I would willingly put him in the same situation again. But it is definitely heartening to know that the Doctor's common sense follows him in the Bridge as well as in Sickbay.

I will be continuing to visit the planet, firming up the groundwork on which our future dealings with the Ornae, the Lahit, and the ;At will be conducted. There are a lot of questions to be asked, and the Master has been endlessly helpful, especially with problems of linguistics and idiom, always a stumbling block. At least we have answers for some of the questions we came with. But some of the answers are obscure, and are going to require long and careful study to be eventually understood . . . if ever they are at all.

"WHAT KIND OF BUG IS THAT?" McCoy said, pointing upward.

"Doctor," Spock said patiently, "your inaccuracies are showing. A 'bug' is specifically a member of the order—"

"I don't mean *bug* bug, I mean *that* bug," McCoy said. The bright-colored creature that he was pointing at came to rest on a branch far above their heads, and looked at them with little bright eyes like sparks of flame.

"It has no name, I fear," said the Master of the ;At. "It flies; it's bright; it seeks certain kinds of trees to pollinate. That's all I can tell you of it."

It was a very early morning, no more than an hour or two after sunup. The light came lancing sidewise through the branches of the forest as McCoy and Kirk and Spock walked together along a forest path, and the Master went with them in its silent way.

"You are great namers, you people," said the Master. "Soon everything here will have a name, if you have your way."

"And will we? Have our way, I mean?" McCoy said.

"Oh, not in any way that matters," said the Master. "No creature needs to keep your naming, if it doesn't care for it. Their true natures are known to them; that's sufficient."

They went on a little way in silence. Kirk was deep in enjoyment of the morning, untroubled by the Master's obscurities. "Gorgeous," he said, as they came out into another clearing, this one surrounded with trees from which cascaded great fragrant veils of flowers, all transparent as water, and dusted here and there with golden pollen.

"They are fair," said the Master, with great satisfaction. "Most things are, this morning. And your ship was the morning star, the first one we have had. A pity it will be to lose it."

"Others will be back," McCoy said.

"But none of them is ever again the first," said the Master. "No matter; memory remains blue. And at least you will be here for another week."

"Yes, we will," Kirk said, "but I don't remember telling you so. Did someone else mention it?"

"No indeed," said the Master, "but you must stay here at least a week."

"I must?"

It paused—or rather, simply stopped keeping up with them. "Surely you must," it said. "Or rather, your ship must. For it was about a week ahead in your time that I took you. Having checked your time measurements, I can say that for certain now."

Kirk thought for a moment, then said, "Of course. The *Enterprise* still has to answer my communications from the planet surface. That must be why Uhura sounded so puzzled."

"Yes," said the Master. "And the young Klingons that I brought into that time, to see how you would react to your great enemies when alone, must be sent back to their ship then. The commander of *Ekkava* will be here for at least that long. But I daresay they will desire to be out of the area shortly thereafter."

"Is that a guess?" McCoy said. "Or are you going to find some clever way to manage it?"

"There's no difference between the two," said the Master, sounding faintly bemused.

They walked on through the clearing, breathing the scent of flowers clear as water. "One thing, sir," said Kirk. "When we spoke—will speak—later this week, and you made your choices. Will make. *Damn* these tenses!" McCoy laughed. The Master itself made that low rumbling that Kirk had quickly come to recognize as laughter, for the Master laughed often.

"You had been to, or seen, or somehow experienced, *this* future. You had to have already known that I had been able to keep the ship from being destroyed in the battle with the Orion pirates."

"But I did not—and *you* had not, not yet. And had I known and shared it, that very knowledge could have made you careless, or rather it could have taken the edge from the fear that is your weapon when you defend your ship. Even had I known, I would not have dared tell you."

"But you had to know! You were in the future!"

"That's so. But neither of us yet knew what the present would *do,* you see. The present is everything —more important than the past by far, and the ground and nursery of the future—even when you are in the future. The present is dangerous, almost too dangerous to tamper with."

"Yet we inhabit it," Spock said.

"Yes," said the Master. "This is a source of wonder to me. But how other worlds are run must remain a mystery to me in some ways. In any case, Captain, I told you no more than you needed to do your work . . . and no less than would enable you to manage it."

They paused near the other side of the clearing, where a path ran farther into the woods. "Sir," McCoy said, "are you glad we came?"

"Glad? That would be hard to say. You have had a child, Doctor. When she first began to set out into the world on her own, how did you feel?"

"Nervous," McCoy said. "Afraid for all the things

that could go wrong. Yet at the same time—" He fumbled for words. "It was what I had been working for," he said. "To see her her own woman, grown, and happy, and doing well. To see her taking her own chances, and becoming things I would never have suspected—"

"Exactly so," the Master said. "Just these past few days, the changes have been great. Already the Ornae speak to me in words I never heard them use. Your language is enriching theirs. I think some of them may go out into space someday, with your people. And the Lahit are becoming more talkative, more open. There is no telling where it will all lead. Changes . . ."

"Sir," Kirk said, "I doubt that there will be many of our people coming here at all. Only a few scientists, linguists, and so forth. We would not want to ruin such a perfect place—so simple and peaceful—"

There was a brief silence. "And paradisaical?" the Master said. "And have a few paradises been spoiled and ruined in your people's time? I see there have. Your concern does you credit. But you need not be overconcerned for the simple pastoral creatures of the Galaxy's edge, Captain," said the Master, and there was a slight edge to the amusement in its voice. "News does travel, by ways that might surprise you. And your guilts aside, paradises are hardly in short supply.— But no matter for that. It is noble of you to worry that your own culture, your many ways of being, might drown ours out. Indeed, that was *my* concern at first. But I have since laid it by. If I have done so, you may well put your own mind at rest. In my estimation, you are not strong enough to do anything but enrich us . . . and it is my only business to know our three peoples here. Later, much later, in some thousands of years, you may come up with something that might actually change one or two of our own ideas. But not just yet."

Kirk said nothing—feeling, as if it still hung over him, the shadow of immense age and power that had lowered over him in the field. *Our intentions are good,* he thought. *That's worth something. But what makes us think we understand everything that's going on around us? In fact, it's the* not *understanding that brings us out here again and again. Mystery is much more interesting than knowledge . . .*

They walked on, into the woods. "I have no doubts about the process of our meeting and our negotiations, Captain," said the Master, as it followed them without moving. "There were many subtle ways you might have tried to affect my decision. But you used none of them; and you intended to use none of them, as I know. And in our own histories, which include the future, your coming had been predicted . . . yours, or that of someone like you. The time had come for growth. So . . . we grow. But never think that is *your* doing," the Master added, sounding amused. "The history being written here is ours. And as for who is doing the writing—" It trailed off in something that sounded suspiciously like a chuckle.

"Sir," Kirk said, "whatever we do, we will keep our interference here at a minimum, and we will be as careful as we can with your people."

"What of your own people?" Spock said. "The other ;At seem rather reclusive."

Kirk got the distinct feeling that the Master was smiling at them. "So they have been, in their time," he said. "Mr. Spock, I am the only one of my kind here at the moment. There are many others, but this is not their place."

Kirk raised his eyebrows. All their scans of the Master had come up blank; and they couldn't get a physical sample of its manifestation—you might as well try to get a cell sample from the skin of the *Enterprise.* The Ornae and the Lahit might have the same basic genetic makeup, but there was no evidence that the Master had anything to do with them at all—another place where the initial survey had gone wrong. The Master was a cipher. "To be the only one of your kind here—" he said. "Do you find it lonely?"

The Master laughed. "With a whole planet to watch over, and two whole species? Hardly. And now another species, for whom the responsibility does not obtain. There are good times coming!"

"The responsibility?" Spock said.

"To guard, to protect." The Master paused on the brink of another clearing. "There are marvels happening elsewhere, that is clear. To have some of them come here will be a great pleasure."

"Sir," McCoy said, "have you considered space travel yourself?"

It was silent for a moment as they looked out across the open space, full of long, waving blue-green grass, waist-high and jeweled with dew, so that the whole field glittered with every breath of wind. "Who doesn't think occasionally," it said, "of leaving his post, and doing something else, some other job, better? But sooner or later, if duty matters, it keeps you where your given word put you. No, Doctor; this is my charge. Here I stay. But perhaps," and the Captain got the impression that it was looking specifically at Dr. McCoy, "you, who know my charge, and your people, will come back this way some time."

Kirk thought he heard something like wistfulness in its tone. He would have liked to tell it yes. But telling this creature the truth had become a habit. "We're not our own men, sir," he said. "We would like to come back when we're done here. Perhaps we will. But it depends on the Powers That Be, and on what they decide."

"So it does," said the Master. "But I'm used to that." Its voice was cheerful.

On they went, through the grass, getting wet to the waist, and not caring. The Master disturbed never a blade of the stuff, and dislodged never a drop of dew. "Nice trick, that," McCoy said, just a little put out what with one thing and another. He had never been a morning person at the best of times, and this was a bit early for him.

"You will manage it some day," said the Master. "I shouldn't worry."

"Not unless I lose a lot of weight, I won't," McCoy said.

They came to another patch of woodland, with an odd sort of luminescence showing through it. "This way," said the Master, and led them down one more path. This one was narrower than most; soft fern-leaved trees and bushes brushed at them as they passed through the blue-green twilight. The trees were thick enough to make a roof here, and the only light came from ahead.

"This is something I wanted you to see," said the Master; and they came out of the woodland, suddenly and finally, onto the beach. The soft brass-golden light of the early sun, caught in the orange haze, spilled over the blue water and caught in the combers as they tumbled onto the peach-colored sand.

McCoy smiled. "Thank you," he said.

"I thought perhaps you might like it," said the Master. "Just one of many boundaries. I thank you for crossing mine, and defending it."

"Sir," Kirk said, "you're welcome. And I thank you for your hospitality to us."

"Oh, as for that," said the Master, "one has to be courteous, after all. You never know whom you might find yourself entertaining—"

It laughed, and vanished.

"Mysterious creature," Kirk said after a while spent looking at that remarkable sunrise. "I'll be sorry to leave."

Spock looked out at the golden morning for a decent interval. "Well, Captain," he said finally, "I think Lieutenant Uhura will be wanting me to come look at her translator algorithm. We finally have the Lahit pronouns and verbs sorted out."

"Go on ahead, Spock," Kirk said, and the Vulcan turned and was off back into the woods, heading about his business.

"No use trying to keep him when he has things to do," McCoy said, looking out over that morning sea.

"Nope," Kirk said.

He walked off to one side, where a big boulder sat half-buried in the sand. "Excuse me," Kirk said to it, brushed it off, and sat down.

McCoy ambled over, bending down once to pick up a shell from the sand and turn it over in his fingers. "Playing it safe, are you?" he said.

"Bones, I'm no geologist. All the rocks here look alike to me, and I'd prefer not to sit down on one that might speak to me. At least, I won't do it without introducing myself."

"Strange place, this," McCoy said, sitting down in the sand beside him.

"I don't know," Kirk said. "Odd, yes. But not as strange as some we've been to. The things that have happened—now, *those* have been strange."

"You're telling *me.* You going to hide off in the bushes somewhere and watch yourself appear in a few days?"

He made a face. "Probably not. Being in one place in one time is enough for me. The Master can do things his own way."

"Never did find out how to pronounce his name," McCoy said.

"You were a little busy," Kirk said. "Bones—I have to say I'm sorry. If I'd known anything like that was going to happen—"

"Oh, Jim, never mind. How could you know? Forces were being manipulated in ways we couldn't understand. Considering the whys of it all, I can't say I mind. If the price of bringing this planet into the Federation was me being terrified out of my mind and dead tired for two days, I think that's pretty cheap. Don't you?"

"Well—"

"And don't forget the learning experience."

Jim chuckled.

"No," McCoy said, "seriously. I always knew that ship was yours; but the knowledge was abstract. It's concrete now. And it was easy to criticize from behind

288

the seat. But I've been in it now. When nothing's happening, it's lovely. The rest of the time—I'll keep the job I know."

Kirk nodded.

"All the same," McCoy said, "one of these days I'm going to have an excuse to make you scrub for an operation. *Then* we'll see who's got the flexibility on this ship."

"No, thanks!"

They sat in companionable silence for a while. Kirk looked out at the morning, and sighed. "I'm going to hate leaving this place. There's something very— relaxed about it."

"Serene," McCoy said. "Enchanted, almost."

"Protected," Kirk said. "Yes."

"That's the Master, I think," McCoy said, and he looked thoughtful. "Long may he wave."

"Others of his kind, he said . . ." Kirk took a deep breath of that morning air. "I wonder where they are?"

McCoy shook his head. "All over, if my suspicions are right."

"Suspicions?"

"Oh, not really. Just a funny thought, a joke. I was thinking of a particular quote, back there," McCoy said, "and he picked it out of my mind and agreed with it, and thought it was funny. Something about being careful about being kind to strangers—because many thereby have entertained angels unawares."

Kirk smiled, and nodded.

"Who knows what people all those years ago might have thought they were experiencing," McCoy said, "when sometimes they brushed up against wise creatures of great age, and great power—nonphysical creatures, good beings—who sometimes passed through Earth in their travels, touched a life or three, passed on? And there are legends of creatures like that all over the Galaxy, in all different kinds of forms. They get called by all kinds of different names. On Earth alone there are a hundred names for creatures who act and talk like the Master of the ;At, if they don't look exactly like him. And there are all those legends of 'live' standing stones, too, that walk and talk every now and then. Anyway, if this is something that some one of my distant ancestors occasionally mistook for an angel, I must say I understand their confusion. And it has a sense of humor, too. What more could you ask?"

Kirk tilted his head to one side. "An interesting theory. Another species like the Preservers, perhaps? But traveling the worlds in various shapes, and devoting themselves to caring for whole planets, whole ecologies? It's not such a strange idea. You could make a case that the Organians have been doing something similar." He grinned, rather wickedly. "And what if they weren't aliens? What if these creatures really *were* angels?"

"Then I'd be especially glad about the sense of humor," McCoy said, "because dealing with us and our like, they'd need it."

Kirk laughed and got up. "Come on, Commander," he said. "Enough theories. According to regulations, I have to debrief you on your period of command. Now, about forgetting to put your shields up in the middle of combat—"

"Aren't you due for a physical?"

"Oh no," Kirk said.

"Oh yes—!"

They headed back through the trees, into the blue-green twilight. Behind them, over the sea, the *Enterprise* rose and passed over, a morning star again.

And if somewhere a stone smiled at it, no one noticed.

STAR TREK®

THE GREAT STARSHIP RACE

by Diane Carey

When a friendly, alien people called the Rey make contact with the Federation, they are thrilled to learn the galaxy has a large number of intelligent races. To bring the myriad cultures to their world, the Rey host a celebration - inviting spacefaring peoples to send representative ships to compete against one another and the Great Starship Race is on.

As the Federation's flagship, the *U.S.S. Enterprise* under the command of Captain James T. Kirk, is sent to compete. But the event takes a dark turn when a Romulan warship arrives and demands to join the race. Soon, Kirk and the Romulan commander are engaged in a deadly game of cat and mouse and, for Kirk and his crew, the race becomes a struggle for survival. Faced with treachery at every turn, Kirk must protect his ship from relentless attack and prevent the annihilation of an entire world.

STAR TREK®
THE ROMULAN WAY

by Diane Duane and Peter Morwood

They are a race of warriors, a noble people to whom honour is all. They are cousin to the Vulcan, ally to the Klingon, and Starfleet's most feared and cunning adversary. They are the Romulans - and for eight years, Federation Agent Terise Haleakala has hidden in their midst.

Now the presence of a captured Starfleet officer forces her to make a fateful choice - between exposure and escape. Between maintaining her cover - and saving the life of Dr. Leonard McCoy.

Star Trek authors Diane Duane and Peter Morwood lift the veil of mystery from the Romulan Empire and, in a startlingly different adventure, reveal the hidden truth about one of *Star Trek*'s most fascinating alien races.

THE WOUNDED SKY

A pretty alien scientist invents the Intergalactic
Inversion Drive, an engine system that transcends warp
drive - and the *Enterprise* will be the first to test it!
The Klingons attempt to thwart the test, but a greater
danger looms when strange symptoms surface among
the crew - and time becomes meaningless.

Now Captain Kirk and his friends face their greatest
challenge - to repair the fabric of the Universe before
time is lost forever!

MY ENEMY, MY ALLY

Ael t'Rlailiiu is a noble - and dangerous - Romulan
Commander. But when the Romulans kidnap Vulcans
to genetically harness their mind power, Ael decides
on treason. Captain Kirk, her old enemy, joins her in a
secret pact to destroy the research laboratory and free
the captive Vulcans. When the Romulans discover
their plan, the Neutral Zone seethes with schemes and
counter-schemes, sabotage and war!

For a complete list of Star Trek publications, please
send a large stamped SAE to Titan Books Mail Order,
19 Valentine Place, London, SE1 8QH. Please quote
reference ST36.